Love Will Find A Way

ALSO BY JUANITA TISCHENDORF

Playground In My Mind
Fiction - Thriller/Suspense

Body Of Evidence
Fiction - Thriller/Suspense

Don't Look Back
Fiction – Thriller/Suspense

The Selfie
Nonfiction – How To

Over My Head
Nonfiction - Biography

An Unfair Advantage
Nonfiction – Biography

The Madman The Marathoner
Nonfiction – Biography

Love Will Find A Way

Juanita Tischendorf

Copyright Page

This is a work of fiction. Names, characters, places, and incidents are products of the author's imagination or are used fictitiously and are not to be construed as real. Any resemblance to actual events, or persons, living or dead, is entirely coincidental.

First Edition

Library of Congress Cataloguing-in-Publication Data has been applied for.

ISBN: 978-1-928613-37-4 Love Will Find A Way (Hardcover)
ISBN: 978-1-928613-38-1 Love Will Find A Way (Paperback)
ISBN: 978-1-928613-41-1 Love Will Find A Way (Ebook)

DEDICATION

I made my first trip to San Diego, via Coronado Island, a two-mile drive from cosmopolitan downtown San Diego. The visit was to see David and Nygra who are a loving and endearing part of my family. The time spent in Nygra's presence lead to me writing this book and the need to write this poem of dedication to her.

She let go without a word, she let go. She let go of any fear or judgments or any indecisions, she just let go.

She let go wholly and completely without hesitation or worry. She let go for all the right reasons and asks no advice or reason. She just let go.

But what she left behind was all the cherished memories, and all those who loved her. She left behind joy as well as sorrow and words of congratulations and applause for all that she has done and shared with those she left behind.

In the space of letting go, she let it all be. She had a small smile on her face of accepting peace. A light breeze blew through her and the sun and the moon will shine forevermore for those she left behind

Epigraph

Our existence is but a brief crack of light between two eternities of darkness.

Vladimir Nabokov (1899 - 1977)

Preface

Trinity walks idly around the room stopping to look at a picture of a scenic view that she imagines hangs in most homes on the lake. It is that picture of the two white Adirondack chairs sitting cozily on the shore and the sun casting a shadow replica in the sand. It makes her smile.

She continues her survey of the room, stopping at an end table where she picks up a family photo of two boys standing with kites snuggly held against our bodies. This too makes her smile.

She now knows that Parker is either married, divorced, or a widow. This explains the exquisite decorating skills obvious in the rooms.

It is a big room and she senses that the paraphernalia laying around on tables and chairs is far from the normal aura of the room. Again, she smiles.

Trinity slowly twirls around, pausing as she spots the bookcase. One can learn much about a person from the books they read, she thinks to herself. She walks over and sees that the books are paperbacks which tells her that this is more a vacation residence than a permanent one. She picks up one paperback to inspect it closer.

That does not make sense, she thinks as she leans forward. Behind the paperbacks there are hardcover books. Who puts paperbacks in front of hardcover books!

Curious she pushes the paperbacks aside and a sense of numbness comes over her as she pulls out and reads first the title of the book she has exposed. "Questions and Answers on Death and Dying: A Companion Volume to On Death and Dying, by Elisabeth Kubler-Ross."

Trinity pulls out another. "In the Face of Death: Professionals Who Care for the Dying and the Bereaved, by Danai Papadatou."

Unable to stop she grabs and reads another title, "Spiritual Perspectives on Death and Dying, by Bernice H. Hill, Ph.D."

Stunned into silence she stares at the book spines. She cannot move from the spot as she focuses on the books until something snaps in her head. "What the hell…!"

Trinity stares at the books she holds in her hands. At first, she is paralyzed by what they insinuate, but then she is infuriated. She rotates and heads toward the master bedroom, rushing toward the bathroom door.

Parker is in the tub ignorantly soaping away happily when Trinity kicks the bathroom door open.

"How could you," she screams. "How the hell did you find out. Who gave you the right to snoop around in my life!"

Shock is written all over Parker's face as he turns quickly, losing his balance and almost hitting his head on the back of the tub as his heels slide forward toward the faucet. "What are you talking about?"

Trinity ignores his reply. "Why did you do it? I loved you, you sneaky bastard and here you were playing some sick sympathy game."

Trinity, her arms laden with the heavy books, shifts them to one side as she throws them one by one at a stunned Parker. Her message delivered, she runs out the bathroom.

Dodging to avoid getting clobbered, Parker reaches over the side of the tub to pick up one of the books. He reads the title and pales. It doesn't take much for him to realize why Trinity is upset.

"Let me explain, please." But his words fall on death ears as he hears the sound of the front door slamming shut.

Trinity is gone, and he is sure she isn't coming back.

DRAKE PARKER

Epigraph

Love has no desire but to fulfill itself. To melt and be like a running brook that sings its melody to the night. To wake at dawn with a winged heart and give thanks for another day of loving.

Khalil Gibran

SPRING 2016

1

I panic the moment Dr. Henderson, shakes my hand, and calls me Drake. No one that knows me calls me by my first name. To everyone I am 'Parker'.

The fact that my dear friend Dr. Martin Henderson is calling me by my first name, makes me anxious.

"Please, take a seat Drake."

I have trouble following Martin's request, but I manage to do as he says, then watch as he moves to his chair behind the big mahogany desk.

Dr. Henderson, known to me as Martin, I think looks much older than me with his gray hair showing just a sprinkle of the raven black it once was. He sports a manicured beard and a mustache that is totally gray and the fact that he has his glasses dangling from a strap around his neck just accentuates his elderly appearance.

I continue to stare at Martin as he nervously shuffles through papers. This is another sign to me. I know Martin well and he is always prepared and organized.

I watch as he tries to smooth out a piece of paper and see it as his way to stall for time. Only I can't take it any longer. "Come on Doc, it can't be all that bad. Give it to me."

Dr. Martin Henderson looks at his friend, Parker, and clears his throat. "Because you complained of stomach pain, I decided to do a little more during your yearly checkup."

"Yes, I know. I also remember that you mostly yelled at me for putting off my physical. Time got away from me Doc and it was not until I felt that pain, did I finally make it in. What is it three; four years later?" I add with a nervous laugh.

"Yes, I'd say that is about right." Martin hesitates, trying to find an easy way to say what he has to say.

"I mentioned to you that I felt something that lead me to believe you might have an enlarged gallbladder. That's why I did a biopsy and sent you to get imaging testing done."

"Yes, and I did that. You should have gotten the results by now."

Martin is quiet, and I stare at him trying to read his expression. Only I can't as Martin's head is lowered. Finally he looks up and I see his eyes remain slightly lowered, his lips squeeze tightly together above his manicured gray beard.

"So, do I have an enlarged gallbladder?"

Martin straightens in his chair. He has known Parker for some time, ever since high school when he was the nerdy guy and Parker the fun loving popular one. Even to this day he couldn't fathom how or why Parker had taken the time to befriend him. He admittedly was so different from the kids that Parker usually hung around with.

But Parker did take him under his wing and as a result he was accepted. That acceptance allowed him to come out of his shell and experience being a part of the popular crowd.

Martin leans back in his chair thoughtfully. He knew that it was the friendship with Parker that made his school years memorable and he had thanked him over and over for it. Now, he only wished he could give something back to this man instead of bad news.

He knows Parker will take it hard. This is a man who has little practice with bad news. He is a happy go lucky person with an overabundance of self-confidence. He does not live in fear because he believes things will work out for the best. Only what Martin must divulge is the cruelest thing to tell his patient; his friend.

Martin keeps his eyes focused on the paper in front of him, so Parker can't see the smirk on his face. It's an oxymoron to be using nothing but kind words for a stock broker. Having seen Wall Street no one would say or think of their agent as kind or even a friend, but Parker is different in that he loves people and wants to do his best for everyone. Parker is the real thing. And now, Martin must be the bearer of bad news.

"Martin! Doctor, where did you go. I'm waiting here."

Martin shakes his shoulders and stretches his neck. No matter how much he wants to ease the blow, with Parker he must give it to him straight.

"I um, I have…" He starts, then quickly he blurts out. "You have gallbladder cancer."

My mouth drops open as I lean back in my chair staring at the ceiling. I lower my gaze so that I am looking directly at Martin. "That can't be right. I feel fine. I get a stitch in my side is all." I pause, then add. "Cancer! I have cancer?"

"Yes, I'm so sorry Drake."

Martin calling me Drake again meant there is even worst to come. I try to remain calm, I remind myself that Cancer IS a bad word but there are more things that can be done allowing more chances for recovery. I must not jump to conclusions just yet.

I breathe deeply and then my breathing quickens as I think no matter what, it does not take away the fact it's Cancer. Not an automatic death sentence, but, yes for some it is.

"Stop it Parker," I say silently as I try desperately to calm myself before interpolating.

"Okay, if I have cancer… What type of cancer is it again?"

"It's gallbladder cancer."

I bob my head up and down. I know nothing about gallbladder cancer or for that matter, what a gallbladder does. What I do know about cancer in general is there are stages of cancer. My pain is sporadic and not that bad so how serious can it be.

"Okay, I have gallbladder cancer. People can live without a gallbladder, right?"

"Yes, they can." Martin pauses before adding, "But in your case, surgery is not an option."

Not an option! The room swam around in front of me and I leaned back against the chair waiting for it to stop.

This is not happening. I look at Martin and I see he is having trouble telling me this. I pray that this is some kind of joke or I am having a bad dream, but I know neither one is true.

I am Parker, the guy voted most likely to succeed in high school, the one who others wish they could be. I have good looks, am in great shape…

I stop myself. Once my life was perfect. I had a great job, children and a loving wife… No, I won't think about that now. I need to concentrate on the present.

"So, I want you to explain to me what I am facing here. I mean, how long do I have?" I stop to choose the proper words. "Tell me what stage?"

"Come on Parker. I know people hear the word, and the first thing we think is that we are going to die. What you should be thinking about is how you spend the time you have left. Gallbladder cancer life expectancy is a statistical number. Do you really want to know this instead of what treatment is available to you?"

Without hesitation I reply, "Yes, I really want to know."

Martin is on his feet now moving around the office as if trying to get his bearings straight. He turns back around, sits down and with determination says," Okay then, you have Stage IV gallbladder cancer."

I nod my head. "Go on."

One look at Parker and Martin knows that he won't let him off easy.

"Okay, then, well, your cancer has metastasized to other parts of your body and, well, surgery is not an option at this point."

I grit my teeth trying not to allow any sound to pass through my lips. When I am sure I am in control I say, "So, it's my fault for waiting so long?"

"No, no, Drake, Gallbladder cancer has a poor prognosis, mainly because it is difficult to catch the disease early. Gallbladder cancer is difficult to detect and diagnose because there aren't any noticeable signs or symptoms in the early stages and symptoms that are present are like the symptoms of many other illnesses. It's location behind the liver also makes it hard to detect. Even if you had kept your appointments it might not have been discovered. It is nobody's fault. However, though we can't remove the gallbladder there is palliative treatment."

"Damn it, Martin, stop calling me Drake. Each time you do I know before you say it, more bad news is coming my way."

"Sorry."

"Okay, so you said, palliative treatment. Don't know what that means." The word sounds promising and I allow myself to hope.

"Yes," Martin says. "It's specialized medical care focused on providing relief from the symptoms and stress of the illness. The goal is to improve quality of life for both you and the family."

About now, I am willing to settle for any crumb of hope. "Okay, I'm listening. Tell me what I need to do."

This is harder than Martin imagined. He is a doctor for God sake and must tell many patients bad news. He takes a deep breath then continues.

"Palliative care is provided by a specially-trained team of doctors, nurses and other specialists who work together with you and other doctors to provide an extra layer of support."

The disappointment can be heard in my voice. "So, you're telling me it's a bandage and there is nothing medically to be done for me?"

"No, I… This is a form of treatment".

Ignoring his reply, I ask, "So, Martin, how long do I have?"

"Nobody can say how much time you have, but with adequate medical therapy, there's a good chance you can survive for many months."

"Months! We're talking months here!"

"Sorry."

"How long, Doc, take a guess."

Martin takes a sip of water and then clears his throat. "Maybe a year."

I try to remain calm, though deep inside there is turmoil.

"You're telling me I'm going to die."

"We all are going to die, Parker."

"Yeah, but not as soon as I am.

It is not fair. It is like someone has pulled the rug out from under me and not slowly either. First, dealing with the separation I thought was the worst that could happen. I love my family but must admit that I was not the best husband, but I am a good father. I tried but failed often to please Cameron. Even when she threatened to throw me out I didn't believe she would. No, it wasn't until after she made good on her word that I began to feel a loss.

I was not happy with the way things were, but the irony is that despite my own dissatisfactions with parts of our existence together, I did not want a divorce. I had at once scrambled to salvage our marriage, citing family and finances, and was prepared to agree to anything to keep our world intact.

Yes, that's what I thought, only that proved to be a reaction to the shock, and not being prepared.

So, my life has turned upside down again, and I am not prepared. I look at Martin.

"Okay. Give me a synopsis so I know exactly what to expect."

"I don't understand what you mean."

"I mean..." I announce finding I am having trouble breathing. "What do I do. What do you think I should do?"

Martin leans toward me. “Medically, it’s up to you. You can decide to treat the cancer as aggressively as possible, hoping to extend survival or improve quality of life. You can opt to decline treatments that are not likely to be curative to avoid side effects that may be uncomfortable or dangerous. It’s your choice.”

“Come on Doc. Give me some hope. I’m only forty-five years old.”

At that moment, Martin wished it was him instead of Parker. It hurt so much to disillusion his friend. He manages to make a suggestion. “Well, you could have immunotherapy.”

“What’s that?”

“An attempt to stimulate the immunity so your body can rid itself of the tumor and prevent further spread of the cancer.”

Hope must have shown in my eyes, forcing Martin to add, “You are wondering if it will save you? I must be honest. It will not. It has spread too far for us to do anything but try to arrest the growth and give you more time.”

I think about this. “So will I be in pain?”

“There will be pain, but when the pain begins there are treatments that will help.”

I am unaware I am shaking my head back and forth, back and forth until finally I look up, “What can I expect? I mean what kind of pain.”

“It’s different for everyone. Gallbladder cancer sufferers describe it as a gnawing pain, rather than a sharp cramp or ache, and it radiates toward the back. It can incapacitate you, but…” Martin pauses to take a sip of water. “There is something that we can give you for the pain.”

I am listening, but it is like I am hearing him from a distance, explaining all the possible treatment alternatives. I no longer care to control my expression as a fog settles around me removing all positivity from my mind. This is the big one and there is no light at the end of the tunnel. It would be dark from now on. I am going to die.

Finally, I manage a smile. I know it is hard for him to tell me this. This man is my friend as well as my physician.

There is silence between us now and I finally stand and watch Martin follow suit.

Martin reaches out his hand and I take it and draw him towards me. I pat him on the back, then draw away before I become overwhelmed.

I manage a weak smile before walking out the door.

2

Martin is worried. He has tried several times to reach Parker with no success. He's not answering at his office or his cell. Finally, with no other choice he dials Parker's home number. The phone is picked up after the second ring. The voice on the other end is his wife's.

"Hello, Cameron? Is Parker home? This is Martin."

"No, he's not, Martin. You know you dialed the house phone?"

"Yes," he says puzzled.

"I guess he didn't tell you."

"Tell me what?"

"We're separated."

Martin is silent. "I'm sorry to hear that Cameron." Another awkward pause. "Do you know how I can reach him?"

"No, he didn't tell me where he was staying, and you know Parker and cell phones. He probably hasn't charged it in days."

"Thanks Cameron."

Martin hangs up wondering what to do next. Knowing that Parker is handling this alone, scares him even more. For a moment he wonders if he should have told Cameron, because from the sound of her voice, she's unaware of Parker's situation.

Martin knows that legally he can share this information if, in his professional judgment, he believes that Parker will not object. But knowing they are separated, he hesitates. Instead he tries Parker's office again.

The phone rings five times and Martin is just about to hang up when he hears, "Hello, can I help you." Martin is shocked and happy to finally hear a voice on the other end.

"Hello?"

"Oh, sorry, yes, this is Dr. Henderson and I am trying to reach Mr. Parker."

"He's not in right now."

"When do you expect him?"

A brief silence follows, and Martin can hear whispering in the background. Finally, a male voice comes on the line. "We haven't heard from him in days, Dr. Henderson, is it."

"Yes, that's right."

"We have not been able to reach him on his cell." There is silence on the line.

"Honestly doctor, we are worried about Parker. It's not like him to be out of touch this long."

"I see, well, thank you for your time." Martin hangs up.

Martin paces around his office trying to figure his next step. Has he given Parker enough time to absorb the fact he has cancer. Should he give him space and maybe let him reach out. He just doesn't know.

He wants to help. He wants to tell Parker he can't handle this alone and what comforted him through rough times before his cancer diagnosis is likely to help ease his worries now, whether that's a close friend, religious leader or a favorite activity. He wishes he had told Parker this before.

Now that he knows he hasn't been to work, it worries him even more. Work could help his psyche.

He continues to pace, unsure what to do next. He pauses to look out the window of his office and his mood changes. He clicks his tongue and smiles. He knows where Parker is staying. No doubt he's at his vacation home on the lake. Why would he be anywhere else when he has that house sitting empty.

It's a beautiful day for a drive, Martin thinks as he stands waiting for the elevator. When it comes, he takes it to the lobby and hurries out to his car where he takes a moment to decide what he'll do. Confidently he backs out of his parking space and heads toward the lake.

He's not in a hurry so takes the scenic route instead of the expressway. It allows him to think a little longer about what he is doing. By the time he reaches Parker's home on Lake Ontario, his plan is in place.

He parks a little way down the street from Parker's house and climbs out. Cautiously he goes up to the front door and peeks in. He sees evidence that someone is in occupancy. There is empty cans and litter on the counter and though the shades are drawn, he can peek through the sides easily. He moves to several windows and finally works his way onto the deck in back where the windows are not covered, and he can see throughout the premises.

He's definitely there, Martin thinks, even though he can't see him. He stares inside a while longer and not seeing any blood or signs of Parker doing any damage to himself, he heads back to his car.

No one seems to have noticed him snooping about but Martin walks gingerly to his car. He checks his rearview mirror and seeing nothing coming, he pulls the car out onto the road and drives away.

He takes the expressway back downtown to his office, feeling better than he did on his way out. He now knows how to contact his friend. By the time he reaches his office he has made a decision to wait and phone Parker later when he wants him to start his treatments.

SUMMER 2015

3

Because it was unseasonably warm that May it turned out to be one of the busiest times of the year to go camping. Factor in that we arrived late at the camp ground to find that everywhere the trees were not the camp grounds were packed. It was the perfect setting for a marital explosion.

"So now what?" Cameron asked.

I checked myself, not saying that if she had been ready and not rushing about at the last minute, we would have been on time.

"Well, we have two alternatives, we can drive around a bit and find a place to pitch our little home away, or give up and return to our proper, sensible, comfortable home."

"Just drive," she said.

Cameron was quite stunning; even in her outdoorsman clothes and little makeup. Her long brown hair, gray green eyes above high cheek bones made her face dramatic in any light. Those perfect dimensions of her face allowed her to pull her hair back tightly or let it frame her face with equal attractiveness. Now as I stole a glance her way it frustrated me more to see that look of annoyance did nothing to dim her beauty.

I was furious with her for making us late and it would be great to have her look like the evil witch. But no, with her lips tightly closed she managed a smirk that accentuated her dimples and cheekbones.

I faced front and concentrated on my driving. We advanced slowly going deeper into the park. Everyone knows the front spots were the best but those were no longer an option.

We passed families all around sitting by fires eating dinner. The smells of burning wood and cooking meat made my mouth water. I was very hungry as I surveyed the areas we passed for an open spot.

There was nothing. I was about to give up hope and turn around when I spotted a perfect camping spot. I could not believe it.

Cameron could not believe it either. "What," she said. It is a miracle no one has taken it. The grass is thick and green and relatively flat. This is nice," she said, actually giving me the first smile since leaving home.

I did not know it, then, but that smile would change drastically by morning.

From experience, I knew that dusk is, traditionally, the worst time of the day to try setting up a campsite because you cannot see a damn thing. The best time is the fourteen hours of good, solid, tent-pitching sunlight leading up to it. Only that was not possible as we had wasted the day doing everything but getting ready for the camping trip.

By the time we all climbed out of the car, everyone was irritable from hunger. Jonathan, our eight-year-old had no interest in camping whatsoever, once he learned there would not be any place to charge his cell or video gamer. He is more like his mother with brown straight hair, and even down to the tight lip smile, but has skin, like me that tans easily. Jonathan could be very mouthy when he was not getting his way and that time, I thought was near since his battery had to be drained by now and there was no place to recharge.

"Okay, everybody," I said. "All hands on deck. We need to set up camp."

No one moves. "I'm not kidding, guys. You will be sleeping on the ground with no tent over you unless you get a move on."

Nolan, our twelve-year-old was the peace maker of the family and the one that usually got the rest of the family to take part or forgive a wrong doing. His short brown curly hair, full lips and even his attitude matched that of mine.

It was recognizing how adult-like Nolan acted that allowed me to see what Cameron and I were doing to the kids by openly displaying our disinclination.

Ignoring them, I go to the van and quickly retrieve the bag with the tent in it. I carry it over to the spot that looks most level and begin unpacking it.

Nolan yells out, "Come on Jonathan. Put that thing down and help. Mom, can you get me the bag of stakes out and I'll help Dad with them."

Cameron nods as she walks to the back of the SUV and begins handing out the supplies until she finally finds the bag of tent stakes.

Stepping out of the back of the SUV, Cameron hands the stakes to Nolan, then we diligently worked together pitching the tent by the headlights of the car that didn't allow for reading of the instructions, which lead to disagreements until Nolan couldn't take it anymore. "It's not helping to complain. We need to get this thing up."

"Either that or tell me now and I will pack our shit up and go home." I added.

Those words were enough. It took longer than it should, but finally the tent was up, and we finished unpacking.

"What is for dinner, honey?" I asked Cameron.

"Grab the canvas bag out of the back of the SUV. It has the groceries in it."

I opened the back hatch to retrieve the bag, but it was not there. I double checked to make sure before calling out, "It must be out already."

"It's not out here," says Cameron.

"We're starving," Jonathan announced blatantly. "What are we going to eat?"

I looked at Cameron, who was looking at me. "Don't start," she said. "You rushed us so fast. It's not my fault."

"I didn't say it was your fault."

I stood there trying to figure out what to do. The camp store had closed hours ago, and it was too late to consider packing up so there was only one thing to do.

Disappointed and hungry we crawled into our tent. "What's that smell?" Nolan asked.

"I'm not sure, probably the tent. It hasn't been used in quite a while. Just go to sleep."

We zipped into our sleeping bags and as luck would have it, fell instantly asleep.

The next morning our mood had not changed. In our rush to get to the campsite we had left behind not only the weekend's supply of food but had also left the bowls and plates. Knowing the camaraderie of campers, even if we were invited to join our neighbors for breakfast we would be expected to have our own utensils.

We finally all agreed on one thing. We were going home.

Together we shoved the blankets and pillows back into the back seat, the tent and sleeping bags into the hatch, slammed the doors shut and headed back the way we came, passing tent after tent as we made our way through the campsite that was laid out in a circle around the area where we had pitched our home away from home.

"Nolan," Jonathan asked "what's "S-E-P," pausing as he reads the ending and adds, "T-I-C."

Upset, I was only half listening as I stared out the window. Several nearby campers were looking at us and laughing. At first, I thought I was being paranoid. After all, it was a long weekend, and everyone was in a good mood. But the more I looked around the more I was sure they were laughing specifically at us.

"Nolan! What does it spell?" yelled Jonathan, raising his voice this time to show he wanted an answer and wasn't going to let it drop.

"What are you talking about?" Nolan asked.

Jonathan spelled it again, then pointed to the sign that was right next to where we had pitched our tent.

As it dawned on Nolan, he yelled out, "Pull over dad. Look at the sign."

By the tone of his voice, I did not hesitate but pulled over next to a wooden sign and read it. I read it once and then again making sure I had read it right. From the look on her face, I knew Cameron was reading it too.

That sign explained how we lucked out finding a lush green grass area to pitch our tent and it explained the smell. It also explained the laughter. The sign read, *Septic Treatment Run-off.*

Trying not to draw any more attention, I eased forward and drove looking straight ahead until we reached the entrance to the park. At that moment I did not want to give up yet, so I asked, "Why don't we go to the beach house instead."

"No…." said Nolan and Jonathan in unison. "We want to go home."

"Come on kids. We don't get that much time together."

Jonathan instinctively turned away from me and said, “Mom. Please.”

I started to protest but stopped myself. With a sigh I looked at my wife for support.

Cameron just gave me a sour look in return.

I looked away and found myself begging. “Cameron, we could just give it one more try.”

Cameron shook her head. “This whole trip idea has been a disaster. I am with the kids. Let’s just go home.”

The smell of the campsite lingered, even with the windows wide open. I drove, squinting into the sunlight that forced me to finally pull off the highway and get my sunglasses out of the glove compartment. With the tension already high, I did not dare ask Cameron to get them.

As soon as the SUV stopped, the back doors opened, and the kids climbed out.

Cameron yelled for the boys to get back in, but they did not listen. She climbed out of the car and snapped at them. “I said, get you butts back in the SUV.”

I watched as the boys ignored her running into the woods near the side of the road. I couldn’t much blame them. We smelled terrible and not only with the stink of the septic.

I sat there thinking that I was a young man and deserving of some joy in life. Somehow our life together had soured, and I couldn’t figure out how to get it back on track. I worked a lot, but that was so we could have a better than average lifestyle.

I looked at my wife, her face distorted with rage at me and now at the kids who were not listening to her. She was three years younger than me but not very flexible in her way of thinking. I had been surprised when she had actually suggested the camping trip. I had taken it as a sign that she wanted to get the family back together. Only now as I sat there I doubted that it was no more than wanting to control my time with the boys.

It did not help when she turned and started yelling at me. "What was I thinking. This was such a stupid idea."

I had not meant to say it, but it popped out. "Not one of your best, that's for sure."

"Don't be sarcastic, you idiot. You wanted us to all be together. Well, we are together. How do you like it?"

I watched as she walked toward the boys, already taking out her cell, which fueled my next move. This should not surprise me. We had been going our own separate way for quite some time.

Strangely calm I reached into the side pocket of the car door and took out a road map and studied it. Something about doing this made me feel better. Slowly, before I realized what I was doing, I climbed into the SUV and I turned on the ignition. I looked out the rearview mirror to see my wife and sons standing there with their backs to me. My mind churned away on its own as I reached across the seat and turned on the radio.

The calming voice of the announcer soothed me and before I knew what was happening I pulled away from the side of the road, picking up speed until the image in the rearview mirror was only of highway.

4

How could I do that! Sure, at the time it seemed like it was what Cameron deserved, but now thinking clearly, I knew it was oh so wrong! I had been selfish and only thinking of myself. God, my sons were there too. It was bad enough doing it to my wife... but my sons.

At least I had not procrastinated and went about apologizing the very next day. And I meant it too.

I can't help but smile, remembering that fateful day of apologizing. Cameron was upset…no, Cameron was ballistic.

"Who do you think you are… Just who do you think you are."

"Cameron…"

"There is nothing you can say or do to apologize for your actions."

"Okay, I understand that, but I want to apologize anyway. Answer me this. When you took out your phone and made a call, was it to Alexander?"

"That's none of your business."

"Just asking."

Cameron stares at me, all the anger apparent in her eyes. "So, if it were. Huh."

"Well, that is what I thought and knowing you had a way to get home, is probably why I did something so stupid. I guess I did not like the idea you had someone to depend on. Someone you would rather contact than try and fix what was happening to us."

It seems a reasonable statement for me to make, but obviously not to Cameron as she leans over and picks up a vase that sits on the corner table. A vase that I gave her on one of our anniversaries. She swings it toward me, but with cat like reflexes, anticipating her action, I ducked in time. That just make her madder. Before she could reciprocate, I was out the door.

All I could do was walk out, throw my hands up in the air and find my sons to asks them to forgive me.

They were in the yard tossing a ball back and forth. As soon as they saw me, Nolan and Jonathan came running.

I fell back on the ground with my two-favorite people in the world, laughing and hugging me. Finally, the three of us got to our feet. "Dad, why are you here?"

I cleared my throat and said, "Because I love you and I owe you both an apology."

I could see the puzzled expression on their faces. Almost in unison they said, "For what?"

"Boys, for leaving you and your mother at the side of the road that day."

Jonathan looked at Nolan and then they both looked at me. They were laughing.

"I don't understand. What is going on."

"Oh Dad, you did the right thing. Mom was ballistic and if we had all been in that car together it would have been…."

"So, wait, you aren't mad at me?"

"No. We just wish you had taken us too. We love mom, but she can be impossible." Nolan said, laughter still apparent in his voice.

I was surprise and happy to find that my boys weren't mad at me at all. They thought it was funny.

"But you don't know what happened, huh?" Jonathan said.

"Something happened," I asked, feeling worried.

"Dad you should have been there. Me and Nolan were running around in the tall grass and trees when Nolan fell, got up and started shouting and jumping about. I didn't know what was going on but figured he was trying to scare me, so I laughed. He was slapping his head and swinging his hands."

"Mom finally heard me, and she came running. She ran like she thought Nolan was dying and was not watching where she was going. Suddenly she just disappeared and when she came back in view she had all kinds of grass and dirt on her."

"Dad, I couldn't help myself. I laughed so hard I almost peed my pants."

I laughed with him now, almost seeing what he saw. That is until I asked, "So, what did your mom do?"

"Oh, Mom just called Alexander and he came and got us."

Yeah, that had taken the humor out of it. I knew Cameron had started seeing someone and I did want what was best for her, but it still left a sting. Even more so when I realized that my boys, my sons, liked her friend a lot.

It wasn't easy to stomach, but the more I thought about it, the more I had to be happy for her and for the boys. I knew they still had a good home with Alexander and Cameron and from what they said during my visits with them, they not only liked Alexander, he liked them too. That was all good.

The fact that Cameron had told me about Alexander before they moved in together made it easier too.

As if sensing how I was feeling she comforted me by saying, "Okay Parker, so the marriage is over, but your sons will always be your sons."

I leaned back on the chair rails and smile again, thinking that if I hadn't left and we had all climbed back in the SUV it would have been the worse drive home in history.

I admit I made mistakes and Cameron whether she would admit it or not, had made just as many. We tried, or at least I thought we had but the myth of my friend who toasted us at the wedding came true. "Marriage is a three-ring circus: engagement ring, wedding ring, and suffering."

I stood and stretched my body. I poured myself another cup of coffee and carried it back to the island. There I sit looking around.

I am lucky. Cameron doesn't put restrictions on when I can see my sons, so I see them as often as I like. Though I have given her the house, I have our beach house.

I stand up and walk over to the windows at the back of the house. How many separated, or divorced men can say that they moved out of their residence and into a 4356-sq. ft. house perched along the shores of Lake Ontario.

5

I remember when we purchased the house as a summer get away for the family. We spent a lot of time here during the summer and sometimes on winter holidays, but as the boys got older, they wanted to be around their friends and didn't want to stay at the beach for long periods.

Once we toyed with the idea of selling, but it was a good investment and we could afford to keep it. So, we did.

Being parents of two active boys the luxury of "couple time" tended to disappear. There seemed to be less time, less communication, less sleep, and less privacy so since the boys were older, and our neighbor was willing to fill in, we thought even without the boys, we could vacation here.

We actually tried it once; just the two of us. I had envisioned evenings of uninterrupted sex and days of spending quality time with each other. Well that did not happen. Cameron spent her days out on the beach while I preferred the deck where I could have a cold one and keep out of direct sunlight. Nights she managed invitations to visit other beach dwellers. The time we did spend alone was sleeping.

"Ah…precious memories." I laugh aloud. So here I am in my new home away from home, where just outside the door at the end of my backyard is a sandy beach that goes for miles and miles in either direction and just beyond it glistens Lake Ontario. Only now I am having trouble enjoying myself.

What happened to my ability to have fun? Was it all wrapped up in my children or could I recreate a good time without them. I go to the counter and pour myself another cup of coffee.

I remember when my boys and I had flown kites, right down there on the beach. I remembers the first time I came home with kites. Cameron was different in those days and she laughed, but it was a sweet endearing laugh as I called out to the boys to show them what I had brought them.

They were young then, probably a little too young for their own kites just yet, but when my father had taught me, I had been young too.

So, after lunch, I gathered up the kites and we all went out on the beach. Cameron stood with Jonathan and I had Nolan by my side as I went over introductory details of flying the kites.

As I talked I watched my sons and could see the eagerness in the boys to get started so I demonstrated a bit more and then said, "Okay, who wants to fly a kite?"

Those first joint flights with us helping them left us all laughing so hard. The kites seemed to have a mind of their own. During the first attempt the boys tried to out run each other and ended up tangling the lines.

This happened several times before first one and then the other child managed to dip their kite in the lake too far off shore to recover.

Many frames were broken, and new kites purchased, but it was good family fun. The first time Cameron and I allowed the boys to do it on their own was a great day.

We sat on the porch watching them as they easily got their kites up in the air. Jonathan picked up on moving the kite in big lazy figure-eights, which frustrated Nolan. He being the oldest thought he should figure it out first.

The problem was that Nolan tried too hard. He would get excited and pull hard and the kite would jerk around fast and crash; usually in the lake.

Before we left that summer to return home, both boys were like pros getting their kites to gracefully curve around. Then, bring their hands back even, making the kite straightened out.

The first time Nolan mistakenly flew his kite in a complete circle, his brother was impressed. He could have kept that admiration going but being Nolan when he noticed that his flying lines were twisted around each other, he panicked, and the kite sailed straight down into the sand.

Yes, they had mastered the art, but then electronics took over and the kites were forgotten. I wondered if anyone flew kites anymore.

SUMMER 2016

6

I left Martin's office that day with feelings of shock and disbelief. What Martin tells me has left me incredibly jarred, turning my world upside-down. One minute I am a successful stock broker and the next minute I am, dying. It can't be real.

If it is real, my life has changed. In the course of an hour, my lifetime has been dealt a shocking and traumatic blow that changes me forever. I snicker at the irony and feel my throat tighten. "Forever," I manage to squeeze out. Well that won't last long."

"Someone, please tell me I am dreaming!"

I look up and realize I am standing on the sidewalk of a city street crying and talking to myself. People will think something is wrong with me. I laugh again which sends a fresh batch of tears rolling down my cheeks.

Unsteadily I make my way to my car and laying my arm on the roof to steady myself, I pause. I feel eyes on me and look around to see several people have stopped and are now openly staring at me as I dig in my pocket. "Don't' worry. It's my car. Go on with your damn business."

I manage to get the car door open and climb in behind the wheel where I sit for a moment waiting for control of my faculties before starting the engine.

Carefully I pull out of the parking space and onto the road, not sure exactly where I'm headed. It doesn't really matter at this point.

At least I am not crying anymore as I put distance between me and my doctor's office. I make a turn and find myself on Park Avenue. It's not exactly a route I usually take, but as I drive a little way I see a sign. It reads Schuber Liquor Store. Without hesitating I pull the car over and climb out.

Inside the store is small and inviting as I make my way around the displays until I have several bottles selected. I carry them upfront and carefully place them on the counter.

"Looks like someone is having a party," the man behind the counter says. I look up to see a big, beefy man with hardly any neck. He has a pleasant smile on his face.

"Yeah, I'm having a party all right," I manage to say hiding sarcasm in my voice.

I return to my car and start driving toward home. In this aftermath of receiving bad news, I am finding it difficult to breathe. There is an actual tightness in my chest and I wonder if I'm having a heart attack.

Desperately I focus on my breathing as I take several deep breathes trying to ward off the fear so that I can concentrate on driving.

I drive staring straight ahead, trying not to think about anything except getting myself home. When I finally pull into my driveway a sense of relief settles in. I reach up and press the garage door opener and slowly drive forward.

Once inside the garage I climb out of the car and press the button. By the time the garage door is closed, I have managed to get my purchases out of the trunk.

I shift the merchandise over to my left side so I can reach into my pocket for my key. "You idiot."

Putting my keys in my pocket was stupid. Everything about this day is stupid.

Here I am fumbling in my pocket for my key again. "Damn. What the f--k."

Finally, my fingers wrap around the keys and I quickly pull them out of my pocket. I stare at them, trying to get a grip on the one I need. When I do, carefully I get it in position so that I can put it in the lock.

By now my tears of anger mingle with the others that I have tried to hold at bay. I can barely see with the tears brimming in my eyes, so it is no surprise I miss judged the key settling into the lock. When I go to adjust my hand to turn the key, the keys fell to the floor.

I am now so far gone in my despair that I lean over, but instead of picking up the keys, I slid down until I am sitting on the step. The storm I was holding back releases and I forget everything except how deeply tormented I feel. My fist pounds the step as I desperately try to release the pain.

Drained I reach over and pick up the keys and work myself into a standing position. This time the key slides easily into the lock and the door opens.

7

I am barely in the house when I take the bottles out of the box and line them up on the counter. I won't be answering any doors or phones or checking any texts.

I want to discourage any outside attention, so I walk around closing all the drapes and douse the set lights in the family room. The car in the garage and no sign of life in the house is what I'm aiming for.

With a bottle and glass in tow I head upstairs. I drag myself to and from the shower and swipe my underarms with deodorant before climbing into bed with my new companion.

The drapes in every room closed so that not an ounce of sunshine could invade my space though I spend most of the days in bed, barely eating, but drinking until I am numb. It is so much easier that way to keep from thinking. I cannot bear to think about anything.

Sometimes I go downstairs to grab something to eat, but then I return to the safe environment of my bedroom. I drink until I can hardly find my way to bed, but I find that it is not enough to stop my mind remembering. So, I drink until I pass out.

I manage to ignore the signs of hunger for a while, but eventually my body again betrays me, and I must eat something more than a pickle or a few prunes. I order pizza; lots of pizza at one time so that I don't have to contend with outsiders.

The food goes down and the food comes up again, but I ignore it.

I do not worry about the trash that builds up. There are pizza boxes everywhere. When the garbage can is full, I allow the excess boxes to litter the counter.

This is my existence for weeks after getting the news. But eventually I am forced to accept the fact that no matter how drunk I get I cannot forget.

At that point I find that I want to cause something or anyone else to suffer as I do, so I bang my fist against walls until they are bruised and sore. Then I resort to throwing things. Anything I can find I throw. It is like the action seems to move the pain away.

The phone rings continuously, but I do not answer it. My cell chimes, and I ignore it. My bed is my oasis and I only leave it to get food, drink or to go to the bathroom.

I allow myself to cry and I cry a lot, too. No, actually I howl. My eyes hurt, my body aches from all the heaving as it releases as much of the liquor as it can. And, my heart breaks because I do not know how to make myself feel good. All I can muster is to feel sorry for myself.

I don't shave, I don't bathe but it doesn't matter since no one sees me. I ignore calls coming in on the land line and since I don't charge my cell, it eventually remains silent. I am alone.

Did I still have a job? I didn't know or care one way or the other.

Yes, I admit spending a lot of time mired in self-pity. I walk around the house in a funk thinking about my family who no longer wants or needs me until finally I face the bare facts. I can waste what little time I have feeling sorry for myself, or I can decide to live. That moves me out of my funk.

I am not going to go out of this world with regrets. I am going to live.

Not wanting to waste another second, I run downstairs and search through the office until I find a tablet and pencil. I sit down, leaning on my fist just staring at the blank page until ideas present themselves. Once I start, the ideas keep coming until I have quite a bucket list.

I lean back and pick up the page, reviewing what I have recorded, and I smile.

"Now that's what I'm talking about," I utter. That night I sleep soberly like a baby.

The next morning, I watch as a weak morning light strains through my drawn curtains and I drag myself into the bathroom, ignoring the voices in my head that whisper I am being silly. I am a grown man and should act like one. "Yeah," I said, "a grown man who is dying."

I am shocked when I see my reflection in the bathroom mirror and I have to pause not sure it is me I see. The man in the reflection has a shaggy beard with pieces of food, and yes, vomit in it. My nose hairs are out of control as are my eyebrows that give me a fierce expression. I look up at the hair falling in complete disorder, adding to my demented appearance.

"Wow, what a mess." I get to work. I grab the waste can and shave over it, afraid this much hair will clog the drain. When I am done, I pluck my nose hair and give my eyebrows a trim. I feel confidence growing inside me as my true image appears.

I take off my clothes, my nose wrinkling at the smell of my body that hasn't seen water in weeks. I start to climb in the shower, stop and look around the bathroom.

"This is disgusting." Grabbing a towel from under the sink I put it around me and go into the bedroom; afraid I will forget if I don't do it now.

I pick up the extension and go through the directory until I find the number I need. I place the call and then wait. The phone rings twice and then I hear, "Hello?"

"Hello, this is Mr. Parker."

"I've been trying to reach you Mr. Parker."

"I know, Alice." I pause, then plunge ahead. "Alice, I'm going out this afternoon. I wonder if you can come and give the house a good cleaning. It's a mess."

"Sure, Mr. Parker, no problem."

"And Alice, I'm sorry about the mess."

I hang up the phone wondering what she will think when she sees the mess for herself. I head back to the bathroom and climb in the shower.

I take a long hot shower, sensing the release of endorphins that make me feel like a new person. My body is stiff from lack of activity, but the hot water relaxes the tension in my muscles. By the time I step out I am a new person.

I dry myself off, standing in the steamy room. Then using my towel, I wipe off the foggy mirror.

I am smiling as I gather up my clothes and put them in the hamper before opening the door and going into my bedroom to get out some clean clothes. When I return to the bathroom the steam has settled and I get out my hair dryer.

My mind is working overtime as I dry my hair and put on deodorant. I take one last look at myself before leaving the bathroom and going back into the bedroom to get dressed.

By the time I enter the kitchen I am a changed man. I set up the coffee maker, play back the messages on the land line and put my cell on the charger. When the coffee maker is ready, I fix myself a cup and continue listening to the messages that have accumulated during the past weeks. Finally, I hear Martin's voice.

"Come on Parker. If you need to talk, you can talk to me, but do not try to do this alone. You aren't alone."

I scroll through the list of calls; too many to count and find another from Martin.

"Parker, I set up an appointment for you on Tuesday at eleven o'clock at the cancer center. Call me if you can't make it."

I grin thinking it's just like Martin to take the lead. I check the date on the message and realize that the appointment is for today.

"Okay, a little change in plans. First stop; the center then I can do my own thing."

8

At the back door I step out on the deck and am startled by the brightness of the day. I shade my eyes and stare out over the lake where the sun reflects like diamonds on the water surface. After a bit my eyes adjust to the brightness.

It's going to be a beautiful day and though I'm anxious to get going, I reluctantly turn around and go back inside.

In the garage I press the garage door open before walking to the car that has been sitting in the same spot for so long it has a light coat of dust on it. "Hello, old friend. Let's get out of here," I say

I climb in the car, put on my sunglasses and then slowly back out of the garage as if doing it for the first time.

Soon I am on my way. My first stop will be the cancer center to keep the appointment set up by Martin.

***

"The stage of gallbladder cancer is one of the most important factors in evaluating treatment options. The doctors here use a variety of diagnostic tests to evaluate gallbladder cancer and develop an individualized treatment plan."

I sit there, giving them my full attention.

"Are you aware there are staging guidelines developed by the American Joint Committee on Cancer."

"Yes, I know that," I said, "I'm Stage IV."

"Yes, that is true, but Gallbladder cancer stages are based on three categories: T, N and M."

I start, "ah…"

But the doctor anticipating what I am about to ask, says, "Let me explain. T describes the primary tumor size. N indicates if the cancer cells have spread to local lymph nodes, and M is whether it has metastasized."

I nod letting the doctor know I understand. I feel like I should ask where I stand on the scale but I'm pretty sure I know the answer.

"So, do you have any questions for us?"

I think for a minute and then reply, "Not really."

I want to leave, but remind myself they are doing their job, so I sit quietly.

"You are the center focus of our treatment. You will be assigned a team of cancer experts who work together, to tailor a plan designed just for you."

The doctor, whose name I have already forgotten drones on. My mind wanders as I am on overload and not really interested in spending more of my day here. If they were to say there is hope that I could be cured, well then, it would be important. Only there is no hope. It is just a matter of comfort for me and delaying the inevitable for my family. So, talk on I think to myself. What was his name? Ah, yes, Dr. Hahn. That was it.

"Mr. Parker? Mr. Parker? I asked if you have any questions?"

With difficulty I bring my thoughts to the present.

"Sorry, No, Dr. Hahn, you don't have to sell yourself to me. You came highly recommended by my doctor, Dr. Henderson, so just tell me where and when and I'll be there."

"It's not a matter of selling myself. We are sharing information on how we can help you."

I can't tell if I offended him or not, but I really didn't care.

That ended the first visit and true to my word, I will keep every appointment until death do us part. Not funny I think, but it's true.

Only it's not over yet. The subsequent visits are with different doctors of the team for different parts of the treatment. They are all kind enough and well-meaning so I pretend interest in what they are doing.

So, this is my life, or should I say death, for now.

When I finally leave the center I need a drink, but I refuse to give in. Instead I drive to the grocery store.

Pulling into the parking lot of Wegmans I feel like my old self, not my cancer self. It's actually comforting to be here. I park and climb out of my car, feeling like I am about to embark on an adventure.

I smile at everyone I pass and when one woman pauses next to my cart and smiles back, I quickly hurry down the aisle not wanting to give her the wrong impression.

I load my cart with a variety of foods that I like, along with the necessities of milk, eggs and bread.

I deny myself nothing as I go down each aisle gathering whatever suits my fancy. I have quite a load by the time I'm ready to checkout.

I scan the front of the store for the shortest line and then maneuver my cart behind the last person before moving from behind my cart to do some checkout shopping. I pick up some candy bars, a magazine and breath mints. As I turn to go back behind the cart I see the woman who smiled back at me and quickly look straight ahead, pretty sure she hasn't seen me. I'm not ready for any interactions just yet.

Check out goes smoothly and soon I am pushing my loaded cart out to the parking lot.

I find I even enjoy pushing the cart on this beautiful day. The sun is shining, bouncing light off the roofs of the cars and I can feel the warmth of the sun on my face. When I reach my car, I pop open the trunk and masterfully unload my groceries, then push the cart into the cart return before climbing behind the wheel and going on my way.

The mesmeric beauty of the day makes my heart swell. Everything catches my eyes on the drive home. It's like I am seeing it all for the first time. The trees, the flowers, the fluffy clouds in the sky are hypnotizing. I understand I am witnessing it all for the first time with admiration and not taking it for granted.

When I finally arrive home, I pull into the garage. There I sit for a moment looking out the rear-view mirror, watching the garage door lower and close out my view. Then I climb out of the car and go to the back to open the trunk.

With the first bags in my hands, I open the door and step in; at once sensing that Alice has been here. Not only is the garbage gone, but the air smells clean. I look around with admiration. Alice has been the housekeeper of our lake home for many years and knows more about our habits than we do. She has opened the windows, letting in the fresh air and because she is used to cleaning the house, I can't help but laugh. I can just imagine the look on her face when she opened the door.

I make three trips and finally all the groceries are in. I then go about putting everything away. I notice that Alice has taken it upon herself to throw out the spoiled food in the fridge. I pause, put my hands into a praying position and say, "Thank you Alice."

In short order, I am done and take a walk through the house to enjoy the cleaning Alice has done.

On the drive home I made a promise to myself. I need to be in control of my situation and that I can accomplish by reading up on my cancer. So once the groceries are taken care of, I get a glass of water and go over to the computer. I visit site after site, taking notes on recommended books to read. When I feel comfortable with the choices, I go to the Amazon site and place my order.

It takes some time as I don't want to duplicate the books I already have, but when I am done, I sit back feeling proud of myself. I look out the sliding doors and smile. "It's time to enjoy the weather," I say to myself as I walk out the door and sit on the deck.

The sun sparkles on the surface of the lake and seems to beckon to me so I stand up and walk to the railing, looking up and down the stretch of beach. It is deserted. I sit on the steps and takes off my shoes and socks and lower my feet to the sand wiggling my toes. It feels good. I stand up and walk down closer to the edge of the water, admiring the view before turning to walk up the beach.

I cannot help but enjoy the sun as it warms my skin, glad that I don't have to worry about burning. I walk for quite a distance and then spin around back toward home. By the time I reach my deck, I am starving. It's time to fix myself something to eat.

For the next few days, I take walks, watch tv and keep my body and mind active. All my early frustrations are there, but I am able to contend with them now.

Each morning I am more in tune with myself. When the books I purchased arrive, I stand in the kitchen eagerly opening the packages. I want to understand and make my own choices and to do that, I need knowledge. I listen and trust the doctors, but I want to play a role in understanding what my body needs, even if it is only to alleviate pain.

So now along with watching television, taking walks, eating and sleeping, I sit on the deck reading. When I get bored with reading about cancer, I grab a short book off the shelf and read that for entertainment.

No one bothers me. The only person who stops by is Alice and she is like a ghost. I barely know when she is there unless we happen to pass each other in the house. She enters and leaves silently.

My work, friends, and even my family seem to have given up on trying to reach me. I don't blame them, one can only waste so much time trying to reach someone who doesn't want to be reached before the message is clear. That is fine with me. I need this time alone.

I am not aware of time as it passes. I find the books very detailed and I read them, cover to cover. When I finally put down the last book, I stare out over the lake thinking to myself. If I had doubted needing help with the pain, I was now onboard.

I carry the book back inside and stand in front of my desk. I have been keeping the books in the drawer, probably not wanting Alice to get suspicious. I need a better place for them and carry an armload over to the bookcase.

Like most summer places the shelves are lined with paperbacks that have been well read over the years. Only these are hard cover books that I hold in my arms. I stare down at the books, then at the shelf. I slide aside some of the paperbacks and realizes that the shelves are deep.

"That'll work," I say, then put the books on the shelf, pushing them as far back as they will go, before moving the paperbacks over until they rest in front.

9

I wake up the next morning feeling fit as a fiddle, making it hard to believe that I am dying. My body feels rejuvenated and there is no pain to signal anything but good health. This makes it easy for me to get started on my list of important things to accomplish.

I am up early and take care of my morning rituals before going downstairs to make myself a good hearty breakfast. I have cooking skills and I put them to good use, not worrying about calories or fat; just eating what I like best.

When the coffee is ready I pour a cup, carry it and my plate over to the island. I am just about to dig in when the phone rings. My head pops up with the fork halfway toward my mouth. It has been so long since hearing that sound that the ringing startles me. I'm not surprised since I figured that sooner or later my family or my job would try again to contact me. No matter who it is, I am not going to answer it.

My first sense is guilt, but it passes. From here on out my life is going to be lived to please myself. If it is family calling, they will understand. If it is work, I will not allow myself to stress. Besides I have saved enough money and time to grant myself a little freedom.

I look around as if expecting someone to be there. Then I laugh. I laugh so hard that the food on my fork flies across the room. Still laughing I rip off a piece of paper towel and clean up the mess, then force myself to finish eating the food I have fixed.

Done, I carry the dish to the sink, rinse it and lean over to put it in the dish washer. Before I can stand up straight, I am laughing again. "That is what they probably will think. I am just taking some time off." If they only knew.

I am still laughing as I go out the door. I have more shopping to do.

It is afternoon when I return home, feeling delighted and proud of myself as I carry my package inside. I have purchased a DJl Phantom 3 professional Quadcopter Aircraft, 3-Axis Gimbal; an expensive and advanced design drone, but what the hell. I have also purchased my license and now have to learn how to fly it.

Carefully I take out the drone and search for the instruction sheet. I anxiously read through the information. Every now and then I nod my head.

"That isn't too difficult." I continue to read. "Oh Damn, why didn't they tell me this first."

I read out loud, "It takes 2.5-3 hours to charge a remote controller Phantom 3 Professional or Advanced controller, and 4.5-5 hours to discharge them while they are connected with a mobile device. It takes longer if there is no mobile device connected. Charging time for Phantom 3 Standard's remote controller depends on which charger you are using. If you use a 1.5A charger, then it takes about 2.5 hours for a controller to be fully charged. Otherwise, charge time differs according to the charge current."

I read it aloud a second time before I finally feel I understand it. Then I am disappointed that I am not going to do any flying right away.

The waiting is upsetting me, only because this was my plan for the day. Flying my drone. Instead I walk around nervously picking up a vase and staring at it like I've never seen it before. I go over to the sliding doors and swing the drapes back and forth until I am afraid the rod will break. Finally I walk into the kitchen and make a decision. Instead of pacing through the house, why not go for a drive.

I have always enjoyed driving. I like it when I can just get behind the wheel and drive with no destination in mind. It clears my head not having to think about anything. Now as I slide behind the wheel, I feel nothing, not sad, not worried, not anxious.

I open the garage door and back out, letting myself just go with it and I am content. I drive pass older homes sitting majestically beside planned community homes.

With the sun reflecting off the hood of my car, it all looks magical.

I see a sign welcoming me to Webster, yet the view remains the same, just not so much water to see. It's like I am all alone in the world and I like it like this.

I notice the change as I continue my drive. Now the homes are farther apart and there is lots of open land. "It's okay," I say as I strain to see a sign letting me know my location.

I continue driving pass field after field with only a few houses spotting the landscape. I can't recognize anything or see a street sign. "Where the hell am I."

I look around and finally give up, taking the GPS out of the glove compartment. I pull over to the side of the road and wait. When it finally comes up, I look at the roadmap, moving it around until I am able to recognize a landmark.

"God, I'm in Fulton." I laugh. "Time to turn around." I've been driving for over three hours. I go to the next intersection and with the help of the GPS find my way to the main road to take me back to Irondequoit.

When I finally pull into the garage, I am no longer thinking about the drone, I'm thinking about my stomach. I am starving. I go to the fridge, stare into the cavity until I find what I am looking for. I take out luncheon meat, cheese, tomatoes, mayo and take it over to the counter before going to retrieve some bread. Happily, I create my masterpiece, get a plate to put it on and back in the fridge I grab a beer.

I'm so hungry I can't wait and take my first bite at the counter, then carry it out to the deck, thinking it is too nice a day to be inside.

Outside I sit and while I eat I am entertained. I watch the seagulls flying over the water and glimpse a couple trying to hold hands as they run down the beach. I turn and stare down the other direction and see a couple sunning themselves on the shore. From no one in sight earlier, the beach is becoming populated.

"Okay, let's get the show on the road," I announce finishing my lunch. I take everything back inside and clean up after myself. Then it's time for the main event.

Not one to practice in front of others, seeing the couples on the beach makes me nervous so I come up with a plan.

I read the instructions again, then go to get the drone that is now fully charged. I stick with the basics first as I try controlling my maiden flight in the living room. It doesn't go so smoothly at first. I manage to take out a couple of vases and put several chips in the walls before I am finally able to control the flight patterns.

"Now for the real thing," I say as I gather up the drone and head outside. I am surprised when I find that it has cooled down quite a bit, so I leave the drone on the deck and go back inside to put on a sweatshirt and a pair of dockers then head back out.

The drone in hand I am ready. The instructions say I have at least 20 minutes of flying time and I plan to use every minute of it. I know drones can travel almost anywhere – the only limit is their battery life. I can't help smiling. I am as happy as I can be until I find out the hard way the limitations of my expensive DJI Phantom 3 Drone.

All is going well, and I am comfortable with the controls, maneuvering the drone into several patterns effortlessly. I am confident enough to allow the drone to fly straight over the lake. I fly it up high, enjoying the feeling of being in control and then it happens. The battery starts to die. The one thing I knew I was supposed to keep in mind was the time.

It could not have happened at a worse point as the drone hovers way out over the lake. I know it is hopeless, but I am not about to give up. I have to try.

I strain not to panic as I begin fumbling with the controls, wishing I had read beyond just the basic instructions. It is hopeless as I watch the drone head to its watery grave.

I know it's crazy, but I can't stop myself as I start running into the lake, feeling the coolness of the water as it works up my body. I am almost totally underwater before I stop, no longer able to see the drone or know exactly where it went down.

Slowly I make my way back to shore and head toward home, turning around wondering if maybe it will float to the surface. It doesn't.

10

I hear it and open my eyes and see that an unrelenting rain is falling. It falls rapidly and with force, in copious quantities that I know won't stop soon.

My new motto is to make the best of every day so I jump out of the bed, humming a tune. In the bathroom I even attempt to mouth a few words, "I'm singing in the rain, just singing in the rain."

By the time I enter the kitchen to start the coffee, I am in a good mood, humming and dah, dah, dahing my way as I pour my first cup of coffee. I go to my desk, sit down and retrieve my bucket list.

I can't help but smile as I read the items deemed important for me to do. Each item brings back memories; some cherished, other's not so wonderful, but still a part of me. It's funny how even the most muldane task now has value.

I stare across the room through the sliding glass doors. "A rainy day." I know exactly how I will spend the day.

After the fiasco of yesterday with my drone, I know exactly what to do. Something with no danger or loss attached to it. "Clean out the attic."

I chuckle recalling the last time I tried to organize the family for an attic clean up.

Since purchasing the beach house the attic had been nothing but chaos, a potentially usable space that seems to provoke an argument every time we head upstairs to tackle it. We blame each other.

I look across the room and can hear and see my family during that request of long ago.

"It's your stupid baby toys Jonathan," Nolan says.

"No, it's not. It's those Sego games that nobody plays anymore."

"Okay sons, come on. Here, I'll start." I'd pick up a lamp that hadn't been used, ever.

"Not that, Parker. That belonged to my great grandmother. I have to keep it."

"But… Forget it. How about this?" I question as I lean over the baby bed tucked in the corner.

"Are you crazy. All our kids slept in that bed…"

I can smile at that now, but then, well, I was irritated and unpleasant to live with the rest of the day.

I lean back in my chair thinking about it and decide that the junk in the attic needs to go. I've always wanted to put a desk up there because it's the best view in the house. Now I can claim that space and enjoy it while I can.

I grab a box of large garbage bags, and a broom and dust pan to take with me as I makes my way up to the attic. I open the door and look around. Doubt begins to creep in as I scan the room. An impossible feat and I start to turn around, but then turn back with determination. What else have I got to do. I've lost my drone so I won't be manning any flights in the future. May as well tackle something I can do. Determined I begin.

I am surprised when I am overcome with the memories attached to an old baseball cap, followed by puzzles that have been well used and now have missing pieces. "Is this how they felt."

I stand up, shake my shoulders and start again. "It is not going to get the best of me."

Every single item in the attic has a memory attached to it. If I let it get to me, this attic will never be usable space. "Come on Parker, get a grip on." Slowly my resolve overcomes memories and I forge ahead.

I can feel the heat of the day as it warms the attic and I know soon I will have to stop so I work faster. There are countless plastic tubs, an old chest, old toys and furniture no one wanted any more. The big items I manage to slide to the front of the attic near the steps, and those I can manage I take down to the landing. I push forward, working from the far corners of the attic where the big items are.

"Why did we hold onto a battered double-bed frame and this dusty rocker," I say as I stand and stretch before moving them forward.

I look at my Fitbit and see that it is noon. I swipe across the face and see that I have accomplished the daily requirement of steps.

I am dripping with sweat but feeling quite satisfied with myself as I look around at the items I have moved to the front for disposal. I decide to call it a day, but before I do, I sit in the dusty old rocker and take out my cell. For the next hour I take a photo of each item, search the internet for an idea of pricing, then post them on Craig's List.

I am about to make my way downstairs when something catches my eye. Over in the front corner of the attic I see something and get up to take a closer look. It's an old kite.

A smile spreads across my face. I remember now. I purchased it for the boys the last summer we were all here, but they were too interested in their electronics to play with something so ingenuous.

Now as I look at it I chuckle. "Now that's more my speed." I make my way cautiously across the attic floor space and lean over a piece of picket fence to get hold of the kite. I check it over carefully and find it to be all in one piece.

"Great." Already I know what I will do later today. As I hurry toward the front of the attic, I trip on a wooden train car. I try my best to stay on my feet, but it's impossible; especially because I refuse to take a chance on my prize possession being damaged. I land hard on my butt.

I sit there a moment, a little dazed, but otherwise fine.

The kite is fine too so I carry it downstairs, thinking I should take a shower next, but decide I'd do that later. Right now, I want to take advantage of the rest of the daylight and try flying my kite.

Just like riding a bike, I still remember how to fly a kite. In no time I have it airborne and it looks pretty against the blue sky, something that cannot be said about a drone.

I watch the kite as it commands the sky at first, but then it begins to lose altitude. That is not a problem. I begin to run up the beach guiding the kite by the string, trying as hard as I can to keep it up in the air. I remember doing this with my boys when they were young, but there is a difference. I cannot run fast or long enough to keep the kite up high.

I give it my best shot and for a while the kite soars as I look over my shoulder running until I must stop to catch my breath. I lean over trying to breathe and the kite spirals downward. I try with all my might to run further away from the shoreline, hoping to land the kite on the sandy beach instead of in the lake.

"How stupid," I reprimand myself for allowing so much of the kite line off the spool so that I could get the kite up high, which unfortunately carried it further off shore.

I manage to stand and salute as the kite lands in Lake Ontario, floating at first, but then disappearing too far out for me to consider retrieving.

"So long my friend," I say as I leans over and gasps for breath.

I try to ignore the fact that my gasping is continuing much longer than normal, but finally I am able to straighten.

"Can't fly a drone nor a simple kite. Pitiful man, just pitiful."

Dejected I turn and slowly begin the walk home. It is then that I notice I have an audience.

I shade my eyes and squint, trying to make out the figure standing near the gazebo. I try not to be conspicuous as I make my way toward the back of my house. As I get closer I can tell that it is a man and he is in his twilight years. I continue to peer in his direction trying to decide if I know him.

The man stares openly at me, his eyes shining, and his cheeks lifted as he smiles. His face is wrinkled and the hand that lies on his arm looks arthritic. His gray hair peeks out from under his baseball cap and matches his beard that reaches almost to the shoulders of his green flannel shirt.

I am practically across from him now and wonder if I should speak, but the sun is in my eyes and compromises my vision. When I can see clearly again, I notice that the man has moved from his standing position and is now sitting on the bench, further up the beach, but he still seems to be staring in my direction. But maybe not.

I have a good view of him now and I am pretty sure I don't know him. I am also pretty sure this stranger has been watching me for some time and probably greatly entertained by my unsuccessful kite flying. Maybe he also witnessed my crash landing the drone. "Glad I could entertain you, my friend," I mumble.

I travel the rest of the distance home, unaware at first that I still have the ball of kite string in my hand.

I walk to the edge of the water and start to throw it in the lake, but stop myself. Instead with the string in tow, I carry it with me home.

As I draw closer I see that there is someone sitting on my steps. At first, I frown, then shading my eyes I see clearly that I know this visitor.

"Paul". "How the hell are you Paul," I say walking toward him. "How did you find me?"

I had not told anyone where I was staying. I was going to wait until I adjusted to the idea I was no longer living in my home and being a father. I wanted to also wait until my family had forgiven me for leaving them on the side of the road. This last thought almost made me laugh aloud as I can still visualize that moment looking through the rear-view mirror.

Paul Parker forces a smile as he watches his brother close in on him. He is nine years younger than Drake, but he looks to be the same age. Their features are quite different though as he has a square face, blue eyes, close cropped black hair, full lips and a light caramel complexion where Drake's face is rounder and his eyes are dark brown.

"Come in, come in, let's get a beer and catch up."

"Okay."

I hurry ahead inside to get two beers out of the fridge and then direct my brother back out on the deck. Though it has cooled off, it is still too nice a day to spend indoors.

After all that running, I am ready to relax and once we are comfortably seated, I ask, "So, what's new and exciting in the old hometown."

Paul leans back in his chair. "Nothing much". Not much happens at home. It's quiet and predictable."

I could believe that. We were raised in Penn Yan, New York, a village with a population of 5,000. It has always been an attractive tourist area because of its grape vineyards, but for business, the only real game in town is Birkett Mills continuing its tradition of providing worldwide buckwheat products.

I nod my head, wondering why Paul after college returned to Penn Yan and what made him want to own a winery after spending his childhood picking grapes for money.

"How's the winery doing, Paul."

Paul hesitates before saying, "It's good, Parker. I can't complain."

I look at my brother and we both smile. It's quiet as we enjoy the warmth of the day and our beer; each having our own private thoughts. It is Paul who breaks the silence.

Cautiously he says, "Cameron's pretty upset with you." He pauses. "You should call her".

"What so she can yell at me some more for leaving her on the highway like that. I'm sorry I did that, but I couldn't take it anymore. Besides she had her phone and I knew she had enough contacts that she could call someone to get her and the kids." I then add, "Besides, I did apologize to her and the boys. The boys accepted my apology, but I'm pretty sure Cameron didn't."

"Parker, that's water over the dam. She is over that. No, she's just worried about you."

I take a deep breath trying to calm myself down. "How are the boys."

"They're fine, Parker. They want to see you."

I finish my beer and turn to Paul. "Paul, I have something to tell you."

I do my best to not make a big deal of it as I tell him about my cancer and what the doctor has said. Paul listens closely and I can read his thoughts from the expression on his face. "Come on Paul, I accept it and you have to accept it too. It's important to me that you don't let it get you down."

"How am I supposed to do that, brother. You're telling me I am going to lose you." He chokes up.

I give him time, then change the subject. "Come on, it's getting cooler out here. Let's go inside"

I walk across the deck and open the door with Paul on my heels.

"Are you hungry."

"I could eat something

Inside the room is cool but inviting. My brother and I head for the kitchen. I open the fridge and retrieve luncheon meat, cheese, tomatoes, mayo and onions while Paul walks over to the pantry to get chips and a bag of rolls. We place everything on the island.

"Okay, go for it," I exclaim.

We smile at each other, comfortable and happy to be together. Then I start to laugh.

"What's so funny?"

"Nothing, I was just remembering what it was like when we were younger. We were always playing tricks on each other. I was remembering the time I went to the bathroom and took a candy bar with me."

I start laughing and hold up my finger until I can continue. "I sat in there for so long there must have been a ring on my butt before the chocolate melted enough in my hand to look like poop."

Paul recalls and starts laughing too. "I remember."

"I said, Paul, you used all the toilet paper and then I opened my hand and wiped the chocolate on your face. You freaked out."

I am chortling hard now and say, "I almost wet myself laughing."

"Ha, Ha. I remember it well," Paul says trying to control his laughter. "It took a while, but I did get even. Remember that day walking back from the bus stop and making it up the long driveway. I was ahead of you and my backpack swung against the flowers along the drive and set off a bunch of angry bees."

Now it is Paul's turn to curl over with laughter as he tries to finish his story. "I ran as fast as I could and saw you running behind me. When I reached the house, I hurried up the stairs and pushed the door quickly to get inside before you caught up with me. I locked the door and stood there watching as the bees attacked you."

"Yes, and then I watched as Mom attacked you when she saw her child covered with bee bites. I couldn't wait to tell her what happened."

When we finally caught our breath, we ate our sandwiches. The rough parts were over. Brothers can talk to each other about almost anything comfortably except each other's money and each other's families. There needs to be a buffer for that.

"So, what are you going to do now?" Paul asks.

I thought for a moment before answering. "I am going to do whatever I please. Like yesterday I flew a drone for the first time."

"You did? That sounds like fun. Always wanted to do that myself."

"Well, honestly, it was fun at first but quickly went downhill. The damn thing is now out there at the bottom of the lake."

I can see that my brother is trying not to laugh. "Think that's funny. Well, today I tried flying an old kite I found in the attic. That too is resting on the bottom of the lake with my expensive drone."

Paul cannot hold it in any longer. He breaks out in laughter, spilling his beer and watching as the tomato slices I added to his sandwich, slip out from the bread and land on the floor.

"Sorry," he says, still laughing as he retrieves the slices of tomatoes.

I know my brother well and as I peer at him I can tell that Paul has something else on his mind. "What is it, hmm. What are you thinking about."

Paul clears his throat and walks over to stand beside me. He reaches into his pocket and pulls out a folded sheet of paper. He lays it in front of me.

I turn to face him and ask, "What is this?"

"Just look at it, please."

I slowly unfold the paper and look down. "Gilda's Club of Rochester". I look up at my brother.

"Read it. Read it aloud so I know you're really reading it."

I gaze at it again, then start. "Gilda's Club provides a meeting place for men, women and children living with cancer, along with their family and friends."

I pause. "What is this?"

"Please Parker read it."

"Okay. We join with others to build social and emotional support as a supplement to medical care. Free of charge and non-profit, Gilda's Club offers support and networking groups, lectures, workshops and social events in a non-residential, homelike setting. Gilda's Club is funded through the generosity of private individuals, corporations, foundations, and grants."

Again, I stare at my brother. "I support this group Parker. It's the best."

"I'm not going to ask how you found out or if Cameron and the boys know too. I figured I could not keep it from the family so I'm not mad. I just need to find my way through this before I talk to any of you."

"I know brother and I accept it. I will let your family know you are all right, but you need space for now."

I nod. Shortly thereafter, we say goodbye.

11

After the visit from my brother, I start thinking about day-to-day affairs, like being able to eat, drink and watch television because to me these moments were not mundane, but important. That's how it gets when you know your time is running out.

Just as thinking about how to address my family was important, every thing I do takes on more meaning. Each day is relished because life is short for me, and I am beginning to understand and accept this.

So, I like being around people more though I don't understand why. That is my goal for today once I've attended to my morning rituals I go outside.

Hiking up the beach in Charlotte is interesting and fun. I especially like to leave the private beach areas behind my house and the neighbors and check out the public beach areas. There I watch the swimmers who spend more of their time laying in the sand on blankets than enjoying the water. I can see women who self-consciously undo the back of their bikini tops and lay on their stomachs, hoping to get a no tan line on their backs. I find it humorous for some reason and grin as I continue along the boardwalk knowing that no matter how many times I make the trek I am bound to find something attention-grabbing or see someone new on the beach.

On this morning, the board walk is occupied with people sauntering with a friend and oblivious to those around them. Others sit in the gazebo playing board games. I pause to watch a chess game taking place across from two other people in their swimming attire, playing checkers.

I see frisbee players having fun laughing and throwing the frisbee out of reach of the other catcher, who reciprocates by making them race to catch the return. I find myself wishing I had that kind of energy. If I did, I would still have a kite and a drone.

I turn around abruptly. "Oops, excuse me…"

"That's okay," said the girl, smiling. Shading her eyes, she looks up into my face. "I've seen you on the beach before, haven't I?"

"That's possible, yes." Taking a good look now, I wish I had said something interesting. The girl is pretty and quite well built, judging from her bikini body.

"Mind if I walk with you," she inquired.

"No, I would enjoy the company. My name is Parker,"

"I'm Missy."

"Hello Missy."

"Hello Parker."

We have gone about twenty steps when Missy asks, "What is your sign?"

"My sign."

"Yes, silly, your zodiac sign."

"Oh, it's Taurus, I think." I didn't know for sure, but that sounded masculine. "What's yours?"

"Oh, mine is Cancer," she said brightly.

I sucked air in. I tried not to glare at my innocent companion as I said, "I've got to go now." I hurried away, ignoring Missy yelling after me.

Sure I have outdistanced my companion, I turn around and leave the boardwalk, wandering across the grass. Seeing Abbotts across the street, I realize I am hungry and what better treat than an ice cream cone.

The line is long but moving quickly. There are people alone and others with a husband or boyfriend with them. Then there are the families with the children impatiently waiting to get that ice cream. This is my entertainment as I move slowly to the window to place my order.

Finally, I am at the window. "Can I help you," the teenager behind the window asks sweetly.

"Yes, I want a soft swirl in a waffle cone." She turns around and I add, "Sorry, I also would like sprinkles on it."

"No problem."

While I wait I grab extra napkins and when I am handed my ice cream in a waffle cone of deliciousness it makes me happy again.

Each lick brings back good memories that stay with me as I make my way back home.

I count the cone as lunch, and concentrate on what to do next. I decide to go for a drive.

It is a perfect day for a drive and when I am almost back home I hit something. I pull the car over in front of my neighbor's house and get out, walking to the front of the car and there he is; my neighbor's dog.

I don't know what to do and I'm afraid to move him so I hurry up to the door and ring the bell. Lucky for me, my neighbor, Harold is home.

"I am so sorry. So very sorry, but I hit your dog."

His expression changes from that of 'glad to see you' to questioning my words.

"What did you say."

"I hit your dog, just now. Can you come with me?"

Harold says nothing as he follows me to the curb.

"I pause, confused."

"What is this, some kind of sick joke."

"No, Harold, I hit him. He was laying right here."

We hear the bark and see his dog, jumping about in the yard. Harold goes over to him and checks him over. He sees a reaction as he touches his dogs side, but it is just a minor twitch.

"He seems fine. I'll take him in and have him checked, but he seems okay. I can see where your car hit him, but you must have stopped quickly."

"Can you forgive me."

"Parker, it's okay. My dog is okay, and I appreciate you coming forward."

We shake hands. "If there is any injury or any expense, let me know. I'll gladly pay for it."

Harold just smiles and turns back to his dog.

I spend the rest of the day inside, putting things in order.

It is a cool beach evening with the smell of flowers intermingled with people having barbeque on the grill. I sit on my porch looking and listening to the sounds around me. When the phone rings, I go in to answer it. It is Harold letting me know that his dog is fine. The vet tells him that it was more of a nudge than a hit. Harold tells me not to worry.

The sky is gray and as I stare out in the distance, the lake seems gray too. There is a cool breeze gently moving the hedges and sending out their fragrance. As I stare into the distance I finally know what I want to do.

I get up and go back in the house, grab a jacket and a book, then lock the back door and head out the front. I take my time, walking down to the local restaurant, enjoying the evening air.

The restaurant is warm and full of happy people; including the waitress who shows me to a table near the back windows so that I can see the lake. I gaze around the room wondering what these people are dealing with in their life. Were they as happy as they appeared or did the atmosphere make them happy?

When the server returns, I place my order, then stare out the window, watching the fisherman sitting idly on buckets with their line over the railing, waiting patiently for a nibble. It makes me feel good to see them.

"Excuse me, sir." I sit back, putting my hands in my lap. I watch as the waitress places my food in front of me. As soon as she leaves, I pick up my fork and start eating. It tastes great. I eat slowly enjoying each mouthful and when I finally finish, I make sure I leave a hefty tip on the table, before going up front to settle my bill.

I am surprised when I step outside to find it is dark now and it has grown even cooler, but I don't mind as I slowly made my way home. I peer out into the gray night, following the sidewalk, thinking about life and how much people take it for granted. Not me. I am going to take it all in from here on out.

At home, I put the book I had taken with me and not even opened, back on the shelf and then go into the bedroom to change. Sitting in the dark in my pajamas, I turn on the tv and watch one of my favorite shows.

12

The next few days pass slowly and I begin realizing that I am fooling myself if I think I can handle this on my own. I read everything I can find about cancer and even find information on what I should do in order to accept my prognosis.

In the weeks following that day, hearing that I have cancer, I slowly recover, only to have a setback. The shock has begun to wear off, but other feelings have emerged. I try to suppress them, but they won't go away. I feel sad one day, wake up in a panic on other days and fight bouts of depression, the likes I have never known.

I remember something I read about practicing certain techniques. I think for a moment and I recall it was in a pamphlet I got from Martin. I walk over to the desk and search the drawers until I find it. I read the bulleted points.

- Practice relaxation techniques.
- Share your feelings honestly with family, friends, a spiritual adviser or a counselor.
- Keep a journal to help organize your thoughts.
- When faced with a difficult decision, list the pros and cons for each choice.
- Find a source of spiritual support.
- Set aside time to be alone.

- Remain involved with work and leisure activities as much as you can.

"What the heck." I start breathing slow and deep. It doesn't specify how many times to do this so when I feel I am relax, I stop and look at the next item.

I read on, admitting that there is no way, just yet, I can do any of the other items. I have never kept a journal or liked writing anything down so this and the pro and con list is a no go. I sit down in my chair with my eyes close. When I open them, I look at the rest.

It is important to share these feelings with people whom you trust. "Not ready for that just yet."

Continue working, "No." Enjoy leisure activities that give me pleasure. "Done that."

I am not about to continue working since time is now precious and it's my time, not the companies.

What I do though is continue to keep my appointments and do whatever they suggest even though I know it is just putting a band aid on my illness. There is no cure, but somehow it does help to know they are there for me and will be there when I need help in managing the pain.

I come to the realization that there is something I am missing and that something is a way to heal my soul. As I ponder ideas it becomes apparent that this can only be done by someone who really knows what it is like. Someone who has cancer and is also facing death.

How horrible is that. But it is true. My cancer peers are the ones who can help me.

I go into the office and sit at the computer. I open the desk drawer and pull out the card that my brother gave me. I turn it over and over in my hand until finally I lay it on the desk in front of me, click on google and in type gildasclubrochester.org in the search engine. I press enter and then lean back on my chair and wait.

For the next half hour I read the information on the website. Everything I read says this is a legit operation for men and women living with any type of cancer.

It says, 'We have a small group setting, moderated by a licensed facilitator'. That appeals to me.

I surf the internet and locate information from real people who have been to Gilda's. I'm pleased with what I find.

One person writes, 'It's a place to share concerns and laughter as you learn how others cope and respond to the challenges of a cancer diagnosis'.

I think about that, then say, "What the heck. Can't hurt." I jot down the address, date and time of the next meeting and set a reminder. That decision made, I spend the rest of the day packing the car with cast offs from the attic and taking them to Goodwill where they will serve a purpose instead of cluttering my attic.

The following Tuesday evening I walk up to a red door on a brick building. I look around. "Stop it Parker. What does it matter if someone is watching." I move up closer to the door and push it open. I step across the threshold of the building on Alexander Street that is waiting to provide me comfort.

Inside it is well lit and colorful with many doors. From what I have read I know there are a lot of activities going on so it stands to reason they would have designated rooms. I continue down the hall and I find myself standing in front of the door of the room where the cancer group is meeting.

I start to push it open but stop. I take a deep breath and try again. I open the door and step inside.

At first, I just stand there looking around. I see there are several people already inside. They are standing over at a table that has a coffee urn and cups. I give myself a few more seconds.

I pull my eyes away from the social group and check out the rest of the room. In my head I pictured a gymnasium with metal chairs in the middle, arranged in a circle. Not so. It is a comfortable size room with winged back chairs, a coffee table with what looks like magazines, and several end tables strategically placed near the chairs.

"Hello. I haven't seen you before."

I jump, surprised when I hear a voice behind me.

"Oops, sorry, didn't mean to scare you. I'm Alice."

I turn and plant a smile on my face. "Sorry, I was deep in thought. Didn't hear you come up."

"So," Alice says, sticking out her hand, "Welcome."

"Thanks. And in reply to your question, Yes. I'm Parker and this is my first time here."

"Well, you can get coffee or tea," she says moving her arm from her side and pointing at the table, "and a snack. On the end of the table you will see a marker and a name tag."

"Oh, okay. Thank you."

I walk gingerly over to the table, fix a cup of coffee and take two cookies. I move to the edge of the table and fill out a name tag. I paste it over my shirt pocket, like I see the other men have done.

As I head over to the meeting area others follow with their coffee and snacks. Everyone is smiling and saying, "Hi." I take this as another good sign.

When we are all seated, light banter is going on between individuals that I assume have met before. The atmosphere is comforting and I feel myself relaxing.

The door opens, and all eyes turn in that direction, watching as a tall woman, made taller by the high heels she wears makes a grand entrance. Her hair is pulled back into a ponytail that bounces with each step. She wears black rim glasses that hide her eyes at first, but when she finally reaches the group, I can see they are hazy blue. I put her at somewhere in her late forties or early fifties.

No one says a word as she sits down comfortably in one of the open chairs. "Hello everyone. My name is Jennifer Platt." As if on signal, the door opens again and a man enters. He is short, heavyset with grey hair and a smile that accentuates the winkles on his face.

"Sorry friends. I got delayed a bit." He looks over the group, smiles and adds, "My name is Howard Williams." Instead of coming to join us, he walks over to the coffee table and fixes a cup.

Somehow his motion has us all looking seriously at each other as if judging him for wasting our time. Once Mr. Williams is seated, Ms. Platt welcomes each person individually. I hear my name being called after she talks with Mr. Rodenhouse who is a new member too.

"Yes?"

"Mr. Parker, you are new here. I want you to know you are welcomed and we are glad to have you with us. I am the facilitator and Howard," she turns toward him then back to me, "is an Oncologist, here to answer any medical questions."

I nod my head and say, "Thank you."

She continues, "Most of you have been here before and are aware of what we do but let me ask Mr. Parker and Mr. Rodenhouse if they have any questions before we begin."

"Mr. Parker?"

"It's just Parker. Not really, I found a good overview on your website. I did miss one thing though."

"Yes, what was that."

"Why it's called Gilda's Club."

I try to ignore the smirks on the faces of the others seated around the room.

"It's one everyone asks. The name is in honor of the comedienne Gilda Radner, who battled ovarian cancer in 1989, It is our legacy to her and a point from which we can look back and realize how much more can be done for those diagnosed with cancer today."

I like that explanation and now remember Gilda Radner. "Thank you."

"You are so welcome. Now, Doug, do you have any questions."

An elderly man in the front row slowly raises his hand as if making sure everyone knows it's him. The lighting in the room did not do justice to his wrinkled face and sallow complexion. His eyes were barely visible beneath the fold of skin above them. But his mouth spoke volumes. It was easy to tell that he has adjusted to the truth when in a surprisingly strong voice he says, "I am here because I am old and I'm dying."

A hush falls over the room as each person looks in his direction. I can feel the love and instant connection felt in their gazes and I am impressed by how easily he announces this to perfect strangers. and I again feel comforted.

"We are all dying a little at a time every day," Jennifer says. "and none of us are ready. I'm glad you're in the class. Here you can relax and talk freely among friends, away from the pressures of daily life and without having to be guarded or act normal about having cancer."

Suddenly the entrance door opens. All eyes sweep in that direction to watch as a gangly young man burst into the room. He tries to step forward, but flies back against the door, his coat edge locked tightly in the frame. Shaking, he quickly turns and pushes the door open; hesitates as if wondering whether to ward off the embarrassment by just leaving, then turns back around looking confused.

In a shaky voice he says, "Is this the painting room…I mean the room where we paint?"

At first I hide a grin, trying my best not to appear judgmental, but when the first sound of laughter fills the room, I can't help but join them. So much for tact, I think as I watch the man flee the room.

To focus the group, Jennifer informs us that there is a class tonight that is using paints to express grief, tension, fear and anger. This is especially helpful to young people who are dealing with cancer and unable to openly express their feelings.

I can feel the shift from jovial to understanding fall over the rest of the people in the room. This should have settled me, but I can't stop the need to laugh. It's like a bomb inside me that needs to explode. The more I try not to laugh the more I want to. I look around to see who else is trying to suppress laughter, but everyone I glance at seems to have sobered after hearing the man's situation.

Why are they being like that, I wonder. If we can't laugh at ourselves then what else is there. I let go. My body is completely out of control in a fit of laughter my extremities flail aimlessly, as I gasp for breath, collapsing hard against the back of my chair.

I stare at the stiff faces around me as tears roll down my cheeks, not caring what they think. Out of the corner of my eye I see a woman sitting off to my left. I can tell before she does, that she is going to laugh with me.

"Sorry," I say to the group as I quickly get up and leave the room.

13

I'm feeling good even though the last report is that the cancer has spread to other parts of my body. I have been aware that there are no methods to permanently cure my metastatic gallbladder cancer so the goals are to slow the spread of the cancer, shrink the tumor and extend my life for as long as possible. I now have a palliative care team to help relieve symptoms and side effects.

What they are doing is working because my pain is minimal so I decide to give kite flying another chance. I purchase a brightly colored kite made out of a plastic instead of the paper-thin material of my old one and after eating lunch I goes out on the beach for its maiden voyage.

It's not a great day for kite flying, but I try anyway. I run and sing, ignoring how hard it is to get the kite in the air as it dances around barely above my head before it falls into the lake.

"Damn."

I don't even try to retrieve it, instead turn and walk down the beach toward home.

I sense movement off to my right and turn to see the same old man I saw before. I stare openly in his direction and see that he is slowly shaking his head back and forth. I can't help laughing as I continue on my way.

Back in the house I get out a beer and sit at the island staring out the window, wondering what I should do next. I admit I do know what I should do, but I hesitate.

I finish my beer and walk to the back door to stand for a moment, wanting to just go out and sit on the deck instead of dealing with reality. Finally, my senses kick in and I move into the front room where I keep my laptop. I turn it on and ignoring all the email message notices, I open up a word document.

It's quiet as I commence typing.

My sons, I am leaving this for you to read after I am gone. Forgive me for not being around you more in my last year but someday you will understand.

I stop typing after the word *understand.* When I was a kid I hated it when someone told me that I would understand someday. It is a stupid thing to say.

I thinks about my sons and question if they will wonder why I never left them a letter that addresses their questions and articulates feelings about life.

I ponder that thought. They still have their mother and from the way things are going, they will have a step father to guide them. Why would they need some dead man to give them advice?

Angrily I give up. I close the laptop and just stare at it before finally leaving the room. In the kitchen I get out another beer. I admit that I am feeling restless and guilty that I couldn't write the letter.

I can't force it because the only reason to write such a letter is to say something important and enlightening that is personal for their eyes only.

"Give yourself a break Parker. You can write it later." I have now broken two of the rules for cancer patients. Number one is to write the letter and number two is to not put things off until later.

I know it needs to be done, but I can't do it now. I turn on the television and surf through the channels until I find a football game.

14

I find myself sitting on the curb trying not to get too hyper. "When was the last time I had a flat tire," I say to myself as I call Triple-A.

I look around, hoping for a better place to wait, but there is nothing. I am in the middle of nowhere with no restaurant or even a gas station. "Figures," I grumble.

I'm thankful there is enough of a shoulder so that the car is totally out of the driving lane, so I do not have to worry about getting side swiped.

Not seeing any alternatives for comfort, I open the passenger side door and leaving it open, climb in to wait for the tow truck.

***

I was twenty-four when I and Cameron got married. She was twenty-two and beautiful. She was the second person that I had fallen in love with.

My first love came into my life when I had just turned 18. She had red hair, a high squeaky voice and not much of a figure but I had the biggest case of puppy love for her anyone could ever have. It was my freshman year in college and she was all I thought about all year even though I could not get a date with her.

During my sophomore year my fraternity brothers were getting pinned and engaged right and left. I thought it stupid to make permanent commitments like that when we were all experiencing being on our own and learning about life. How was a man supposed to know who else was out there and what possibilities were yet to be discovered?

Still I was interested in the red-haired girl. Only I admired her from a distance and she would never know how she filled my heart and soul during those first years of college. Eventually she faded out of my life, though she never really was a part of it.

I played it smart. I graduated from college without any prior commitments and knowing what I needed to do if I was to become a stockbroker. While my fraternity brothers were taking time off, I got an entry level position at Scottrade. I needed at least seven hundred dollars to sit for the exams and this would meet two requirements. Once I passed the exam I had to work at a firm within two years from the date I passed the test or I would have to take them again. Luckily, I was able to get in at Scottrade

I wasn't rich, and my family had struggled to help me pay for college. I couldn't ask them for more help. So, while my friends partied, I sat for the General Securities Representative Exam, Series 7 and passed. Then being new to the securities business, I studied and sat for the Commodity Futures Exam.

Knowing I wanted a position in New York I sat for the Uniform States Laws Exam and the Uniform Registered Investment Advisor Exam. It took time, but when I finally interviewed I was immediately hired as a stockbroker at Scottrade. I was on my way.

When I met Cameron, I was a successful young man by anybody's standards. I made good money, wasn't bad looking and the coup de grâce; I was ready to settle down.

But I did lack an education in one area…dating. I hadn't dated since high school and a lot had changed since then. I also had lost touch with my close friends, so I couldn't ask anyone for advice. Though I was ready to get married, I hadn't a clue how to go about it.

We met each other through mutual friends and hung out a lot, but slowly realized our friendship was turning into something else. So, we decided to have an official date.

That first date we met for brunch, which turned out to be the best first date idea for someone you already kind of know. I actually wasn't sure if we were on a date until the day turned into a day-long excursion around the lake and Durand Eastman Park, just talking and enjoying each other's company. From then on, we were together every chance we got. I was smitten and when I finally got the nerve to ask her to marry me, she said, "Yes."

We went on a cruise for our honeymoon. It was the first time I realized how comfortable a person can be with someone they love. A year later Nolan was born and four years later came Jonathan.

I had worked hard all my life so that I could give my family everything. We got a dog and purchased a four bedroom colonial and furnished it with the help of an interior decorator. The boys went to the best schools and I sprung for expensive class trips and sports events. We were living the American dream.

***

I am startled awake by the beeping of the tow truck as it positioned itself in front of the car. It takes me a minute to remember where I am and another to focus. Finally, I get out of the car.

"Hi guys," I say. "I need a tire change, not a tow."

"Yes, we know. We'll have you back on the road in a few."

I nod, close the car door and move back out of the way. I take out my cell and look through the messages. I then check out the news.

"You're all set Mr. Parker."

"Thanks guys."

"You're welcome."

I wait while they climb back into the tow truck and pull back on the road. When they are out of my sight range, I finally climb into my car and ease back on the highway.

There is literally no traffic as I continue driving. It is so relaxing to just steer; especially in the outskirts of the suburbs where there is great scenery and little traffic to contend with. Of course, it kind of bites you in the ass when something like a flat tire happens, I reflect.

Now, back on the road, my thoughts return to my family. We did have some good years of marriage. That wedge between us happened slowly. So slow it was not noticeable in many ways until it was too big a gap to close.

In subtle ways Cameron seemed to change. She used to love going to carnivals and ride the roller coaster with me and the boys. We would each take one and climb into the cars near each other. I would hear her scream and laugh with our sons. Once we were back on the ground she would give them playful punches and tell them to stop laughing at her.

When the boys were big enough, she stopped going and it was me alone with them who went to the carnivals. Even a simple family outing was something she would say, "Why don't you and the boys go."

Cameron had majored in art history and loved to paint and visit museums. It was not my thing, but I would always go with her. I loved to hear her tell about the famous paintings on exhibit or talk about the way the painter showed light and shadow. But as far as I knew, Cameron hadn't gone near a museum in the last ten years.

I wonder if it is me that has changed or whether I am responsible for the change in her. I feel like the same person I have always been, but maybe she sees a difference.

It's funny I am thinking about this now and I wonder why I never asked her what was wrong or why she never talked to me about it. What I did know was that I and Cameron loved each other, but out of habit over the last four or five years of the marriage our passion died and with it the need to be with each other.

It was quick, yet shocking when the last bond between us simply separated and the final string was gone.

I was pulling into my driveway when I thought about our conversation to try a trial separation. We both knew there would be no trial about it. We would never get back together as a couple. Any contact would be because we were still parents.

How did I feel about that, I wondered. At the beginning of the separation I would say I was devastated, but now…

Still thinking about what use to be, I return home. I contemplate what went wrong with our relationship and decide it was because I loved Cameron too much from my head and not my heart. I thought about how she was at twenty-two and then at thirty-five. She was two different people. That had me wondering if the red headed girl would have changed too.

I stood at the fridge filling a glass with water and deliberated. Would Alexander and Cameron start out as two crazy in love people who got married and lived happily never after or would they have the magic to make their marriage last.

"Good question," I mutter in the quiet of the house. "Good question, but it doesn't matter". I would not be around for the final chapter.

I drink my water, leaning on the island and just like that, I decide it's time to see the family.

I take my cell out of my pocket and call Cameron. She picks up on the first ring.

"Cameron, I was wondering if I could stop by this evening and talk to you and the boys."

There is silence on the line, but then finally she says, "Yes, of course Parker. I have been waiting for you to call."

That done, I feel satisfied with myself.

15

Dr. Martin Henderson's office is the same as it was on the day I got the results of my lab test but Martin now seems more relaxed as we sit and talk.

"How did it go telling the family."

"Quite easy since they had an inkling something was wrong." I pause, "Don't worry, I know you didn't tell them. Cameron just knew something was wrong; maybe not how bad it was, but she knew."

Martin nods.

"Talking to the boys was a lot easier than I thought it would be." I added. "It was like the words just flowed from me and they seem to understand."

"It's easy to forget kids have a lot less preconceived fix on how things ought to be. You tell them something honestly and they nod while you wonder if they have heard you. Then, before you can turn around they are talking about something they made in school."

"Yes, you're right. It's like we translate the meaning differently than they do. Life and death are not white and black in their world." I yawn and then apologize. Cameron and I had stayed up most of the night talking.

Martin raises his eyebrows then asks, "how did it go with Cameron."

"God that was one weird conversation to say the least. She was ready though, I have to hand it to her. Most men would be upset that their wife was planning for their demise, but not me. Cameron and I had to check the details of our taxes and insurance and stuff. We even talked about whether it would be best for us to get the divorce or continue as we have been knowing that she would soon be a widow."

Seeing the expression on Martin's face, I quickly added.

"I know that sounds horrific, but I didn't want to go through a divorce and neither does she. Why not admit this was a blessing in disguise."

Martin leaned in toward me, then bluntly said, "You still feel guilty because you're dying don't you."

At first I am shocked by his outburst, but realize it is true. "Yeah. That plus I am still a little angry about that."

"You know how little sense that makes don't you."

"Yeah."

Martin shrugs and starts putting papers into a big manila envelope. When he is done he hands it over the desk to me.

"What's this?"

"Copies of lab reports and your medical records with all my notes. These are in addition to what I sent earlier. You can have your Oncologist contact me any time of course, but I want them to have a good background on you from the start."

"Are you saying I won't be seeing you again, Martin."

"No, we're still going to get together." Martin gets up and goes over to his desk. "Oh, yes, here are a few books you might want to read. One is on cancer itself and the other has terminal cancer patient stories of coping."

I keep still about the fact I probably already have the books, but trying to add a little humor I say, "Thanks, but I don't know when I can return them. I may never pass this way again."

"Keep the books. That's funny. You know there's probably only one other thing that I can do for you".

"What?"

"Take you to Red Robin for a turkey burger. That's still your favorite place, right?"

"Yes, it is."

"Well, let's go."

16

That night I laid in bed for a long time thinking, unable to sleep. My mind is in turmoil, going over all the changes I know I must deal with until finally I drift off.

The next morning my resolve is the first thing that comes to mind as I go about getting myself ready for the day. When I pour my first cup of coffee, I carry it with me to my computer and wait while it boots up.

Words tumble in my head. How do I say it best, I wonder. As I click on the Word program, surprisingly it all becomes clear.

Words cannot begin to express how deeply sorry I am for the hurt that I have caused. There is no defense for what I did to cause our separation.

First, I apologize to you Cameron and Jonathan and Nolan for my actions that lead to our separation. There's not a single day that goes by where I don't wish I could undo the damage I know this caused, and I am so happy that you, Cameron found happiness again.

To my family, I apologize for the trauma you faced and may still feel. I know that current circumstances can make this an ongoing sentence you serve because of me. I am sorry to my friends who were betrayed by everything I hid from them and all the hardships I caused people by breaking all lines of communication. The cliché "It's not you, it's me", is true in this case. My only defense is that in dealing with the aftermath, I responded toward many of you with bitterness that I should have directed toward myself. I know that I can't undo the animosity I brought our way, but I hope this message will mend what I can now and as time goes on.

To my sons, who looked up to me, I let you down in so many ways. I tried to show my best side to you, but hope that the great memories we had in the past will brighten each day. I want you to both respect your mother, Alexander and each other. Our separation came not because I don't love the three of you. I do. It happened because I was living a life that lacked empathy and viewed everything through a self-motivated lens.

I don't have much time, but the time I have I would like to know I can share it with all of you. You are in my life, my heart and my thoughts.

I am so thankful that all of you have been a part of my life,

Parker

I let out a breath as I lean back in my chair. I know I should read it through for errors, but decide against it. In a sense I am leaving it all up to Cameron to share with those concerns as well as our children. I save a copy and then open up my Outlook and create a new message to Cameron. I then cut and paste my document into the body of the email.

I lean back hard against my chair and stare at the email. "It has to be done now."

Slowly I move my mouse over the screen and press, Send.

TRINITY HUNTER

Epigraph

You have to walk carefully in the beginning of love; the running across fields into your lover's arms can only come later when you're sure he won't laugh if you trip.

Jonathan Carroll,

SPRING 2016

17

Dr. Glenn Scott recalls the first time he met Trinity. She had told him that his eyes seemed intense behind his glasses as if he was trying to see through her. He had heard that before. He based it on the fact that he had a habit of trying to study each patient as they entered the room. His eyes being dark, reflected their image and thus giving the impressing that he was looking through them. At least that's how he saw it.

Today in preparation, Dr. Scott has set a fresh box of Kleenex on his desk. He is just about to take a seat when the door opens, and Trinity walks confidently into the room, her thick dark hair bouncing. He tries to avoid looking into her almond shaped eyes, knowing they will be twinkling with anticipation, but he can't avoid seeing the dimples appear in her high cheek bones when she smiles widely in his direction.

He has known Trinity for some time now and over the years he learned a lot about her. She had shared with him that she had been the best athlete in her school and even now one could see that she had a spectacular athletic built. She was five feet eight and a half inches tall and she always wanted that half inch to be recorded on her chart. She'd even check to be sure it was there saying, "Someday when I'm old and shrinking I want proof of how tall I started out in case there is a contest to see who has shrunk the most, I have that half inch recorded and it could be the winning factor."

That's Trinity, a person who is seen as a fast talking, take charge business woman who can be pushy at times. Few get to see her fun loving nature side, but all who meet her see her as a woman who is very sure of herself.

Dr. Scott shifts in his chair and plasters a smile on his face. He has been in this seat before, giving bad news to a patient, but it bothers him now, more than ever before because Trinity is not one to expect bad news and he hasn't a clue how she will react. This is a thirty-five-year-old woman who is about to learn the worst that can happen to anyone.

This is like the time she told him her sugar level was high because the day before she had been a contestant in a pie eating contest for charity. He had added that her blood pressure level was up too. To that she responded, "Think about eating pies, lots of them until you want to vomit, but you don't. Others do and that should be a mark against them. But, oh no, it was not because I got second place, while the guy next to me who had vomited more than once, won. I was so mad I picked up the pie I was eating and smooched it into his stupid face." To that, Dr. Scott could think of nothing to say.

He keeps a smile on his face as she walks toward him and takes the seat in front of his desk. Once she is seated, she tilts her head to the side, her lips pressed tightly, her eyes lifted and then straightens her body so that she appears taller. He knows that body language is saying, well, what is it. He takes a deep breath and begins.

"Trinity, I called you in because we need to review your test results."

"Okay. Fine. So, did I pass with flying colors?"

His throat tightens and he fights to keep his facial expression blank.

"No," he clears his throat, "well, not exactly."

***

I can't help hearing the hesitation in Dr. Scotts tone. It scares me, but only a little as I ask, "Should I be worried?"

Dr. Scott hides his eyes, trying to decide the best way to tell her. But there is no best way.

"Trinity you have a desmoplastic small-round-cell tumor. It is an aggressive and a rare cancer that primarily occurs as masses in the abdomen."

I am silent.

Dr. Scott is not sure she is hearing what he says. "It's rare; especially rare to discover this type of cancer in an adult female. It is considered a childhood cancer that predominantly strikes boys and young adults."

He wished he hadn't said all that, but he couldn't help it because there is no reaction from Trinity and he doesn't believe she is listening to him and he knows her well enough that not laying it out precisely will be the wrong path to take.

***

Actually, I am not able to absorb all of what I hear. I take my time, wanting to react intelligently. What comes out is far from that.

"What? What did you say."

"You have cancer."

Yes, she has heard right. I look up. My eyes glance around the doctor's office which is small but growing smaller by the minute until it looks as though there is not enough room to move around.

This can't be right. I don't have cancer. No way, not me. I stare at Dr. Scott with a grimace expression. Reaching at straws I tell myself the doctor is kidding, trying to make me pay for not keeping my earlier appointment. Yeah, that is it. My mind drifts back as I run my hand over the lump that had appeared quite some time ago.

It was small and hard and I knew it was there. My ex-husband knew it was there and so did my internist. Of the three the only one who showed any concern was my ex.

"What's that?" he asked. "I don't know," I said. "It's a lump," he said. "Think you're right." "Are you going to have it checked out?" "Sure," I said, and went to sleep.

I didn't rush as there was more on my plate at the time than getting a little lump looked at.

First I visited my internist, who said she wasn't exactly sure what this was and told me to contact my MD, Dr. Scott, who in turn said he wanted more tests and sent me to see a sarcoma specialist.

That should have set off alarms, but it didn't. That's what happens when you are in denial. I had no idea what a sarcoma specialist is, and I planned on going online to find out, but I had not gotten around to it. Now I am seated in Dr. Scott's office hearing the results of the tests, or at best his interpretation of the tests. Thinking that way makes me feel better.

"Trinity?"

I pull myself back and appropriately ask, "A what?"

"A desmoplastic small-round-cell tumor."

I let it sink in. He said a desmoplastic small-round-cell tumor. That doesn't sound threatening at all.

"Trinity, this is a rare tumor and not many family physicians or oncologists are familiar with identifying this tumor. I had a suspicion so that's why I had you see a sarcoma specialist. I called you in as soon as I had his results.

I am quiet, thinking. How can this be. I take good care of myself. Yes, sometimes I have to cancel an appointment or two, but I get around to it eventually. I try to eat right and don't smoke. I do like a little wine now and then, but nothing stronger.

I know this isn't helping, so I ask, "Okay, so what now?"

Dr. Scott hands me a pamphlet. "Here, Trinity, this is where I'm sending you next.

I take the pamphlet and look it over. It talks about the sarcoma center he is recommending for further treatment.

"Good. I'll look it over and give them a call."

"Trinity, you can't hold off. I want you to contact them immediately. The prognosis depends upon the stage of the cancer and from the reports I've received, your situation requires immediate attention."

I have been reading while he talked.

"Hey, doc did you happen to read this pamphlet. It says only 1 out of 100 lumps that are presumed to be harmless lipomas turns out to be a malignant sarcoma."

Dr Scott just stares at me. "If you consider our starting point is that of using probability to express the chance that an event of interest occurs, then a probability of 0.1, or 10% risk, means that there is a 1 in 10 chance of the event occurring. Here they are saying 1 out of 100."

Dr. Scott starts to interrupt her, but she raises her finger.

"I know what you are going to say, but answer me this. How many patients have you seen with this diagnosis?"

"No one. Just you. But…"

"No buts. So 1 out of 100 is pretty good odds. I can't be that unlucky."

One look at the doctor and I realize that he thinks my situation is critical and it makes me angry.

"Well I'm sorry but I think you're wrong."

Dr. Scott looks at Trinity and says, "I wish I were, but the report says I am right". He pauses. "Let me go over this with you."

"The report is wrong. You're wrong." I conclude dismissing the entire subject with a shrug. I know I am reacting to the shock and not the reality, but I didn't care.

Dr. Scott allows me to vent. I stop trying to be the authority, take a few deep breaths and listen.

"Okay, say you are right. What are my chances of beating this. And, be honest with me, doctor."

Not wanting to be negative, but knowing he must encourage Trinity to seek treatment immediately he says, "The prognosis is poor as you are in Stage IV. Like I mentioned, the tumors have grown large in your abdomen and metastasize to other parts of your body."

Dr. Scott looks once again at the lab reports trying to think of what to say next, but he can't add anything more to what he has already told her.

"I'm so very sorry Trinity, but the reports are accurate. You have cancer."

His words swirl around in her head. Stage IV! Positive! Metastasized!

I blurt out. "So what are you saying, exactly? Are you saying there is no hope for a cure? If that is what you are saying, how long do I have—five, ten, maybe fifteen years?"

Dr. Scott clears his throat. "No."

"No? No what? How long?"

He forces himself to look directly at her. "Maybe a year."

Trinity leans back hard in her chair as if someone pushed her. There is a stunned look on her pretty face and her eyes glare at Dr. Scott as she says, "It's out of the question," I reply with a fake laugh. "You got your files confused. The lab must have screwed up."

I can't sit still any longer so I stand up and pace around the room in front of his desk.

"Trinity. The report shows Trinity Hunter as the patient. I know this is a lot to take in, but it is important that you act quickly."

I can't believe it. I start ranting. "Five years I loved this guy. I wasted five years on him and what does he do. He calls me to tell me he got married a month ago."

I am not making sense, nor do I care. I pace faster and my voice raises several octaves until I am yelling. Through all of this Dr. Scott remains quiet.

Suddenly I stop and lean down to pick up my purse.

Dr. Scott, thinking she is planning to leave, starts to stand up, but before he can, he is startled when Trinity throws her purse against the far wall. Lipstick, gum, her cell, pens, and other items spill out.

I am shocked at what I did, but it felt good. I keep from looking at the doctor as I march over and quickly throw everything back in my purse.

But it is not over. I hear myself yelling. "A bunch of god damn stupid tests. You have me sitting in your tacky waiting room with the striped wallpaper and the back issues of National Geographic and Redbook then when you finally drag my ass in here you tell me I have a rare cancer and you try to tell me I'll be dead in a year."

I continue to rant with tears now spilling down my cheeks.

"You sanctimonious little juror. You think you're the only doctor in the world." I whirl around, charging out of his office and slam the door hard behind me.

Dr. Scott is frozen, unable to react and when he finally does, he hurries to the door. He hears his nurse trying to calm Trinity and speak to her. Though he doesn't hear what the nurse says, he does hear Trinity's responds.

"Make another appointment. You stupid old witch. Shut up and stay out of my way. Don't tell me to make another appointment. Why don't you go somewhere and get that wart removed."

I hate myself for being so mean, but I can't stop the rage consuming me as I turn and quickly walk across the tiled floor, my high heels echoing with each step until I reach the door of the reception room. I swing my purse over my shoulder and push the door open, watching as it closes behind me.

No one moves. The front reception area is almost full, yet there is complete silence. Dr. Scott walks gingerly, but is unable to reach Trinity before she sashays across the tiled floor to slam the office door shut. In the now silence of the reception area, a picture falls to the floor. The glass shatters and everyone in the reception room recoils.

18

I don't know how I drove home that day. It is all a blur. I have one thought in mind and that is to put an end to this day as quickly as possible, so I swing into the first open parking space in the vicinity of my apartment. I barely stop the car before climbing out and hurrying to my apartment door.

Did anyone speak to me on my way there? I don't know because I am in a world of my own.

Inside I look around as if expecting everything to have changed somehow. But it is all as I left it that morning. That infuriates me, and I swipe my arm across the counter sending condiments napkins and my leftover coffee in my morning cup, to the floor. It doesn't break!

"Damn!"

I hurry into the bedroom and take off my shoes, fling them across the room. I pull back the covers and climb into the bed, staring up at the ceiling until gratefully I fall asleep. That is how I ended the worst day of my life.

I am up early the next morning, unsure if all of this has been a dream until I move slowly across the apartment making my way to the kitchen. I stop as memories flood forward, but I remain calm.

I fix myself some coffee and force my mind to work on what I do next. I've never been in this situation before where I have to feel my way around, but finally I decide what the average person would do. Reach out to the internet.

It is so easy to search for where to start. I type seeking medical advice, afraid to put in 'that word' to tighten the search. I wait.

The first screen of sites to visit is worthless so I ask for more choices. I find a good source and thus begins my day.

By noon I learn that any time you have a very serious or life-threatening disease and the suggested treatment may be risky, or the diagnosis is not clear, it is time to seek a second opinion.

My next search is on how to seek second opinions. I pause to get another cup of coffee and when I return, scroll a bit and click on WebMD.

I have a large sip of my coffee when I read the first line. I *think we all want to be polite and civil and don't want to spark an adversarial relationship.* Memory serves me well as coffee flies out of my mouth and onto the computer screen as I laugh out loud. The last thought on my mind had been being polite.

When I stop laughing at the irony, I read further and see that it is a must to let Dr. Scott know I want to get a second opinion because I need my records, pathology slides and test results to share.

I am in agreement.

I am proud of myself for researching this before going blindly out there wondering what to do or where to go. I even find information on health plans and what is covered.

I lean back in my chair thinking there may be hope as it is not uncommon to have a misdiagnosis. I need hope.

I haven't eaten all day and am beginning to feel the first pangs of hunger. I get up and go into the kitchen and fix myself a sandwich and pour a large glass of water. Once seated I know I am ready and I used the word, cancer, in my next search. Later that day I am into putting not only the word, cancer, but the full name of the cancer diagnosis.

I stumble across a website called Partners Online Specialty Consultations. I click on several links and end up at Partners Online Second Opinions (POSO). I continue my searches, reading with interest. I know there's a lot of junk on the Internet, but sometimes you hit a gold mine.

In one day I have managed to have a non verbal consult. I have visited The Cleveland Clinic, Johns Hopkins, The Mayo Clinic and some less popular medical sites. I am now ready to do a face to face.

I am not willing to waste any time as I make a call to Dr. Scott to obtain my records. He graciously has a packet waiting for me with his receptionist, who seems a little intimidated by my presence. I don't blame her.

Later that day I have three appointments set up. The X rays the analyst blood samples the ultrasounds and the CT Scans all begin to blur together in my mind.

I go from one specialist to another. Sit with medical teams to review their findings, keeping an open mind until there is no denying the opinions.

"You have what is called, desmoplastic small-round-cell tumor."

"Please, no"

"I've read every report and we all support the finding. It's not well known. It's a soft tissue sarcoma tumor and it is rare to find it in adult females of your age."

I have exhausted all possible options. There is no one else to call. It is time I admit my fate. When I first heard that I had a sarcoma, I thought, "But it could be wrong." When I have seen five sarcoma specialist and get the same report, well, it's time to believe.

The next step is to choose who will handle my case. They are all excellent but of the five I felt very comfortable with one. He was the one who pushed aside all the sarcoma talk and said the word, Cancer when I talked about alternatives in surgery and radiation.

During the weeks that follow, I receive books to read. I learn a desmoplastic small-round-cell tumor is an aggressive and rare cancer that primarily occurs as masses in the abdomen, just as Dr. Scott said. Other areas affected may include the lymph nodes, the lining of the abdomen, diaphragm, spleen, liver, chest wall, skull, spinal cord, large intestine, small intestine, gallbladder, brain, lungs, testicles, ovaries, and the pelvis.

"Whew, why not just say, every organ in the body."

I make notes to ask questions about how far my cancer has spread. Exactly to what organs and what can be done to stop the spread.

But the biggest problem I have is accepting why in this day and age I can't find one doctor who can do a simple thing like save my life.

At the last doctor's office, I asked, "Can you buy me some real time with something?"

He had responded, "No."

Wanting to end on a positive note and not show her colors, she asked, "Well then, can you validate my parking ticket?"

19

I am a thirty-two year old woman and I am being told I have terminal cancer. And the doctors, all of them tell me even with treatment my life expectancy is a year or more. That means a year at the most; only they won't say that.

Leaving that last doctor's appointment, I walk down the street holding back the tears and the desire to scream. I keep myself in control by telling myself I must set it all aside for now. And as luck will have it, I find the perfect way to do it. I stop in front of a bar; not an upscale bar, but not that bad either.

I open the door to find itt is dimly lit, and it takes a minute to adjust my eyes before I can see my way over to the bar and find an empty stool.

Once seated, I glance around. The place is scarcely populated and there are lots of empty seats. That is fine with me.

"What can I get you?"

The voice startles me at first, then looking at the bartender I reply, "A bloody Mary." It just pops out, like I knew before I said it. I usually drink wine.

"A bloody Mary it is."

The bartender turns around and I watch as he makes my drink. When he sets it down in front of me, I manage a smile. "How much?"

"That'll be $8.00."

I take out my wallet and hand him some bills. "Keep the change."

He thanks me and takes off down the bar where a man has just entered and sat down.

I turn back around to concentrate on my drink, stirring the contents with the stalk of celery and watching the liquid ripple in the glass. When I finally pick the glass up to take a sip I am aware of another body near me. I turn and see that it is the man who was talking with the bartender.

He smiles and I stare at him, taking in his cheap suit and the stink of too much cologne.

"What is your name," he asks spreading out the words in an annoying way.

"Cancer", I hear myself say. "Ms. Cancer."

The man stares dumbfounded.

"Like the disease," he asks.

"No, I am the disease."

Without another word, the man picks up his drink and moves back to his seat further down the bar.

I finish my drink in silence and know that getting drunk is not going to make me forget . It's imbedded in my mind now. If I sit here and drink until I can't think anymore, all that will get me is trouble. I take one last look around then slowly get off the bar stool and head for the door.

Outside in front of the bar I place a call to Dr. Scott.

"Dr. Scotts office, Lydia speaking."

"Can I speak to Dr. Scott. This is Trinity Hunter."

"One minute."

I am on hold for less than a minute. "Hello Trinity. Are you all right?"

"Yes, I'm fine. I wanted to tell you I am ready to proceed.

That done I head to my car, walking confidently, my mind less cluttered.

When I climb into the car, my hands are shaking so I rub them together and wait. I sit in silence thinking that it is okay to be shocked and emotional; especially since I am facing this alone. But no matter how upset I feel, it is not going to go away, so I have to face it head on. Finally, I confidently turn the key and start backing up.

I drive through the parking garage a different person than when I entered. Here I am an accomplished business woman who has met challenges head on and overcame them. Only this... My heart skips a beat at the realization I have walked into something I cannot handle.

"God, why me?" I say, braking at the garage exit. The reality surrounds me now. I am a cancer patient. The car behind me honks, but I ignore it as my head fills with all sorts of visions. It's like I can feel the cancer inside me reaching out and attaching itself to each of my body organs. "This can't be happening to me!"

I am overcome with an inconsolable crying fit that chokes me up with emotional intensity. I put my head down on the center of the steering wheel while my hands pound furiously on the sides. "Why, why, why."

Slowly I manage to pull myself together and react to the honking going on behind me by wiping my eyes and brushing my arm across my running nose. I put my foot on the accelerator and the car moves forward. At the end of the drive I check both ways and maneuver the car out into traffic.

I drive to my neighborhood Wegmans where I pull into the parking lot and find a place up close to the entrance to park. I take a quick glance in the rearview mirror and see I need some damage control as I work on my face before climbing out and going into the store.

Once inside, I move robotically down the aisles picking up items and stopping at the frozen food section to get a lean cuisine for dinner. I am not in the mood to cook anything.

With my purchases in plastic bags, hanging from each arm, I make my way to my car thinking how wasteful it is to not use my reusable grocery bags and for no logical reason I begin to sob and cry at the same time.

When I've stowed the groceries in the trunk, I slip behind the wheel, looking around at all those people who will benefit from my years of being cautious of the environment and I start to bawl again.

When I finally get hold of myself, I turn the key and head toward home.

That evening I try to eat my meal, but my stomach fights against me. I keep struggling desperately ignoring the pain in my stomach and the hurt in my heart. My stomach wins as I rush to the kitchen sink, vomiting more out than I have managed to put in.

With my head in the sink and my stomach lurching I wonder, who is this girl. My hands shaking, scared to death of what life remains in front of me.

This is not how I saw my life ending. I try desperately to take my mind off my problems as I go into my bedroom and put on a jogging suit and sneakers. I grab my spare key off the hook by the door and step outside.

The warm evening air lifts my spirits as I hurry down the steps and onto the sidewalk. For a moment I stand there wondering what I am doing. Why am I eating lean cuisine dinners and now going for a run. I let out a gasping laugh at the irony.

I run with tears flowing unchecked from my eyes. I run down the sidewalks of East Avenue sobbing uncontrollably as I pass the George Eastman House, where I have to wait to cross the street to continue. I prance around waiting for the light to change, then start running again. I run down Park Avenue in a daze, my eyes so full of tears I can barely see around me. But I have made this trip so many times it doesn't require thought or sight. By the time I reach the Rochester Museum & Science Center, I am calmer and work my way back on East Avenue to head home.

My hand trembles as I struggle to put the key in the lock, but it is not because my mind is on the cancer now, but because I have tired myself out. When I finally cross the threshold, I head toward the fridge, get a glass of water and stand at the sink drinking it, feeling more like myself.

My body is sufficiently warmed and I wipe sweat from my face as I make my way across the room to the wine rack where I randomly pick out a bottle of wine. I take it over to the counter and getting out the bottle opener, I struggle a moment until finally succeeding in removing the cork.

I reach for a glass, then change my mind and go over to the china cabinet, to take out one of my fancy wine glasses. I smile as I pour the wine. "May as well use them," I say out loud.

I take my first sip standing in the kitchen. It feels wonderfully relaxing. Moving around my apartment I stop to peer out the windows then close the shades as I make my way into the living room where I sit in my big comfy chair, turn on the TV and find a *Forensic File* episode. I lean back and allow myself to clear my head as I watch intensely while sipping my wine.

Its late when I finally get up and go to bed, but I can't close my eyes. I turn on my side and stare at the wall, knowing I can't sleep. I'm afraid to sleep and I'm not sure why. I toss and turn until I just get up.

I needed something to help me accept what was eating at me so I opened up the computer and clicked on google. When it opened, I hesitantly typed in the word 'cancer' and waited while the screen filled with articles on cancer, cancer institutes, what to do about cancer, etc. etc.

I opened the first item and started reading and when I finished I opened the next until I had gone through over half of the items showing on the screen. I paused to look at the clock and saw it was after midnight. I had plenty of time, but maybe I should try and refine my search. I thought about it and decided that I would start with finding out what may have gotten me in this situation to begin with.

Sure, it could have just been I was due for some bad luck, but I wanted to know for sure.

Again, there was a lot to choose from so I read the headings and made my picks. I opened a word document and begin taking notes on what I found because if I didn't, I would draw my own conclusions since I felt confident in my personal eating and living habits.

Every now and then a frown appeared as I read and when I felt confident I had covered most of it, I looked at what I had written. Drinking soda, bad for you. Eating fast foods, bad for you. No smoking. bad for you. Eating red meat often, bad for you. None of which I do. "That's no help."

So I turned to finding what is good and my list included eating organic meals, drinking water and tea, and juice, take multivitamins daily, read the ingredients on shampoo and hair care products… "What?" I highlighted the last two.

Days pass and I sit around in my night clothes searching the internet and taking notes. I don't answer the phone or follow any of my normal routines as I search for the whys and the hows of controlling hat time clock on my head.

Some days I become so overwhelmed I indulge myself with a pity party, reprimanding myself for all the things I did not do with my life or my time. It gives me the comfort I need to go on.

I live off wine and yogurt for a disturbingly long period of time, until finally I remind myself that I am a strong person and as a mentally strong person I must face reality because it won't go away. I have to stop thinking that I am suffering more than anyone else. I have to get through this.

That thought makes me laugh, "Well it won't take long."

That seems to do the trick because that night I climb into bed and I immediately drift off. The following morning, I wake feeling like my old self.

I get out of bed and stretch and for the first time I verbalize what I have kept inside. "I don't want to die."

20

Knowing what I don't want helps me to start living again. No more shut in I tell myself as I go into the bathroom. I brush my teeth, staring at my image in the mirror. My dark hair is snarly from lack of care so I search through the vanity and find my brush.

With my teeth clean and fresh I begin brushing my hair. It's like seeing myself for the first time as I focus on my image. I can feel my mood changing as I stare at my dull hair, and sunken dark eyes. I step back from the mirror. "Girl, you've lost weight!"

It's like a dark cloth falls over me enclosing my being from the world around and I start to panic.

Slowly I take several deep breaths, turn away from the mirror. I turn on the shower, moving the lever to hot and wait while bathroom fills with mist. I climb in.

"Oh," I say, "Hot, hot." I make the adjustments to the faucet.

Its soothing as I wash my hair and clean my body, all the time working on what I want to do with this day. By the time I climb out of the shower, I have a plan.

Wrapped in my big fluffy terry cloth robe I traipse into the bedroom and begin opening drawers until I have what I want to wear.

I concentrate on getting dressed but it's not enough of a distraction.

"Alexa, play 'This Girl is On Fire'."

The song fills my bedroom lifting my spirits and I can't help but dance around as I put on my clothes. I can still hear it as I go into the kitchen and get a smoothie out of the fridge. It tastes good as I stand in the kitchen enjoying it. When I am done, I rinse out the bottle and throw it into the recycle bin, then fix my first cup of coffee. The music stops and silence descends.

"Alexa, what time is it?"

"It's one o'clock in the afternoon."

I am shocked. I hadn't realized how long I'd slept and here the day is half over. "Well, I better get a move on," I said gathering up a jacket, scarf, and my keys before heading out the door.

The first sensation to greet me is the warmth of the sun and second was the hint of a breeze, carrying the scent of flowers and freshly cut grass. I climb into my car and carefully back out of the parking space, pausing a moment to admire the flowers that are blooming in front of the apartment building.

I drives carefully making several turns until entering I-490 E. A SUV up ahead is actually driving at the required 55 miles per hour, something that happens very infrequently. I wait for a semi to pass before pulling out in the lane and putting the SUV well behind me, only to find myself behind another slow-moving car. I quickly pull back out into the right lane, pass again, and swing back into the left lane just in time. The semi sounds his horn at me either pissed to be passed or giving me a 'good job' honk.

The further I drive, the less traffic there is. I shift lanes to take I-590 North, wishing I knew a more scenic route, but accepting the fact that I am making good time,

Up ahead I enter my first traffic circle and take the second exit to Sea Breeze Drive. I continue on for a short extent before entering the second traffic circle where I take the third exit onto Durand.

The scenery changes as Lake Ontario becomes visible. I enjoy the view as I progress to Sweet Fern Road, then onto Pine Valley Road before finally reaching Lake Shore Blvd.

There is a dramatic drop in the temperature as I drive along the lake, hearing the waves breaking on rocks off to my right. I roll down my windows so I can hear the sound of the water and the breeze messes up my hair. I love it.

Up ahead I see a parking space and pull over. I can't wait to get out of the car. It's not my first time seeing the view, but it feels different, more inviting to me now. Every one of my senses are alert. The warm air caressing my face, the breeze gently moving around me and the sun shining on the surface of the water that gently moves toward the shoreline.

I stare out at the sea gulls watching as they glide across the sky and wonder if they have always looked this beautiful.

The first twinge of hunger hits me and I wonder what time it is now. All I have had is a smoothie and it has worn off and though I want to just stay here, I regretfully return to my car and start driving down the road.

I know my way around and some of the areas restaurants. Up ahead I see the sign and ease the car into the parking area of the Pelican's Nest. I take a moment to straighten my hair before climbing out of the car.

It's not too busy in the restaurant at this time of day

so I am lucky and given a seat next to the window facing the lake. Most people are going to the food stands and eating on the shore, but I am too hungry for snack food. I've missed having a good breakfast or lunch so I need something substantial for my meal.

When the waitress comes, I place my order and then take in the waterfront view. "Miss, here's your food."

I have been daydreaming with my elbows on the table in front of me, supporting my head as I stare out the window looking out at the lake.

"Sorry," I reply, removing my arms from the table so that she can place the food in front of me.

Everything is good. I am halfway through my dinner when I look up and see a man coming over to my table. I don't want to deal with anyone so I try to look annoyed. At any other time in my prior life I would have loved to see a man approach me; but not now.

Trying to keep a stern look on my face is hard as he draws closer. I guess him to be over six feet and close to my age. He wears a tan linen jacket that accentuates his shoulders and when I look up he flashes a friendly and quite sexy smile.

"Excuse me," he says when he is standing directly beside my table, "but I see you're eating by yourself." God even his voice is sexy.

Taking care to not express any interest I reply, "I am."

"Well, I am too; except for this extremely boring book. Would you join me, so I can stop reading it?"

Good lead in, I think as I smile and wave my hand across the table. I watch as the man takes the seat, thinking he is definitely a ten.

Trying to be conversational, I ask. "So, what is

your book about?"

"It's a fascinating in-depth study on the complete history of scissors."

I can't help but laugh. He has a sense of humor and that's what I need so I join in.

"Well, that sounds fascinating. Always wondered about scissors."

It's his turn to laugh and he does with a deep resonant attractive sound.

His food arrives, and we spend the next fifteen to twenty minutes eating and making small talk between bites. He continues to entertain me with funny anecdotes and the time passes too quickly.

"Well, this has been nice. Thank you."

"I've enjoyed your company too. Do you have to leave?"

"Yes, I must."

I stand and pick up my belongings, then reach for my check. "No, it's my pleasure. Let me thank you for being such a wonderful eating companion."

"Are you sure?"

"Yes."

"Well thank you." I turn and head out the door and once I am on the sidewalk I laugh. This was a first. A stranger who never asked my name or shared one intimate detail, had given me a wonderful evening.

Back on the highway I feel reborn as I drive aimlessly enjoying what is left of the evening. With no plans, I drove all night long down suburban streets and out to the country where there were no street lights to brighten my way. I had no plans or any destination except to just drive. When I noticed the evening changing to light, I checked my gas gauge and headed toward the nearest service station. It would be a day to remember.

21

I gaze out the office window at the trees across the street from my psychiatrist office.

"Trinity, you never talk about your family. Why is that?"

"I don't have a family."

"You have a mother and a father. Tell me about them."

I am quietly thinking. Dr. Thomas Paterson is such a bland name and that thought makes me smile. He is bland, a person with no outward physical description beyond being a man who seems to survive on hearing others talk. He has a broad nose and I assume teeth though I have never seen them because his lips are always tightly closed even when he smiles.

I look up at the top of his head. He does have hair, though it is scarce behind a high forehead.

I decide his name fits his appearance well. I hear him clear his throat and remember he has asked me a question.

"Sorry, I…" I pause. "Please, Doc, I would consider it an act of mercy if you never reminded me again that I have a mother. You can't imagine what it took to become a sane adult with her in my life."

"But…"

"No buts. When I was a little kid I thought she was the most wonderful mother in the world, but then I grew up and realized what real mothers were like..."

"On to your next questions, doc."

"Okay, how about best friends. Do you have a best friend."

"That's a good question. I had a friend. Her name was Monique. She loved to tell me how alone I was with no family or friends. At first it hurt to hear her say that, but I realized why she did. You see, Monique was ugly and unlucky and knowing I am considered to be beautiful and things that I want I usually can get made her jealous."

"Hmmm…."

"Is that all you can say doc. I grew to hate her like every other non-friend I had and so I let her go. So, you can say I have no friends either."

I stood up and walked over to the window. "I would make a lousy shrink."

Dr. Paterson smiled, then caught himself. "I agree. I think you'd make a lousy shrink."

I had been coming to see Dr. Paterson for some time now, trying to understand myself. My need to see him was also one of the items stressed in my research on cancer that I was already doing.

I needed to understand why any joy I felt was always short lived. I wanted to find out what kept me from having any long relationships with woman or men and I was beginning to think it wasn't all my fault. If it was a fault at all. I turned toward the doctor who was examining me with serene but indecipherable eyes.

"So, can you tell me how you feel about learning you have cancer."

My head pops up and I feel anger creeping in. "How would you feel knowing that all the things you put off doing were now out of reach."

"Why do you say that?"

I can't help it. I laugh. "You can't be that ignorant!"

"I'm sorry. I didn't mean that. I guess what is bugging me now is why I am here. Is it because I want to be a well-adjusted corpse."

I look at him and stand. "I don't want to be mean to you. I like you, but this," I say sweeping my arms around the room. "This is not working anymore."

Dr. Paterson stands too, and I am surprised by what he says now.

"I understand. Because we psychiatrists don't encounter as much death among our patients as other physicians, death can become more poignant for us. My training is geared to preparing people for a life not death."

I am shocked at first then an acceptance comes over me. He's right; especially when I am so against any advice he has to offer.

I walk over and open the door.

"Wait Trinity, please take this."

I turn and watch as Dr. Paterson writes something on one of his cards and walks over, hesitantly holding the card

"What is it," I say as I take it. I look at what he has written, then look up in surprise when I read the name on the card.

SUMMER 2016

22

I consider myself somewhat of an expert on the décor in doctors' offices now and prefer the cold sterile type that gave no pretense of snugly warm and comfortable. But this one takes the cake.

The office is located on Park Avenue in Rochester and provides a little respite from the office traffic rush usually experienced in other areas. From the minute I enter I am taken aback by this old brick warehouse building that has been transferred into an almost all windows environment with a waiting area large enough for the philharmonic. Not only is the size impressive, it is all open with wall less office spaces facing the waiting area, allowing the light to shine through with no barriers and no typical ceiling, but one more like you see at a planet fitness; except sporting navy blue base with white ironwork.

Yes, there is the white, but it is offset with grays, tangerines, and even lime green carpeting visible in the offices.

They have converted this corpulent warehouse into a modern day facility with seating areas grouped together and highlighting colors of plum, gray and soft yellow. If one could use the word, 'swanky', that is the feeling I now have.

"Hello, my name is Dr. Proctor."

The voice comes from my left side as I stand in awe, my mouth hanging open and my eyes and mind drawn into the sight before me. Unaware of anyone approaching, I am disconcerted.

"Forgive me. I didn't mean to frightened you."

I recover promptly, chuckle and say "That's okay. I was admiring, ah, the building and didn't hear you come up."

I turn to face the man beside me, expecting to see someone in futuristic attire, but instead receive a pleasant shock.

He is disarmingly handsome. Looking at him it seems odd that he would choose the medical field. He should grace the stage with his charismatic presence.

He wears casual clothing that fits his broad, muscular frame and his curly black hair. Everything about him is noteworthy from his tanned skin, his startling white teeth and beautiful strange eyes, of a clear, pale amber.

He is the epitome of tall, dark and handsome.

I am shaken back to reality when I sense the movement of his hand as he extends it toward me and I take it.

"I'm Trinity Hunter." I say hearing my amazement causing my word to come out shakily. If he has noticed he doesn't show it as he smiles graciously and walking side by side we go halfway down the length of the building before he stops and motions me into one of the wall less rooms.

"Please, have a seat."

I feel like a star struck teenage and act like one as I miss judge the chair position and bend to sit only to end up falling on the floor. I am embarrassed as I see his hand extend and I take it. He easily pulls me up and I successfully place my bottom on the chair seat.

Thoughts run through my mind as I watch him as he makes his way behind a white melamine laminated desk with stainless steel legs. If the aim is to take my mind off my medical situation, the approach has been brilliant.

"So," Dr. Proctor says as he flips through a folder on his desk.

Not up to any more surprises, I stare at tab on the folder. It says, Trinity Hunter- DSRCT. I grin, able to easily translate the code for Desmoplastic Small-Round-Cell Tumor and the spell is broken. I become the fast-talking take charge business woman I have always been.

I interrupt him. "I've read a lot about my cancer, doctor. I know it's a nests of small round tumor cells within a cellular and vascular collagenous stroma and its rare to be found in an adult female. I know it is also known as desmoplastic small round blue cell tumor; intraabdominal desmoplastic small round blue cell tumor; desmoplastic small cell tumor; desmoplastic cancer; desmoplastic sarcoma; and DSRCT. Please feel free to use any of the nomenclatures," I add trying to be humorous.

Dr. Proctor graciously smiles. "I appreciate the fact that you've gotten some reading in on the subject. Thank you for sharing that with me."

"So what now, and please be direct."

"Obviously you are aware how aggressive, rare, and fast spreading this tumor is."

"Yes, I know there is no standard protocol for the disease however, recent studies have reported that some patients respond to high-dose (P6 Protocol) chemotherapy."

"Yes, true." He pauses having already determined that though his patient is trying to be tough, it is only superficial. He has seen this reaction before and he must not misread it.

"Unfortunately, Ms. Hunter, that is not an option in your case."

I am not about to give up. “Okay, what about cytoreductive surgery, or radiation therapy.”

Dr. Proctor shakes his head. “No, your cancer is too widespread. In fact it might even do you more harm than good.”

“I just thought that, maybe...”

Dr. Proctor stood and walked in front of his desk. He sits in the empty chair near me and leans close speaking gently.

“If you know enough to ask the questions you must know the answers.” He pauses. “Trinity; can I call you that?”

I nod.

“Trinity, you have a very aggressive cancer and it has formed multiple tumors in the tissue that lines the inside of your abdomen and pelvis. It has already spread to other structures within your abdomen. You are in the late stages and beyond surgery, chemotherapy or radiation therapy.”

He talks in a soft nurturing voice and I listen. I listen closely, but when it’s time to leave it’s not those words that follow me out. Its wondering how much that desk and this building costs.

23

By the next morning I am feeling revived, having taken care of what needed to be handled consoles me. When I open my eyes that morning my mind and body are relaxed and I can tell it is going to be a beautiful day.

Not wanting to waste a minute of it, I jump out of bed and hurry about getting ready. I enter the kitchen and drink a glass of water before stepping outside.

I take a moment to breathe in the warm morning air and then stretch a little before starting out on my run.

I find myself admiring everything around me as if seeing it for the first time. It's the same route I take each day, but I see things now with different eyes.

I pass Molly Madison who lives on the second floor and she waves at me. I wave back, wishing I had taken the time to get to know her. All the years I have lived in that apartment and I only have a blasé relationship with any of the tenants. We say hi, but I don't know them nor they me.

I start feeling weepy for having missed so much in my life because I had goals that seem silly now. It is clear to me I have little time and the wonderful doctors are only there to help alleviate the pain. They aren't family or friends which is what I need now.

Sweat mingles with the few tears that escape and I wipe them away, determined to get the best out of the day.

By the time I am back at my apartment, I know what I want to do. I grab a water bottle from the fridge and take it with me as I search for the box that holds the old photo albums.

I check the baskets under the bench in the hallway, but to no avail.

"Think, Trinity, think."

I continue searching and finally find what I am looking for on the top shelf at the back of the closet.

Memories flood my mind as I sit on the floor in the bedroom flipping through the old photo album until I find what I am looking for. "Ah, Monique."

I stare at her picture, trying to remember her husband's last name.

It's a quite common last name, but it seems to evade me at first as I test out several until finally I have it. Smiling, I get up, carrying the album with me.

I go over to my computer and put in the name, 'Monique Abernathy'. To my surprise, several choices pop up and I stare at them.

I get up and fill my water bottle, then return to the computer and start working my way through the choices, pausing when I see one that displays a husband's name too.

"God, what was his name…"

I can't help but smile now, remembering how people use to kid me about hanging on to 'all that old stuff'. It was about to pay off.

Carefully I flip to the back of the album where I stash those personal invites to weddings, birthdays and yes, even deaths.

The invites use to come often, but now I haven't had one in a long time and it's no mystery why.

Finally, I locate it. "You are cordially invited to the wedding of Monique Abernathy and Tom Clark."

"Ah, thanks for the internet. Back at the computer I begin my search. With a little initiative you can find anyone and anything on the internet. I keep searching and then finally I have it.

I write down the information and then pick up the phone to make the call. "What are you doing Trinity. What are you going to say to her."

I pause and think, smile at the simplicity of my decision and then dial the number.

"Hello".

"Hello, Monique. This is Trinity."

There is silence on the line and then a voice says, "Trinity, Trinity Hunter."

"Yes, it's me."

I allow her time to absorb the fact of this blast from the past. We had only seen each other twice in over 10 years since college, so she has a right to be shocked by my call. Like young female relationships, we had our differences over the years, and our lives had taken different paths, but we were grown now and hopefully none of it mattered.

I start, "So, what are you up to these days, Monique."

The conversation is full of one word responses at first, but soon we are talking easily, catching up with what has happened over the years, which for her is a lot, but not so for me.

"Remember how we use to talk about the future and I would say I wanted to wait at least 10 years before I got married and had any children?"

"Yes, I remember because I was right there with you on that."

"Well, as you know I got married in my junior year of college and broke the record by having a child. How about you."

"Still single, no kids."

"I have two now."

"Oh, I haven't seen either of your children."

And just like that I add, "Why don't I come over. I'd love to catch up."

I hold my breath.

"That would be fun, but we're moving to Boston and the house is upside down today. There's cardboard boxes stacked everywhere. It's a mess."

"I've seen cardboard boxes before," I try not to sound desperate. Hearing a friendly voice is even more important to me then I realized. At that moment I understand Dr. Scott's insistence to get in touch with loved ones and friends.

"Trinity listen let's have lunch before we move. You know I want to see you, just not today."

I feel dejected but determined to make this happen. I don't have time to put off anything until later.

"Oh, please Monique. I really want to spend time with you and see the kids."

Monique hears a strange tone in Trinity's voice. Trinity has always been so independent and uncommunicable. For Trinity to be begging to see her is so out of character. "Okay, come on over." She gives Trinity the address and starts to give directions.

"No problem, I have my GPS".

24

I waste no time as I dress and head out the door. I take a minute to put the address into my GPS and am on my way.

There is not much to see as I enter I-490 East and turn onto 590 north, but once I leave the expressways the scenery changes to that of residential homes on lush green lots. By the time I turn on to her street, I feel surprisingly settled.

I pull up in front of a contemporary home, park the car and climb out. I wish I had thought to bring something, flowers or wine, but it's too late now. I walk up and ring the doorbell.

The door opens and there is Monique. "Excuse the mess, Trinity, along with trying to get ready to move, I've been up to my armpits in kids."

"Don't worry about it. I'm not judging you." I look around. "This is beautiful."

"Tell you what, I'll give you a quick tour before all hell breaks loose."

I laugh and follow behind her.

"This is a Christian Leighton design home. I'm hoping to find a wide-open floor plan in our new home. Look at the coffered ceilings and with the two kids I love this wide-open floor plan and massive living space. Here's the dining area, and there is the kitchen."

I can barely keep up with her as she hurries through. "Office, and yes, here's the first-floor master with great built-ins. Look at the size of this closet and this bathroom," she says, stepping through another doorway. Before I can take it all in we are out and heading down a hallway.

"Here's the laundry room with tons of cupboards and counter space for storage. There are three additional bedrooms upstairs with two bathrooms," she says sweeping an arm toward the staircase as we pass on our way to the back of the house again. Out here is a pool, patio and over in back a studio or what I use as a greenhouse. That's it."

I start laughing, "That was quick but informative."

Monique laughs as she says, "I know, that's my life, quick and efficient."

We are back in the living room that is full of cardboard boxes. but I am looking at the baby standing in a playpen in the corner of the room.

"Monique she's absolutely beautiful."

"Yes, she is."

I turn to look at my old friend. She has changed for the better in every way possible. I had always thought her to be ugly, but she isn't. Monique is attractive.

I stare openly at her now with her hair tied up in a scarf and wearing a sweat shirt and jeans. Just looking at her I can see the love and compassion she exudes. The way she took the time to show me around and her expression when I mention her daughter was wonderfully soft and loving. She is very beautiful and has the kindest eyes that I have ever seen.

"I hope you don't mind if I continue packing while we visit. I just have so much to do."

"No, no problem. I'll give you a hand."

At that moment ten-year-old Aaron bursts into the living room.

"Mom," Aaron hollers.

Monique answers him and turns back to Trinity. "This will be fun," she says. "He's going through the difficult stages of boys. You know, from ages 3 to 38."

I laugh and soon see Aaron coming around the corner of a pile of boxes. The minute he catches sight of me, his smile changes and the loud boy is instantly attacked by shyness. His eyes drop to the floor and he begins to twist at a button on his shirt.

I watch as Monique goes over to give her son a hug and shoo him off to his own vices.

"Come on Trinity, let's take a break and have some wine. I'll go get us some glasses."

Monique leaves the room and I am alone with Aaron who is staring at me. "Hi Aaron, my name is Trinity."

Aaron just stares, making me uncomfortable so I look across the room at the baby and give a grateful sigh when Monique reappears. I have never felt comfortable around children and it's probably because I can't relate to them enough to know what they are thinking.

"Come on, Trinity, have a seat."

Monique moves stuff off the sofa and we sit down.

"So what is your baby girl's name."

"Oh, I'm sorry Trinity. Her name is Sonja. She's three, but she is tiny."

"Three is a great age." I pause. "For girls that is..."

We both laugh. "Would you like to hold her."

"Ah…Yes, I would," I surprise myself. I am not the baby holding type usually. I watch Monique walk over and pick up Sonja and soon I have a baby on my lap who is grabbing my hair and appears comfortable with me, a stranger.

I continue to hold Sonja as we talk about old times. During the midst of our conversation, Sonja takes her hands and places them on my cheeks, and I have all I can do to keep from crying as she smiles at me. In an effort to get in control of my feelings, I pat her little hands and then hand her over to her mother.

In that moment, Tom walks into the room. He leans over and gives his wife a kiss on the cheek and before she can say anything, he lifts his daughter into his arm.

Monique smiles up at him as she says, "Tom, do you remember Trinity."

As if unaware there is anyone else in the room, Tom looks over his daughter's head and smiles in my direction. "Yes, hello Trinity."

"Hello, Tom."

Just then Tom is grabbed around the leg by his son who runs quickly into the room. I watch as he reaches down to pat Aaron's head and then he looks over at us. "I'll give you two some time alone and take these monsters with me." Soon all three are headed up the stairs.

"I swear," Monique says, "Tom was so happy to have a boy, but I was overly ecstatic when the second one was a girl. That boy has so much energy. I love him, but I do need a break some times."

Monique finished her wine and got up. I followed suit and soon we were back to packing dishes."

We continue conversing about our college days until Monique says, "Hey, Trinity you haven't said a thing about yourself. " C'mon talk to me. Tell me what's going on in your life."

I just smile and shrug like there is nothing much new with me and continue helping Monique pack.

"So where are you living."

"I live in a great apartment downtown on Alexander Street. It's an old converted house and I love it. I'm near everything, including work."

"That sounds nice. Anyone special in your life?"

Not wanting to talk on that subject, I pause and reach into my purse. I get out one of my business cards and write my address and cell number on the back. I hand it to Monique. "Better give this to you know before I forget."

An hour later I am on the front steps and Monique stands in the doorway holding Sonja. I kiss them both.

"Monique, write me when you get settled in Boston,"

"I will. It is so good seeing you."

"You too Monique. My love to Tom."

I start to go then turn back around and look at Monique. "You've got a wonderful family you know."

Monique smiles and gestures away the compliment. She stands in the doorway, watching as I walk to my car and I see her waving as I pull out onto the street.

I drive slowly and stare once more back at Monique. Tears fill my eyes as I drive away from the quiet suburban neighborhood and the happy family of my dreams.

25

Diving away from Monique's I open the window and the flyer falls into my lap. From there it tumbles to the floor.

Keeping my eyes on the road, I feel around and pick it up, planning to put it back on the dash, but something stops me.

Instead I pull the car over and park. It's the flyer that Dr. Scott handed to me that day. I take a closer look at it now. I don't even get pass the title before I burst out laughing. Who titles a session, *Facing Termination Sitting Down.*

I throw back my head, and I laugh. I laugh uncontrollably. It's just what I need as I sit there sniffing to keep my nose from running. After a bit I reach into my purse and get out a Kleenex. I blow my nose and then taking another one, I dab at my eyes.

When I am finally calm again, I stare at the brochure and see that the class is to be held this evening. And just like that I decide to go.

It's interesting and informative. I find that I enjoy being around others who are experiencing what I am experiencing and it relaxes me. I even find it comfortable to talk about my situation. When I leave that meeting, I am not against coming back again.

The next morning while wiping the sleep from my eyes, I stretch and force myself out of the bed. I go into the bathroom and take care of my morning rituals.

Back in the bedroom I turn on the tv, then go about pulling out my running gear while brushing my teeth. I hear the announcer say that the weather report is due in five minutes, so I go into the bathroom, rinse off my toothbrush and fill the reservoir on my water pic. Keeping my head down and over the sink I spray the water through my teeth, while thinking that I might shake it up a bit and take a different route during my morning run.

I grab the bottle of mouthwash, swish a bit in my mouth and spit it out. Next, I grab my brush from the bottom drawer of the vanity and expertly brush my hair into a ponytail and rubber band it while walking into my bedroom to put on jogging clothes.

Dress and ready I stop and stand at the foot of the bed as a thought occurs to me. I smile. Yes, I think. Why not. Instead of running in the neighborhood, why not go to the boardwalk at the beach. No traffic, no streets to cross. It would be fun. My mind made up, I grab my keys and soon I am out the door, ponytail bouncing as I walk with a special lithe in my step.

PARKER & TRINITY

Epigraph

Such is the inconsistency of real love, that it is always awake to suspicion, however unreasonable; always requiring new assurances from the object of its interest.

Ann Radcliffe

Fall 2016

26

The day is warming and the slight breeze coming off the lake as he stands on the deck taking in the view, is calling to him to get out and enjoy the day. It's so beautiful, with the warmth and the scent of the flowers filling his nostrils. He remembers when Cameron decided to plant the flowers and he thought it was unnecessary since they had the lake and the beach for beauty. But she insisted. Right at this moment he's glad she did.

It takes a few minutes but finally he knows what to do on this new day. Parker hurries through the house and into the garage where he climbs into his car. Slowly he backs out onto the street and heads toward the public beach.

He could easily walk there, but he wants the full experience of strolling through the two brick entrance guards at the parking lot entry to Ontario Beach Park.

In minutes he is there, and Parker climbs out of his car. He leans against the fender for a moment staring ahead. He finds it hard to imagine that this very spot was once dubbed the 'Coney Island of the West'. He had seen pictures of the amusement park it used to be, but now it is no more than picnic space just beyond the entrance. Even so the beauty is there with the boardwalk, the white sandy beach and the lake.

Slowly he walks through the opening and the first sound he hears is the laughter of the children. Off to his right he can see children as they wait for their turn to ride the classic Dentzel Carousel that still remains in the park. He smiles as he remembers when his boys were little and never missed a chance to climb on those horses. "Some things never change," he whispers.

Parker walks unhurriedly through the picnic area and on to the boardwalk. He has barely stepped onto the wooden surface when he hears a voice saying, "Coming from behind you."

Parker stops, not knowing which way to move. Trinity, moving too quickly, is unable to stop in time and runs into Parker, knocking him down on the pathway and falling on top of him.

"Oh, I am so sorry." He can hear the suppressed laugher in her voice. "I yelled for you to move over. I did, really."

"I…" Parker started and then looked into the face of the woman who now was trying desperately to climb off him. Her almond shaped eyes twinkled and the grin that escaped emphasized her high cheek bones and dimples.

"Are you hurt?" she asks.

Parker amusingly ran his hand over his body. "I don't think so, but I'm not a doctor. Want to check me out?"

A crocked smile appeared on her face as she finally was able to get up and stood over him. She reached out a hand and he took it, allowing his full weigh to be supported by her and surprisingly she made a little stumble but held firm until he was up on his feet.

"Well, if you're all right, I'll leave you be."

"Yes, I'm fine." He started to add, 'but don't go'.

Parker watched as Trinity jogged ahead of him, her pony tail swinging as she went.

With a shrug, Parker continued his walk, enjoying the fresh air and the activity along the beach. It seems like the whole world decided to make the mecca to the area. Everywhere he looks there are people enjoying the sun and sand.

He paused to watch a group of four throwing a frisbee back and forth. "Not bad," he said to himself as they managed to keep it going with little effort.

He glanced up further on the beach and noticed there was a volley ball competition going on. There with radio station vehicles and someone announcing the plays. Quite a crowd had gathered, but he managed to get a viewing angle.

They were serious players. He thought back to his youth when he could run and play on a sandy beach with little effort. A man next to him who appeared to be close in age said. "Ah, I remember those days", as if reading Parkers thoughts. Parker responded, "Yes, I know what you mean."

He tired of watching and continued his walk until he reached the end of the boardwalk. Trying to decide what to do, he finally stepped off the boardwalk and started across the grass until he reached the entrance to the pier.

He had to make a choice. He could go left and head out into the lake or turn right and walk along the Genesee River.

It was growing hot now and thoughts of the sun beating down on him as he walked out to the end of the pier seemed less inviting, so he turned right and started walking.

He was just about to the restaurant patio area of the pier station when he heard a familiar voice. "Hey, are you watching where you are going." He turned just in time to see the woman who had ran over him, walk face first into the pole at the end of the restaurant patio.

Parker wanted to ask if she was all right, but he couldn't get the picture of her out of his smacking into the pole and whipping her body backwards with hands pressed against the side of her head.

It was too comical and unable to stop it, he folded over in laughter.

"I'm okay." He could hear annoyance in her voice. "Thanks for the sympathy my friend."

With effort, Parker managed to suppress the laughter. "Oh, I am so sorry. These days, everything is funny to me. Forgive me. Are you all right."

The woman softened. "Yes, I think so, but I don't think I can jog for a bit. Mind if I walk with you."

"Sure, I would like the company."

They walked but a few steps when a boat pulled up to the dock and they stopped to watch as a woman climbed out of the boat. Her foot slipped on the dock and her leg fell into the water. Because of the force of her push off the boat, it floated away from the dock and the two of them watched as she slipped in, reaching up with one hand and grabbing the rail on the edge of the boat.

Parker turned toward his companion and found her looking his way. There was no way to stop it as he chortled. That forced her to cackle, and high pitch laughter filled the air as they rock back and forth.

She is the first to stop saying, "I'm going to pee my pants". That made Parker laugh again until finally they were both standing there watching as the woman tried to pull herself up with the one leg that rest on the top edge of the boat. Her bikini bottom got caught on the rail at the nose of the boat and she hung there, screaming, "Matt!"

It was too much and leaning against each other, they let it all out as they watched the comedy unfold.

Finally, a man came around from the front of the boat, laughing as hard as they were, taking pictures with his cell phone as he made his way over to help her out of the boat.

"You ass," she said, "I could have been really hurt and what were you doing…taking pictures?"

"Sorry, but this will go viral. I took a video of the whole thing and uploaded it to youtube."

Trinity and Parker stared at each other again and laughter puffed out of their mouths as they hurried on ahead, until finally they were finally able to control the laugher.

Trinity couldn't resist saying, "I think it's you!"

"Me? What about me."

"You disturb the space around you and cause things to happen."

Parker's forehead creases as he looks at Trinity. "Are you serious?"

Trinity tries not to but can't help smiling. "Just joking you."

No matter how many times he had walked this way, there was always something new to see and enjoy. His new-found friend seemed just as interested as she pointed out things of interest. Finally, they turned around and headed back.

At the start of the pier they stop and turn toward each other and without a word spoken they head out on the pier.

They dodge skateboards and rollerbladers expertly on their way to the end of the pier. The sun is brutal, but they ignore it as they try to find a space where they can walk side by side.

Trinity and Parker take their time and point out every little thing. "Look, over there, the family of ducks," Trinity says pointing off to the left.

Parker shades his eyes. "Yeah, wonder if any of them run into the boats."

He feels Trinity as she pushes her shoulder against his. "Very funny."

Several minutes pass until finally they are at the end of the pier. Parker manages to shoulder through the crowd so that he and Trinity are able to stand at the railing and gaze unobtrusively out at the Lake.

The water is calm. "I've come out here some days and the water splashes over the pier, making it slippery. But not today. It's like a sheet of glass."

"Look over there at the sailboats. I love it when they have those colorful sails, don't you?"

"Yes, I do."

There they stood gazing out at the unending expanse of Lake Ontario. When they finally turn around to start back, Parker asks, "So, what do I call you?"

"My name is Trinity."

"Hi Trinity, my name is Parker."

"Hi Parker."

They continue in silence until returning to the start of the pier. Trinity puts her weight on one foot and then the other as she shades her eyes. Parker nervously takes his hand and rubs his neck trying to figure what to say to keep this day from ending.

"I'm hungry. Are you hungry."

"No," Trinity replied.

"I know a terrific place."

"I do too," Trinity says starting to walk away from him.

"Hey wait a minute."

Trinity stops a few feet away.

"Why so rude. I'm just asking if you want to get something to eat. Nothing more."

Trinity starts walking again, not making a response to him, and before he knows he is even doing it, he is at her side, grabbing her by the elbow and spinning her around.

Surprised by this change in him, Trinity turns and sees he's not smiling.

"Look Miss. You don't have to be rude. I'm not asking you out or making a pass. I have enough on my plate."

"Don't flatter yourself. I have a life too. I just don't want to spend the rest of my day with you."

"Fine."

"Fine."

Parker doesn't want it to end like this. he likes her. She is the first female in a long time that he feels comfortable with. He thinks quickly.

"I am going to O'Loughlin's Silk. It's right over there, across the pier. No pressure, but if you change your mind you can show up, or not. It's up to you."

Trinity doesn't reply as they go their separate ways, each unaware of how it will all play out.

Later Parker sits in a window seat at O'Loughlin's Silk with a beer. Looking at his cell he sees that 20 minutes have passed.

Across the street at an ice cream Parlor Trinity watches Parker. She stares at the side of his head through the glare of traffic that blocks her view from time to time. Parker never once turns and looks in her direction.

She sips her coffee feeling childish now, but it seemed the smart thing to do; especially after he grabbed her so roughly. She had decided to go home and forget about him, but for some reason she changed her mind. So here she was acting like a spy and watching him.

In her mind she goes over it all. They met and she liked him. He invited her to come so it wasn't an actual date; just two friends meeting up. That seemed a safe way of looking at it.

Trinity stood up and went and paid for her coffee. She walked slowly over to the door and pushed it open.

The evening was coming, taking away the light of the day as she pondered whether to continue across the street or not.

At that moment Parker slowly turned and looked right at her from his seat in O'Loughlin's. Trinity knows he has seen her and feels awkward, but then Parker tilted his head stuck out his tongue and if she had been closer she would have seen he crossed his eyes.

Flustered at first, she finally relaxes and goes across the street to join him.

Trinity walks right up to the table where Parker is sitting and stands there. He grins at her but does not move.

"Don't get up," she says as she sits herself directly across from him.

She barely takes a seat when Parker says, "You know what we're going to do tonight."

"No, I don't know what you are going to do tonight. I do know what I am going to do tonight."

"I thought we were friends."

"We are, but I don't even know you and you're becoming a very strange person and I don't know what I'm doing here in the first place."

"Tonight," Parker says going right on as though she has not said a word, "we're going to eat dinner and we're going to do something you secretly always wanted to do but never really had the nerve."

"What's that, Mr. know it all."

"Sneak into a movie through the exit doors."

"I have money to buy a ticket."

"I have too."

"Come on. Do you think in this day and age a person can sneak into a theater?"

"We're about to find out."

So, here's how it works. Either me or you can go in and buy a ticket. Once inside, you need to go to the 'Exit Only' door and open it.

"That'll work?"

"Think about it. The 'Exit Only' doors are used for patrons to exit the theater when the movie is over. While the front entrance is usually crawling with theater employees, these 'Exit Only' doorways are almost always completely void of anyone being nearby."

A smile plays at the corners of Trinity's mouth. "You're right. I have always wanted to do this, but you thought of it so…"

"No, you can be the one at the 'Exit Only'."

They can stop smiling as they place their order and then, while waiting for their food to arrive, they are both deep in thought.

When the waitress brings their meal, they force themselves to slow down and eat like people instead of animals gobbling down the food. They are just that anxious to get on with their conspiracy.

Finally, Trinity says, "I'm finished. How about you."

"Yeah, I'm done." She watches as Parker takes out his wallet and puts a bunch of bills on the table. "Let's go."

The theater is just a short block away. It is one of those small neighborhood type theaters which makes it perfect for them. Parker walks Trinity along the side of the building to the exit door.

"Okay, stand here and when I open the door, step in quickly and then we must hurry to the nearest seats and sit down right away."

Trinity nodded.

Pangs of doubt fill her head thinking it can't be that easy. She whispered. "What if we get caught.

"I'll ask for a comfortable cot for you in the slammer," he laughed.

Parker hurried to the front and purchased his ticket. He went through the theater entrance doors. It is dark and he stands waiting for his eyes to adjust. He waits a little longer for the soundtrack to be loud. A glance around the theater and he sees all eyes pointed ahead so he hurries to the exit door.

The first feeling of doubt descends as he wonders if it could be locked. He tries the door. It opens. Careful not to open it too wide, he peers through the crack. No Trinity.

Parker frowns and leans outside keeping his hand on the door so that it doesn't shut. Trinity is no where to be seen.

"Damn."

He hesitates wondering if he should just exit or get his monies worth. He makes the right choice.

Outside he is able to look farther up and down. He spots Trinity. Sensing she is being watched, Trinity turns in his direction.

She smiles widely as she approaches.

"So. What gives."

"I got scared. Someone saw me standing there and I panicked."

Trinity is silent, then starts laughing uncontrollably. Parker can't help but join her.

“So much for a successful first da…” He stops himself. “sneaking into a movie”, he says instead.

To compensate for the failed movie attempt, Trinity offers to buy him an Abbotts ice cream across the street from the beach. They walk slowly as if not wanting to reach their destination too soon. When they arrive, Parker steps back and allows Trinity to go to the window and make the purchase.

“What do you want, a two-flavor softie?”

“Yes, how did you know.”

Trinity just smiles and then turns back around. When she comes toward him she has two cones, a vanilla swirl for her and a chocolate and vanilla swirl for him.

He takes his cone and they go to the side of the building and sit on top of a picnic table. From here they have a great view of the lake and a huge number of seagulls just waiting for them to drop something.

Silence falls between them as they eat their ice cream. It is still quite warm and humid, and it takes non-stop licking to keep the cones from dripping all over their hands.

“So, what shall we do now.”

After finishing their cones, they cross the street and enter the park to walk over to take a close look at the carrousel. “Let’s take a ride,” Trinity says.

Parker nods in agreement and goes over to the stand to purchase two tickets. There is no one in line so they are able to climb on right away and make their choices. They both pick horses that go up and down as the carrousel goes around.

Parker keeps looking at Trinity wondering what is going on. Why now, did she come into his life. He wonders if it’s fair to her and if he should stop this before it goes any further. Then he selfishly thinks that he deserves some kind of happiness.

Trinity smiles at Parker and thinks, this must be some kind of joke being played on her. How long has she waited for someone to enjoy life with. No one came until now when it was too late.

Once the carrousel stops, they get off and together they say, "Want a beer?"

They laugh and at the same time, say, "Sure."

They make their way over to the boardwalk entrance to the bar. Trinity settles on a Merlot instead of a beer, while Parker orders himself a Goose Island IPA. They take the drinks out to the patio to sit and watch as the boats start coming in for the evening. The heat of the day is gone now and the mild warm breeze of the evening is inviting.

When they finish their drinks they order another.

"Let's sit near the river edge," Parker says.

"You mean the lake edge?"

"No, out there is the lake," Parker says as he sweeps his arm out toward the left. "And here," he adds moving his arm in front of him, "You have the Genesee River."

"Ah, I didn't know that."

Parker smiles and leads the way to a bench close to the river. They sit properly on the bench seats as they look out at the river and the lights going on across the way. There are still boats coming in and still ducks swimming. The reflection of the lights on the water is fractured each time a boat slowly makes its way back to the docks, adding another dimension of pleasure.

When they finish their drinks, Parker takes the glasses back inside then returns to rejoin Trinity.

"Parker, want to walk along the edge of the lake?" she says emphasizing, 'lake'.

"Let's do it. It's just about empty of folks now so we can get up close with no problem."

They walk across the grass and into the sand. "Wait Parker. Let's take off our shoes here." He stops and watches as she plops down on the edge of the grassy area and slips off her sandals. He follows suit and with shoes in hand they start across the warm sand, pushing their feet down and wiggling their toes.

Soon they are walking in the wet sand at the lake edge. Testily they move forward until their feet are in the water. They keep moving ahead until the water reaches the hem of Parker's shorts and they stop to stand there gazing out.

At the same time they turn toward each other and Trinity is about to say something when a wave comes in and knocks them both on their asses.

"You've got to be kidding."

Parker laughs.

"It's that aura of yours coming out again."

"Oh, come on. You'll live."

They sit there and let the water wash over them without regard as they enjoy the coolness of the waves that come, making them bob up and down. Finally, they get up and start heading toward the parking lot. They are almost there when Parker stops and Trinity follows suit. They put on their shoes and Parker. Parker turns to Trinity.

"Well, it's almost time. We can make it out on the pier and watch the sunrise."

Trinity looks at Parker. "You have great ideas. I'd like that."

Without hesitation they turn back around and head to the walkway of the pier. As they go along they are joined by several other couples who must have the same idea of seeing the sun come up over the lake.

They move at a quick clip, not allowing for much conversation as they go until finally they stand at the railing along the end of the pier, sides touching, watching the sun come up each silently caught up in their own thoughts.

Parker can't remember when he has been up all night and stood watching the sun rise. Where did the time go, he wonders, but then he looks over at Trinity.

It's breathtaking. The dark blue sky is suddenly illuminated by an amber globe that casts a line of color above the water edge as it begins its assent. Watching the sunrise, witnessing the fresh start to a brand-new day can't be expressed in words as they stand breathing in the cool morning air.

Parker hesitantly reaches for Trinity's hand and she lets him take it. "It's too early to worry and yet too late to stay in your bed. We are seeing the world before it gets too busy."

"You are right. Watching the sunrise is like watching the world awake, Parker."

Parker thinks to himself that he can start anew and forget what troubles him. He can just look forward to every new thing, can still see and feel and taste for the hours given him.

He doesn't want this to end so as they slowly walk back down the pier he labors on finding another idea to keep Trinity entertained.

"I could use some coffee," he says.

"Me too," Trinity replies.

They veer away from the parking lot and go into the Marina where they find a coffee machine and stand waiting as each cup is filled. Parker takes a sip. Trinity takes a sip of hers. "It isn't bad for machine coffee."

They continue sipping the hot liquid as they head to the parking lot. There Parker helps Trinity as she climbs up on the hood of her car and leans against the windshield. He in turn does the same, sitting on his car. Though not planned, the cars are parked side by side angled a little toward each other.

Holding Styrofoam cups of steaming coffee, they drink in a comfortable silence, tired from walking around all night.

Trinity finally speaks.

"I have had more fun with you tonight than I've had in months."

"I've had just as much fun with me tonight than I've had in months too," Parker says.

"And if I didn't think I'd start to like you so much I'd probably see you again." Trinity added.

"I don't know anything about you, really, except that you just might be crazy. But that's enough, really because well I just can't get involved with anyone right now."

"Who said anything about getting involved."

Showing signs of embarrassment, Trinity says, "I guess I'm flattering myself aren't I. I shouldn't have assumed… Doesn't matter."

"Ah, so, what is this. I mean…"

"I know what you mean. I don't know."

Silence falls between them again. Not wanting to say anything serious, Parker says, "Did you ever not want a new day to start?"

"Yes, I have."

Parker drops his eyes and makes a big deal out of sipping his coffee and Trinity shifts her weight and watches a seagull walking in the park.

The silence between them now is uncomfortable. Trinity suddenly gets down off the hood of her car and goes over to the trash can. She can feel Parker watching her.

"I've gotta go," she says as she stands at the driver's side of her car. She opens the door. "Thank you for this night. Take care of yourself."

She starts to climb in behind the steering wheel, but hesitates. “You are quite a guy, Parker.”

Then Trinity swings her body inside and starts her car. Parker watches with a stunned look on his face. He manages to find his voice.

“Trinity…”

Trinity looks up through the windshield at him, while he reminds himself that he has no right to ask her to stay.

“Don’t…” He mumbles silently.

He waves as he stands watching Trinity back out of her parking space. He continues to watch as she drives to the exit.

When her car is out of view he remains standing there wondering if he has done the right thing. Finally, he forces himself to get into his car. He sits there reflecting then turns on the ignition and heads for home.

27

Trinity wakes feeling wonderful. For the first time since learning of her cancer, she feels safe. Cancer has become like a dark shadow over her existence, waiting for her to be off guard and steel her life away. Only this morning she feels like, well, singing.

She lays in bed smiling and says, “Alexa, play, I am woman.” She wonders if that is the title, but then, the song starts playing. Laying there so peacefully she hums along at first, then getting into the rhythm she twists and turns and sings at the top of her lungs.

“I am woman, hear me roar

In numbers too big to ignore

And I know too much to go back an' pretend

'Cause I've heard it all before

And I've been down there on the floor

No one's ever gonna keep me down again."

Snaking around on her back in bed is not enough. Soon she is on her feet, jumping up and down on the mattress, a stern look on her face as the words sink in and she continues to sing.

"Oh yes, I am wise

But it's wisdom born of pain

Yes, I've paid the price

But look how much I gained"

Her voice takes on a puzzling tone as she stops jumping and stares straight ahead, but the words continue to pour from her mouth, only softer now.

"If I have to, I can do anything

I am strong

(Strong)

I am invincible

(Invincible)

I am woman"

The last lines are almost in a whisper as tears flow from her eyes. In the silence that permeates the room, Trinity looks around, then slowly steps across the bed. When she reaches the edge, she sits and puts her feet on the floor.

Her mind is going a mile a minute and her thoughts spill out. "I am going to make this the best day ever. I am going to take control of my life and my time. You hear me cancer."

As if it is listening, she feels a twinge in her side; just a little twinge, nothing to worry about she thinks. She smiles and gets up.

So, what does one do with a day when they feel on top of the world. That she thinks about as she brushes her teeth, climbs in and out of the shower and gets ready. She flips on the tv and with a cup of coffee in hand, waits for the news.

Trinity leans against the counter, her hair covering her face. When she was 20 she believed that the world revolved around her and on the tv and movies everyone seemed her age too. Life was full of hope and dreams that could be met. She was young, vibrant and, yes, invincible.

She lifts her head, absently pushing back the sides of her hair thinking, even 40 wasn't bad, just different. No longer could she eat whatever she wanted and not gain a pound. Her metabolism had slowed at 40 so she had to be careful what she put in her mouth. If she bruised, it healed quickly when younger and now stayed long enough that she forgot what she did to injure herself. So that was a downside…

Trinity frowns wondering why she didn't enjoy every second of every day during those wonderful age years. She had let them slip by. Now as she looks back she can't help but feel she wasted time by not enjoying each milestone.

She hasn't accomplished all that she wanted to either. There are no children to mourn her passing, no husband to wonder what his life will be without her. She has waited, thinking then it was the smart thing to do, only now…

Trinity shakes her head to remove the unpleasant thoughts wanting to feel the positivity of the morning. She pours herself a cup of coffee and settles down as the weather report begins. It's to be a bright, sunny day with no chance of rain. That brings a smile to her face and once again she feels happy and content.

She starts to turn off the television but pauses when the travel guy appears on the screen. She's always thought there was something wrong with him; the way he held his head leaning toward the side as he speaks and smiling with interest at his current travels.

Trinity shakes her head as she starts to stand, but then she pauses and finds herself actually listening to what he has to say.

First a close-lipped smile, then a full on grin appears. She knows what she wants to do.

Trinity takes her cell phone off the charger, grabs her purse and goes out the door. She climbs into her car and again heads toward Lake Ontario.

This is so unlike her. She could count on one hand the times she has been in that area in the past and here she is heading that way again. Only now it's for a frivolous reason. Well, some may think so, and she would have too...before. She hasn't had any interest in amusement parks for a long time, but now she feels drawn

She considers herself a city girl and as such she worked and played in the city scape. It is strange to find herself heading to the outskirts for fun and entertainment and at her age, going to an amusement park. She laughs.

Seabreeze Amusement Park has been around a long time, but she can't remember ever going there. Why is that she wonders. It only takes a minute for her to answer her own question. Because fun was not part of her repertoire. Being productive was what her life was about. If she wanted to get ahead in this world, she didn't have time to dillydally. She had to push hard and fast. So where did that get her, she wondered. It didn't matter because she would not waste another moment, not anymore.

Trinity continues her drive not needing to use her GPS since Rochester is compact and she has a general roadmap in her head. Just head toward the Lake.

She turns on the radio and the voice of Beyonce fills the air, singing "Single Ladies (Put a Ring On It)". It's one of those songs that knock all thoughts out of your head as Beyonce belts out the tune.

The sun shining, Beyonce singing, "It can't get any better than this," Trinity says. Before she realizes it, she arrives at her destination.

There are plenty of parking spaces and Trinity assumes that is because the kids are at home with their electronics. Which is bad for them, but great for her. She parks and climbs out of the car, grabbing a hat and sunglasses. After paying the admission she is on her way.

Once through the entry gate, she is surprised by the amount of people wandering around; holding tightly to little tots as they meander through the throng of occupants. She forgot that tot generation too young to play video games.

Raised in Chicago as an only child to professionals who paid little attention to childish desires, Trinity grew up thinking that reaching the top in one's professional life was the most important factor …everything else was a waste of time. She can't recall going on picnics, to parks and never an amusement park of any kind. One time when a carnival was in town, she asked her mother first, then her father, if they could go. The answer was, No, on both counts.

Trinity shakes her head, trying to vanish those undesirable thoughts. They have ruled her life and though she didn't like it when she was little, she adopted each and every one of them.

Now as she tries to break free, she has no idea what she wants to do, only that it be fun. The spectacular views and cool summer breezes off Lake Ontario, is mood lifting.

Something is missing. Trinity sits on a bench staring at the crowd, her mind refusing to stay in the present. She looks around and sees the Center Stage where a show is about to begin. "Great," she says as she gets up and follows the crowd in that direction as the Cirque En Vol begins its acrobatic entertainment.

She stands amongst the crowd enjoying the performance and is smiling again as she leaves, stopping on the way at the Gift Shop and looking through the souvenirs before going to the candy counter. She makes a purchase and then heads out.

Trinity wanders toward the Carousel Museum and goes in, enjoying the historical amusement park pictures. It's easy to imagine what it was like those so many years ago when life was less complicated. She sees a sign with directional arrows. One points toward the midway. She walks over and sees there are games called Water Race, Seabreeze Derby, The Poster Game, Basketball, Whiffle Wing, the classic Cat Rack and more. She hasn't heard of any of them.

"Okay," she hears herself say as she finally recognizes a familiar game; Skeeball. She makes her way in that direction and sees two teenage girls laughing and pushing each other as they play the game. She stands there observing for several minutes before moving on.

Trinity sees a familiar sight. It's a photo booth. Before she changes her mind, she climbs in, reads the instructions and then, poses with sunglasses on, hat pulled down over her face, then removes the glasses and squints into the camera with her fingers in a V at the sides of her eyes.

When the pictures come out, she looks at them and laughs. She puts them in her purse and continues on her way.

The next thing she knows she is strapped into a stylized little bucket seat attached to a conveyor belt and finding herself being taken to a series of darkened rooms. Skeletons jump in front of her and she screams with laughter. Further along, strange sounds begin and even stranger apparitions appear. Holding tightly to the rail she continues to laugh, only not as much as she screeches. Then comes the whirling lights flashing from all angles and Trinity wants out.

It's too late.

As the seat bumps around in the darkness she feels a spray of water and if it weren't for the bar in front of her, she would have jump out of her seat.

It's still dark ahead and she fears there is more to come. Trinity at this point would do anything to get out but has to settle on closing her eyes and keeping from screaming at the top of her lungs. Whatever possessed her to enter the haunted house is beyond comprehension now and she prays for the ride to end.

As she is hurled farther into the darkness she hears a dull steady throbbing sound that grows louder and louder. It continues until she can't handle it a minute longer.

Trinity let out a caterwauling scream.

When her car reaches the exit, she stumbles out, wanting at that moment to drop down and kiss the ground, but instead she walks unsteadily down the stairs. At the bottom she pauses to catch her breath and prays no one knows she was the one making the earsplitting sounds. If her face is as jerky as her insides, one look and they would know it was her. Only as others join her at the exit she realizes she's not the only one looking as though they were scared enough to pee their pants.

She lets the people pass her as she takes several minutes to stand there until she finally feels like herself again. There is only a few people left at the exit when she goes down the ram and starts walking to the midway. "No more rides for me," she whispers.

The midway is packed with hordes of people moving as one. Trinity moves into the crowd. She can't see above the heads in front as she presses forward, each time making an effort to move toward the left by sliding through each opening that presents itself until finally she is a few steps from the edge of the crowd. She finds it illuminating, feeling part of a whole even though she has come here alone. Then with one gentle push she makes it to the clearing.

At the outer edge of the crowd Trinity pauses wondering what she should do next when suddenly her forehead wrinkles as she squints. Slowly a smile of recognition forms as she makes out the face across the way. It's Parker.

28

Parker sits at a snack bar patio table in the midst of hundreds of people all of whom are frantically stuffing themselves with hamburgers and French fries.

He is alone and bored, staring at the cup in front of him. He thought that being around people was what he wanted, and at first, it was. Now he feels annoyed by their joviality.

He is about to get up when a little boy about six years old, comes up to him and smiles shyly, holding out a folded piece of paper.

Parker smiles back and hesitantly at first reaches out to accept the child's offering. He looks at the paper in his hand then looks up and says, "What is this, son," but there is no answer because the little boy has taken off as quickly as he appeared.

Confused Parker looks at the paper and unfolds it. A surprise expression appears on his face as he reads. "Guess Who." There is no name written on the paper, but he knows without a doubt who it is from.

Parker stands and twists around. He looks up and then behind him. He doesn't see her. Slowly he scans the area searching for her face in the crowd on the midway. She's not there.

No longer bored, he takes off toward the exhibits, persistently scanning the faces of everyone he passes. "Where are you," he whispers, moving slowly and determinedly through the area, his eyes swiveling from front, to back and each side.

Admittedly he begins to panic, rationally he should have stayed where he was because she knew he was there. Now like him, Trinity will not know his location, he thinks.

So slowly Parker makes his way back to the snack bar patio peering into faces as he moves hoping that one will belong to Trinity. He is almost back to where he started and still he can't find her.

Resignedly he gives up. Parker stands alone watching a man with a bunch of balloons walk along the midway. The colorful balloons bounce up and down and when the balloon man is pass his sight line, he sees her. He sees Trinity.

She is grinning as she looks in his direction, pleased with herself.

Parker starts to shake his finger at her but couldn't keep the happy grin off his face.

As they stare across the distance at each other two things are certain. She has chosen to say hello to him and he has wanted very much to find her.

Parker is the first to move as he walks toward her.

Trinity stands watching him as he closes the distance between them. When Parker is right in front of her they say nothing to each other, but their faces reveal their joy at being together.

Parker looks Trinity in her eyes takes her arm and steers her toward the midway. There is no resistance as they walk as one, side by side, not needing conversation as they pop in and out of shops along the way.

Finally, Trinity asks, "So what are you doing here anyway."

Not missing a beat, he replies, "I thought I might buy the place. I've been thinking about tearing it down maybe putting up a giant golf course. Do you golf?"

"Parker seriously why are you here."

"I could ask you the same thing."

"Touché."

They continue toward the exit and when they are at the gate, Parker asks, "Do you have any plans?"

"No, it's a do whatever day for me. What about you."

"Same." Parker pauses. "Well, we could do whatever together. Want to go to my house?"

"Ah, I don't..." She hesitates before saying. "Why not."

Parker walks Trinity to her car and holds the door while she climbs in. When she is seated he says, "Follow me."

She watches as Parker goes over to his car. He moves with determination and she likes that. When he is seated behind the wheel she takes note of the license plate, in case she loses him, but she needn't worry. She is surprised when a few minutes later he is pulling into a driveway.

Trinity remembers that Parker had mentioned that he lived on the lake, but she thought it was him trying to impress her. Now, as she stares at the house in front of her she says, "Wow!"

She sits in her car waiting while Parker pulls into the garage. The architecture of the house gives it the appearance of a woodland retreat and the beauty of the new landscaping blends effortlessly with the old. At the front of the house, there is a porch with a swing that she can imagine sitting on with a glass of merlot. The front door is massive with planter pots on each side and a copper gas lantern that provides pleasant illumination from above.

She is still sizing up the house when the door opens, and Parker motions her in.

Trinity doesn't want Parker to see how impressed she is, so she stalls a moment, carefully checks her expression before getting out of the car and walking up to the front door entrance.

The vista in front of her includes the kitchen, dining room and main living spaces all viewed from the foyer and each sporting wide plank oak floors and splashes of color everywhere. It makes Trinity feel welcomed before stepping over the threshold.

Parker gestures her forward into the kitchen/dining room combination separated by a huge island. Off to her left she sees a cute built-in bench by the window with a table for casual dining. It is a modern kitchen with stainless steel appliances, and white cabinets that pop against a soft gray color wall.

"Can I get you a glass of wine," Parker asks.

"Hmmm…oh, yes, please."

While Parker goes for the wine, Trinity continues to look around. There is crown molding everywhere and a view no matter where she stands.

Trinity checks to make sure that her jaw hasn't dropped as she takes in the views of this lakefront property. It is right on the beach and where there is water, it is followed by white sand. Closer to the house there is green grass and flowers -- lots of flowers.

Trinity turns to see if Parker is back, but he's not so she checks out his work desk off to one end of the huge room in front of her and the massive book case that takes up one wall, with the biggest tv Trinity has ever seen resting in the center of it all.

She continues exploring and sees a broken kite standing on the far side of the desk and a simple goldfish bowl that somehow doesn't fit in the room.

"I see you have goldfish." Trinity says out loud. "I've got some goldfish too."

"What," Parker said from the back of the kitchen.

"Nothing," she replies wandering about some more.

She has checked out all the main areas so she turns and walks back to the entrance to pick up her purse. She opens it and pulls out a small figurine that they purchased at the park.

Carefully she unwraps the Silver-plated carousel horse and turns it around in her hand. It is a beautifully crafted sculpture. The saddle and carousel pole are said to be accented in brass and 24 caret gold, which she doubted until she saw the price. Yes, it had an ornate design and yes it had exquisite detail and was beautifully elegant but nothing that just sits on a shelf should cost that much.

Parker didn't balk at the price and then she figured he was trying to impress her again. Now, she was confident that he could afford it...very confident.

Parker comes over to her with two glasses of wine. He holds one out to her smiling as he sees she is holding the horse. They had both been drawn by it in the shop; He remembers how Trinity was backing off when she heard the price. But he convinced her it was worth it, and she admitted it was beautiful.

When Trinity takes her glass, Parker reaches out and fondles the horse. She hands it over to him and he turns it around in his hand. She can read the delight on his face.

"You should keep it here," Trinity said.

"No, I want you to have it."

"It goes better here."

Unlike women, men are not as inquisitive and so Parker said, "Okay, so where should I put it."

"I don't know. How about right here," Trinity said walking over to an empty space on the book shelf above the tv.

"Yes, that's a great spot. That way it can be admired often."

She nodded in agreement sipping her wine.

An uncomfortable silence falls between them. They truly have nothing in common and know little about each other. Parker walks over and sits on the sofa and Trinity sits in the chair. The space between them suddenly seems wider than it really is.

Trinity glances around trying to find something to comment on, while Parker thinks hard for anyway to break the ice. Nervously they continue to sip their wine and the silence seems to expand in the room.

Parker finally asks, "so what part of the town do you live in, Trinity?"

By now Trinity's mind has drifted as her eyes take in the environment that Parker is used to. Before she can stop herself, she says, "What the hell am I doing here anyway."

It takes Parker by surprise and not knowing what to say, he replies, "How come you're so uncomfortable."

She has no interest in telling him and just gets up and paces back and forth. She admits she wants to be curled up next to him, and that makes her even more panicky. She doesn't know this man.

"Have you ever noticed how we never ask each other anything about the other," she finally says.

"Yes."

"You hadn't even asked me what my name is she says facing him. How come."

"I don't know," Parker says and takes a big drink of his wine."

More silence falls before Parker unwittingly asks, "How do you like the house."

"I don't want to make small talk about your house either. I don't know what I want." She sits the glass of wine down and picks up her purse. "I'm going home."

Surprised Parker slowly gets to his feet still holding his glass of wine not knowing what else to do.

Not wanting to look in his eyes Trinity just puts out her hand and they stand there feeling stupid as he shakes her hand.

"Aren't you going to say. Thank you very much and I had a nice time." Parker asked jokingly.

"Good bye Parker", she says as she pushes her wine glass into his hands, then turns and goes over to the door. She opens it and walks out into the night closing the door behind her.

Parker stands there by the door, stunned, unable to comprehend just what has happened. He looks down and notices he is still holding both wine glasses. As if in a trance, he walks over to the hall table and sits both glasses down and that motion seems to motivate him into action.

Parker moves rapidly back to the door and opens it. In the driveway, Trinity is just about to get into her car when she sees Parker coming toward her. She wants to climb in, but she is frozen in the act of opening the door as he reaches her, grabs her abruptly into his arms and kisses her deeply.

Her arms dangling loosely at her side, Trinity is at a loss as to what to do. She gently backs out of his arms and looks into his face.

Parker is looking at her, no, looking through her as though he can't decide what to do next. Then, she watches as he wordlessly turns and goes back into the house.

His motion breathes life into Trinity. She poses a moment longer, then climbs into the car, still unable to comprehend what has just happened. Slowly she backs out of the driveway and heads toward home.

###

Inside Parker listens as she drives away. He is alone again. His reflexes sharpening as he turns around wondering what to do next. He needs air, fresh air to clear the cobwebs from his head and get his body into motion so he can think because right now he has no ability to understand his actions of the past few minutes.

It has cooled outside so Parker grabs a jacket and zips it up before stepping out the back door and onto the deck. He looks out across the expanse of the lake and then goes quickly down the steps toward the shoreline.

His shoes are cumbersome on the sand, so he turns back toward the house and on the deck, removes them. Then starts out again.

The sand is warm on his feet as he trudges up the shoreline, walking gingerly at first, then slows his pace, as the wind picks up, causing me to pull up the collar of his jacket. It feels good to disappear in the night and not think about anything.

###

Trinity drives along at a slower pace than usual. She chews on her lip, lost in thought.

God damn you Parker she thinks to herself, damn you. She is mad at him for reasons that she can't understand.

Trinity knows herself. She tries to be flippant and cynical because she is a romantic at heart and it's hard to control those feelings since she likes being with the opposite sex when they show they care.

Parker is getting to her.

Hiding her feelings has been a past time since her teenage years when she found herself to be gullible. The worse of it was that she was smart, only she hid that from others with her shy demure. When it came to romance or attention that she could translate as feelings from the opposite sex, she was all woozy and was an easy mark.

It didn't get any better as she got older. In college it was even harder to control her feelings and she found she could cry at the drop of a pin, which may have been her salvation.

How she made it through all those years without having a breakdown was beyond her because the pent-up feelings pushed to get out as hard as she struggled to keep them in.

So how did she plan to meet the man of her dreams. Well that was figured out for her. Her mother had told her when the right man came along she would know it. But until then she needed to keep her feelings reined in. So she did.

It might have been at the base of her need to keep moving. She traveled a lot, starting and stopping several different career paths, not making her mind up on what she wanted to do with herself. She had a bit of knowledge and experience in lots of fields, but no title.

She wanted to be appreciated for her worth and accomplishments as a person instead of making it on just her good looks; which she had in abundance.

She put herself out there, but she always had trouble meeting men she could really care about. Her well thought out high standards kept getting mixed up with some of her fantasies.

Besides most businessmen she'd meet were either married or dull or both.

She even tried the singles bars and took out a match.com page, but the kind of men she wanted to meet wouldn't be caught dead in the bar or online dating.

Of course, if she had kept in touch with her girlfriends they might have had a chance in helping her find someone, but they were all long gone and married.

The problem wasn't the men, it was Trinity. She wanted to meet some special man in some really special way. She knows it is a silly way of thinking but that's how she felt.

Once she accepted the fact her mate was not out there it made it easy to settle into not allowing or going to places that would encourage involvement. Admittedly she developed a hard shell of protection that made her feel she didn't need anyone in her life but herself.

Then she met Paul Danson.

This was the man of her dreams. He was the best looking, sexiest man she'd ever seen in her life. He was tall, with black hair, gray eyes and beautifully tan skin.

He also had an offbeat sense of humor that really appealed to her. Only that wasn't the clincher. That came later when she found that they actually had gone to the same grade school together. Once hearing his name, she remembered him, but he admitted he didn't remember her.

That didn't matter because as if this touch of fate wasn't enough, after their first date, Paul sent a dozen red roses to her at the office where all the other women looked at them enviously. On the card he wrote. "Red roses for a blue lady."

Some may have thought that sinister, but Trinity saw it to mean that if he had seen the sadness below the surface he was interested in more than the outward appearance.

Paul turned out to be wonderful in bed and a lot of fun out of the bed. They did fun things like go to the zoo instead of a night club. She had to admit they were a stunning couple and people watched as they walked by.

She fell totally in love with Paul Danson.

As quickly as it started, after several months, Paul stopped calling as often and Trinity knew he was seeing other women. They hadn't made any commitments to each other so there was nothing she could say.

She waited for his calls, frantically, seeing him whenever he decided he wanted them to be together, never questioning him or sharing that she was being faithful to him.

By chance Trinity met another woman in the lady's room at the office building where she worked. The woman was crying and at first Trinity felt that pull to keep her distance, but she managed to shrug it off.

"Are you okay? Can I do anything?"

Through gasps for breath she replies, "My boyfriend dumped me. He just walked up and said, it's over and gave me no reason."

The woman is bawling uncontrollably. Trinity cranks off a handful of paper towels and hands them to her.

"Don't worry. If he did that, he is not the man for you. That is so heartless."

The woman moves forward and pushes into Trinity's arms, sobbing her heart out.

Trinity doesn't know what to do. She pats the woman's back. "There, there."

They stand like that for several uncomfortable minutes until finally the woman gets ahold of herself and stops crying. She moves back and beings wiping her eyes and her running nose while Trinity wonders how much of that is on her shoulder.

When the woman has finally pulled herself together she manages a shy smile. “I’m so sorry. I was just so heart broken.”

“It’s okay. Glad to help.”

As if feeling she owes Trinity, she adds. “He is a menace.” Looking directly at her she says, “Whatever you do, don’t fall for Paul Danson. I thought I was the one with his roses and his fun dates. But then he dumped me.” Tears spilled out again as her shoulders heaved and her nose started running. In a daze, Trinity gathered up more paper towels and handed them to her.”

She stood watching as the woman regained her composure. She mentions her name, but Trinity quickly forgets it. “Are you okay,” she asked.

“Yes, I’ll be fine.”

Trinity left the bathroom knowing that she was one of the women that her Paul was seeing. But he had dumped this woman. Maybe because it was her, he wanted; or at least Trinity tried to tell herself that.

Then one day Paul ended the game. He took her to an expensive restaurant and told her he finally felt like getting married.

Even though this is not the romantic way she wanted to be proposed to, Trinity sat up straighter in her chair.

Paul smiling dropped the bomb on her. “So, when?” She asked.

“When what,” came Paul’s reply.

"When do you want us to get married. I mean, I have to have time to plan, you know," she says cajolingly.

"What?" He looks at her questionably, before it dawns on him what she is thinking.

Then cruelly he says, "No, I didn't mean we should get married."

He paused then added, "I am going to marry a woman I've been seeing. Dreamily he says, "She's pretty, 22 years old and is a music critic."

Trinity slumped in her chair dumbfounded as he began to carefully explain how he knows that Trinity would understand and how he hoped they would always be friends.

She couldn't believe what he was saying. Sitting there in a restaurant knowing how she cared for him and telling her he had met the woman he planned to marry and it wasn't her.

Anger replaced the feeling of rejection and Trinity stood, picked up her plate and threw it at him. She stood a while longer just to enjoy the sight of pasta sauce and spaghetti strings falling down his handsome face. Then she turned on her heels and walked out the restaurant door.

She left New York City that day and moved to Rochester, New York. She was done being an idiot and a new place was what she needed.

Well, that wasn't all she obviously needed because shortly thereafter, having a routine doctor's appointment it ended up not being so routine.

Trinity now drove through traffic angry at Parker and angry at herself and not too crazy about the world in general. Parker was sneaking up on her blind side just when she decided to be coldly logical were men were concerned.

But there is one thing she is sure about.

Parker is kind, fun loving and makes her happy. She likes him and time is not on her side anymore. By the time the other shoe falls, she will be gone.

Yes, it dawns on her. That's true. Why not have a little joy while she can.

Trinity reflectively swung the car to the curb, checked her rear-view mirror and swung across the lane, pointing her in the opposite direction.

Three cars screeched to a halt, but Trinity isn't aware as she heads straight back to the beach.

###

Parker has finally stopped walking and sits on a bench in the dark watching the waves. He leans over and fills his hand with sand, then watches as it escapes through his fingers. It starts to rain, but he hardly notices the change as he sits thinking.

Finally, he sits up and looks at the sky. "God, I was getting use to being alone. I need to be alone because I don't have much to give any more. So why, why put temptation in my path. Why." He pauses, then adds, "then snatch it all away…

###

Trinity pulls into Parkers driveway and runs up to the door. It is raining hard and her hair is plastered against her head. She rings the doorbell and pounds on the door. Then she stops and waits, listening for movement on the other side, but the rain is loud and she can't hear anything so she rings the bell and pounds on the door again.

"Hey Parker, c'mon, answer the door. Its me."

Still nothing. Trinity stares at the door and then moves over and peeks through the window but can see nothing. Where could he have gone, she wonders. Ignoring the rain, she moves around the house, then returns and goes to the sidewalk looking up and down. She even peeks into the garage to see if his car is there, but the window is too high for her to get a good view.

She is pissed, but she doesn't know why. This is her fault. She caused this to happen. Again she knocks hard on the door, her knuckles sore. She tries slapping the door, but to no avail.

"Parker, it's me," the tears apparent in her voice but mingling with the rain on her face. "It's me."

Tears mingling with the raindrops, Trinity finally resigns herself. Parker is either not home or avoiding her now. She slaps the door one more time then turns and walks slowly to her car. There are puddles building on the driveway and her shoes slap in them causing the rain to splatter her pants. When she slides in behind the wheel she is soaked.

She sits there, now bawling for all she has thrown away. Sure it was only to be for a short time, but it would have made things easier.

Trinity reaches for her purse and pulls out a Kleenex. She blows her nose, then gets out another and wipes her face. She starts up the car and slowly backs out of the driveway.

###

Parker finally decides he needs to go home. This sitting in the rain is not a sane thing to do. So, he gets up and starts the long walk back home, wishing everything in his life was different. When he finally reaches the house, he climbs onto the deck and instead of looking at the view, trudges inside. He strips right there in the great room and then hurries upstairs.

He walks briskly into the bathroom and turns on the shower. He goes to the sink and puts toothpaste on this toothbrush and starts brushing his teeth. He gargles and spits.

The shower steams up the bathroom before he finally climbs in. The hot water is soothing as it warms his skin. He soaps himself down and turns around in circles letting the water do its job. \

Parker washes his hair and his face before finally stepping out and feeling renewed. After drying himself he slips into a pair of boxer shorts and a t-shirt.

He wants to just climb in the bed, but instead goes back downstairs to turn off lights and lock doors and windows. He picks up his wet clothes and carries them upstairs with him. He puts his wet clothes on the top of the hamper and then crosses the room and climbs into bed. He falls asleep immediately.

The next morning Parker is up and about early. He runs a few errands then keeps his doctor appointment with Martin.

In the doctor's office Martin reviews the lab tests with Parker and asks if he has any questions.

Parker shakes his head. "No, not really, but you will be glad to know I am going to see the family.

Knowing Parker well, Martin hears the downward trend in his voice. "You still feel guilty because you're dying, don't you?"

Parker is not surprised by his statement and replies, "Yes, I do."

"You know how little sense that makes, don't you?"

"Yes."

Martin shrugs his shoulders and begins stuffing some papers into a big manila envelope that he hands to Parker.

"Lab reports, X rays, medical history, and copies of all my notes. Give them to the doctor and tell him he can contact me any time."

Martin pauses and then adds, "You know, there's probably only one other thing that I can do for you."

"What's that?"

"I can take you to lunch. My treat."

Parker looks at Martin. They start laughing as they leave the office together.

After lunch Parker drops off the envelope at the Cancer Research Center and then is on his way to see his psychiatrist. He spends an hour there and admits he feels better after the session. He feels safe in the knowledge that what he says goes no further.

Parker's mood changes and again he feels a need to be around people so goes to the grocery store and picks up a few things. He then spends a lot of time checking out the beer choices before putting a couple six packs into his cart.

He decides to make one more stop. He goes to the liquor store. Parker walks down the aisles wanting to try something different than the normal wine choices he makes. He stands reading the description cards for the wines and eventually a decision is made.

Done, with his groceries and liquor in the back, Parker climbs into the car. The car makes the next stop for him as he drives letting it take him along for the ride. When he looks around he knows where he is going and begins rehearsing what he will say when he gets there.

He slows down as he turns on to his old street. It is then that he begins to wonder if his family will understand. It's not his home anymore so he hesitates, wondering if he has the right to just drop by. He wants to apologize to each of them, but if it goes bad, he does have the cancer card to play.

He parks slightly away from the house, telling himself it is out of respect for his wife and her friend. He gets out and walks slowly. As he gets closer, he can see through the line of hedges that his sons are out in the yard.

It seems unfair for him to interrupt them, so he just watches. His sons look up and laugh. He follows the path of their eyes and sees what they are laughing at. They are flying kites. Parker smiles.

Jonathan sees Parker first and stops, gawking toward the driveway. Nolan follows his brother's eyes and forgetting the kite, the string is released as they run across the lawn and into their father's arms.

29

Trinity drives to Parker's house a couple of nights later, but he isn't home. She waits fifteen minutes before finally leaving.

The following evening she waits a half hour.

Dr. Proctor, the Sarcoma Specialist walks Trinity out of his office, filling her in on the latest tests. His scruffy beard suits him. Trinity finds it intriguing as it softens the whole doctor specialist image of this tall man. He's a well-known specialist in his field, but he obviously has time to spend outdoors because he is tanned and in shape.

He continues with her down the corridors and out to her car. There she turns and interrupts his detailed report.

"You keep talking to me about the extent the tumors have metastasized and what can be done is being done. I want you instead to talk to me about time."

Dr. Proctor has only recently met this new patient, but he knows that she wants an answer and will not give up until she gets one. He looks at her and says, "You have less time than we thought."

###

Parker has started out feeling great but as he heads toward home that feeling drains from him. He has always been instinctively a person who made plans for the future, but that future is so close to completion he has to stop himself from thinking ahead. Not easy.

Anxious to get home, when he finally pulls into the driveway he sits impatiently waiting for the garage door to open. He happens to look at the front door. He can see something white flapping at the side of the door and puts the car into park, climbs out and goes over to see what it is.

Parker reaches out his hand and pulls a folded piece of paper from the seam of the door. He opens it and smiles.

"Parker, where are you." He reads.

It's signed, Trinity and after her name she has put her cell phone number, her home line and an email address. After which she puts in parenthesis, 'In case you have any doubts I want to see you.'

30

His face illuminated Parker pulls his car into the garage and jumps out. At the door he fumbles frantically for his keys nearly dropping them as he anxiously tries to get the key in the keyhole, first with it upside down then twisting it around. He hurries inside and without missing a beat, takes out his cell. He calls Trinity.

"Hello?"

"What the hell is your name, anyway?"

"Parker!"

"Yes its me." I can hear the excitement in her voice.

"What happened to you. I came back, but…"

"It's a long story I'm home now. Come on over." Parker goes over to the wall and turns on the light."

"Is everything all right?" Trinity's voice sounds a little strange.

"Sure come on over." Parker waits listening to the silence on the other end. "Hey, are you there."

"What?"

"This is the best note ever."

There is a silence, then, "Listen, something's come up and I don't think it's wise to see you."

"What are you talking about.". Parker is getting visibly upset, but he manages to keep his voice calm. "Listen, come on over. Tell me about it here."

Another pause. "I don't think I should".

"Come on. We'll talk about it".

"No."

Parker is tired of the standoff and can't help letting her know how he feels.

"Hey, what is it with this on again off again relationship of ours. Trinity you're the one who left the text. Now get over here and have a glass of wine with me and we can make love or do whatever you want to do. Just, let's get on with it!"

In the midst of his rambling, he hears something that sounds like a muffled cry.

"Hey, Trinity, are you crying?"

Defiantly she replies, "No. Why would I be crying?"

He can hear the quiver in her voice. "I just have a cold, that's all. You're right, I shouldn't have left that note."

"Please..."

"Look, I just don't think we should see each other."

Parker started to say something but stops. Again it goes through his mind like a litany that he has no right to ask her. He waits.

"Parker," she finally says, "the thing is…ah…see…"

Her voice trails off.

Parker waits feeling strange. Their relationship, he realizes, is like a bizarre game of stud poker, where you see four of the other player's cards, but never the one hidden until the end. He knows that whatever minor problem in her life was complicating their being together, he had her beat, in spades.

"Parker? Are you still there?" Her voice sounds soft and quiet, like a little girl.

"Yeah, I'm here."

"See…" There is another pause. "Never mind, good-bye, Parker." She disconnects the call.

Parker slowly puts his cell on the counter. It is a while before he starts to move.

The next morning over lumpy oatmeal Parker makes a decision. Flesh and blood people were out. Human contact just wouldn't work not in his particular situation.

He wasn't bitter. It is just that the ideal of embracing friend's family or lovers now was not fair to himself or to them. So he makes a decision.

Once he is dressed, Parker heads out the door to go to his favorite place where he can get involved with people without it costing anybody pain or time.

He arrives at the bookstore feeling calm and almost happy. He is among the lives of many people now, as well as strangers who walk down the aisles staring at the bindings, looking for that book to fill empty hours. Parker can't help thinking that unlike him, the characters in the books will live forever and ever.

He loves novels, probably even more now that he thinks of having an ending. He slowly moves down the aisles, excusing himself when he has to pass behind another browser. Someone drops a book, "Sorry." They say.

As he stands there, he thinks how he would like to write a novel and have it appear on the library shelf. That would give him immortality.

Parker thinks back, recalling how he tried to write a novel on his very first day at the beach house. The title was easy. It even went through the dedication quickly. But starting the first sentence of the novel was a whole different story.

He stared at that first blank Word sheet for over an hour. His fingers were poised above the keys as they nervously awaited inspiration. Parker finally realized the best way to begin was to just begin, so he knocked out a quick first sentence and studied it.

"Let's eat."

That is as far as Parker got on his first day before giving up and going outside. He told himself that he was just going to fly a kite so that he could think more about a plot for his novel.

After several failed attempts he decided he needed help. He found a local class on writing novels and joined it. The first lesson he learned was that all first novels that are destine to be best sellers must have love, war, hate or pain.

That was depressing and so he gave up his novel writing days and stuck to flying kites instead.

After half an hour browsing Parker purchased two paperbacks that he always meant to read and after paying for them he left the book store and stopped at a food stand to purchase a hamburger and a newspaper before heading back home.

That evening he read until 5:30 then browsed online until he came across a movie he wanted to see. Parker grabbed his jacket and left the house, feeling proud of himself as he drove to the theater.

After those first few weeks of becoming a recluse, his doctors were on him to not become a shut-in. They wanted him to socialize. This was socializing, and he would make sure to mention this when he met with the doctor again.

He actually enjoyed the movie but was happy when it ended to go home get a beer out of the fridge and turn on the television.

Parker watched a few sitcoms before turning in for the night. He was smiling as he undressed for bed realizing that he had filled the day with both entertainment and isolation.

He lay there, unable to fall asleep so he climbed out of the bed and went into the living room to fetch one of the books he had purchased. He ran his hand over the title,

War and Peace, by Leo Tolstoy opened to the first page and began to read.

Part 1, Chapter 1, 'Well, Prince, Genoa and Lucca are now nothing more than estates taken over by the Buonaparte Family. No, I give you fair warning. If you won't say this means war, if you will allow yourself to condone all the ghastly atrocities perpetuated by that Antichrist – yes, that's what I think he is – I shall disown you. You're no friend of mine – not the 'faithful slave' you claim to be... But how are you? How are you keeping? I can see I'm intimidating you. Do sit down and talk to me'.

Parker stared up at the ceiling feeling the weight of the book in his hand. He grimace. "The rest of this had better be a little snappier than the opening,"

31

The second Trinity steps inside the nursing home she is sorry she has come. The place smells like old cheese.

It does do something for her though. The wonderful thing about dying young and childless she thinks while looking for the main office is that you don't have to worry about being a burden to your children in your old age. That and having to end up in a place like this, waiting for the end to come.

A stern matronly woman approaches Trinity. "Can I help you, miss?" she asks.

Trinity replies, "Yes, I'm here to help. I called to volunteer."

"How nice it is for you to volunteer to help with the elderly."

The smell is less offensive where they stand. “I’m glad to help. What would you like me to do?”

Please don’t ask me to change diapers or empty bedpans, please, please. This goes through her mind as she waits.

“Well, we need people to read, write letters or just talk with them. Some haven’t had any real visitors in years and love the company.”

“I can do that. Yes, I’d gladly do that.”

Trinity’s first assignment is to read a travel guide and pause to show the nice pictures to old Mr. Walters in room 206. She is told that he use to travel a lot when he was younger and they think hearing about places may bring him some peace in his day.

Once she meets Mr. Walters she understands. He lays in his bed, staring up at the ceiling and doesn’t acknowledge her presence. Trinity has the feeling that anything more involved would be too much for Mr. Walters.

With a sigh, Trinity sits down close to Mr. Walters bedside so that she can show him the pictures as she reads. He is non-responsive and she can’t tell if he is really listening or even enjoying a glimpse at the pictures, but she continues.

Not anxious to start another assignment she sits with Mr. Walters a bit longer, her mind wandering.

The call from Parker had just happened causing her to have a terrible night. She’d stayed awake conscious of the emptiness of her apartment and when dawn finally came she realized the importance of people to her now more than ever.

She decided to throw herself into helping people by getting involved using her time to do her small part to make the world a little better place in which to die.

Trinity had called several charity organizations assuming it would take them a few days to find her something, but an hour later she found herself walking into the nursing home.

She looks up from the travel guide and notices outside the door a patient slump forward with his head on his chest and his eyes closed. She gets up and goes to him. Not knowing his name she says loudly, "Sir, let me help you to your room so you can lay down."

There is no reaction from the man to let her know he hears her. She tries touching him lightly on the shoulder.

He doesn't react. Trinity panics.

She runs toward the nurses station in alarm.

"There's a dead man in the hall."

"What?"

"Dead."

The nurse rushes behind her and when Trinity stops, the nurse moves up beside her.

The nurse takes one look and says, "No, he's not dead. He has just fallen to sleep. He usually does around this time of day."

"Oh, sorry." Trinity can't help feeling embarrassed.

"No problem. You'll get use to it. Let's get you to you next patient, shall we."

Trinity nodded and followed the nurse who stopped in front of Room 219. She followed behind the nurse as they enter the room.

"Good morning Mrs. Mereweather. This is Trinity. She's come to keep you company.

Trinity manages a smile and watches anxiously as the nurse leaves her alone with Mrs. Mereweather who has on a faded cloth robe over a faded floral nightgown. Her gray hair is untidy and her glasses sit at the edge of her nose.

Trinity spends the longest hour of her life listening to the woman say how much she wished she could get a new cat. She wanted it to replace her old cat Cinnamon who was the most beautiful Persian ever, who she got to replace Rosemary her perfect Tabby, who was a replacement for Parsley, her special Calico that she had gotten as a replacement for her daughter who had grown up and left her here.

The woman never stopped talking and though bored, the hour flew by.

From this patient Trinity is introduced to Mr. Conrad. He is a man in his late eighties who sits straight up in his chair. When Trinity asked him if he wanted to watch TV or talk, he didn't answer so she tried a more personal approach by asking him about his family.

That did it. Mr. Conrad came to life. They where interrupted by a nurse who came to give him his pills, but then he talked on about his friends and family. Everyone was dead. "Miss, there is no one left to call me or come to see me--no one." By the time he stopped talking, Trinity was almost in tears.

She next talks with a woman who answers her question by saying she loves to knit, but her arthritis would not allow her to knit anymore. Then on to another who wants her to write a letter to her dead husband and finally a woman who wants her to read letters she keeps in a wooden box. The letters have been well read as she carefully unfolds one after the other, noting the dates they had been sent being some thirty, forty years ago.

Trinity finally made her way to the nursing station where she tells the two head nurses she is going to lunch. She can tell by their expression that they knew she would never come back.

Trinity feels like a failure as she heads straight for the door never looking back until she stands beside the driver's door of her car. She pauses and looks up at the building. "Thank you." She says as she slips behind the wheel. "Thank you for letting me know what I'm going to miss out on."

Driving away Trinity realizes there is an upside to her situation making it confusing because now she doesn't want to grow old and she doesn't want to die young.

She is in a better mood as she drives to the grocery store. Normally she eats most of her meals out because she hates to cook, but tonight she figures she'd breakdown and fix a meal. As she pushes her shopping cart, she picks up her favorite foods and snacks.

###

Parker abandons *War And Peace*. Instead he starts reading a James Patterson novel about Detective Alex Cross. From the first sentence he is hooked and can't put the book down. He reads it in the great room, carries it with him onto the deck and when he gets hungry, he fixes himself something to eat and stands in the kitchen devouring the book along with his food.

He barely notices the day growing dark as he turns the pages not wanting to stop reading. When it gets harder to see the words on the pages, he gets up and turns on the lights. He sits back down, puts his feet up and in minutes he is lost again in the pages.

Parker raises his head. He thought he heard something and he listens, but there is nothing. He starts reading again. Then he hears it again and knows it's someone knocking at the door.

He doesn't want to be disturbed so he sits quietly wishing whoever it is, away.

It comes again, this time more determined.

"Who is it?" He calls out.

"Trinity."

"Who?"

"Trinity."

Parker remains seated, puzzled.

"Trinity who?"

"Trinity Hunter."

He smiles, finally learning her name.

"I thought we were off again," He says trying to sound serious.

"Well we're on again." Trinity says impatiently from outside. "Open the damn door."

Parker doesn't want to stall any longer as he gets up and hurries over to open the door. Trinity marches right in, hardly looking at him and heads for the kitchen carrying two big grocery bags with her.

"What's that?"

"Dinner," she says.

32

This is the life, Parker thought as they cuddle on the porch sofa watching the sun go down.

"It's so beautiful," Trinity says

"When the sun sets, the colors of the sky change from what is normally a light blue, gray or white cloudy sky to darker hues of blue or shades of red, orange, violet and yellow. Scientists say the lower positioning of the sun on the horizon, combined with the molecules and particles in the atmosphere, affect the way and direction light is reflected. When the phenomenon of light rays scattering happens, it results in colorful sunsets and the details of colors and designs on the sky are determined by the wavelength of the light and the size of the particles."

Trinity lifts her head from his shoulder and stares at the side of his face. She can tell that he is about to smile or laugh by the crinkling at the corner of his eyes and the lifting of his angular cheekbones.

"It's a sunset, Parker. Wasn't looking for a scientific explanation."

He pulls her closer and they laugh together. But then Parker grows sad thinking just how many more days will he be able to hold her, or see a sunset again.

"Need a refill on your wine?" Parker says to shake the feeling away.

"Yes, I'll come with you. It's getting a little chilly."

Arm in arm they enter the house. In the kitchen the clutter of dishes and pans from dinner awaits so with a sigh they clean up the kitchen. It's comfortable working together. Parker rinses the dishes and Trinity puts them in the dish washer. As if pre-arranged, he cleans the counters by the sink while Trinity gives the island a once over.

They talk non-stop trying to learn everything about each other in one evening.

When Parker finally fills their wine glasses it has grown dark. They carry their glasses into the livingroom where Trinity opts for sitting on the floor so Parker joins her.

The lamp in the corner of the room that is on a timer, comes on. Parker reaches for the remote, but Trinity grabs his hand, "Let's just enjoy the quiet."

So they do. They sit there on the floor enjoying their wine in the twilight hours of the day. Parker lays back, balancing his wine glass on his stomach while Trinity leans against the chair playing with some kite string.

"Trinity, have you ever been married."

"Came close, but no, never. Worked with some powerful men and dated them but I managed not to do the cliché of falling in love with my boss."

"So who was the lucky man who almost got you."

"Well," Trinity says smiling. "He was a lawyer who had his office just down the hall. He had his own practice and I would walk pass his door every day and then one day he sees me at the coffee stand and we start talking and he asks me out. That's how it started. That cost me five years of my life, waiting around for him."

Trinity takes the last sip of her wine so Parker takes her glass, excuses himself and refills both in the kitchen.

Back in his spot in the livingroom he again relaxes.

"Anyway," Trinity says, "the son of a bitch even dumped me the way they advise in men's magazines. You know, in a classy restaurant so there won't be a scene." Trinity turns with a mischievous smile on her face.

"When I got finished there were little pieces of scene sticking to the walls and ceiling."

Parker has his wine up to his lips when she says this. His hand can't stop fast enough, and wine enters his mouth. He chokes on it in the midst of laughing. Tears run down his face as he puffs out wine and Trinity joins in his laughter. Soon they are both laughing uncontrollably. It feels good.

When they finally manage restraint again Parker asks, "Have you always lived in Rochester?"

"No, I lived in Arizona, then Seattle, which is not a good way to go. I mean, maybe from Seattle to Arizona might be better. I even lived in New York City for a bit, but that was worst. It was not only wet, but the snow…" She turned and looked at Parker. "Don't have to tell you about snow." She chuckled.

Trinity takes a sip of her wine, then mumbles, almost to herself. "Wow, that is the story of my life and it wasn't very interesting."

"No, I found it interesting, sort of…"

Trinity gives him one of her special stares. She keeps her eyes on him and Parker knows what she is waiting for.

"Well…" she says.

"Well, I've got a wife and two kids in Rochester. We've been separated for a while now".

Trinity doesn't react one way or the other.

"Is that what you want," she asked.

"Yes."

"So how are things between you."

Parker exhales noisily.

"Let me put it this way. We were having a lot of trouble, but the finale was quite a scene all by itself."

Parker repeats that day when he drove off, leaving his family by the roadside. He keeps his eyes on Trinity so that he can read her feelings about what he did. He is glad that Trinity doesn't react with distaste or anything but sympathy as though she understands his actions.

Parker adds, "Then I had to tell my two boys something I should've told them a long time ago."

"So what was that. The facts of life," Trinity says teasingly.

"Yes, you can say that. I told them at least one of them."

There is a comfortable silence as each deals with their own private thoughts.

"So what do you do Parker. So far I know you lay around the house a lot."

Parker comes up on his elbow. "I fly kites on the beach." He smiles at Trinity. "You either work at home or you are on a sabbatical too. At least, I think that's the case. I am taking time off from a very stressful career."

"What's that."

"Stock broker…and, don't say anything. I've heard all the jokes. What about you."

"I've got some money saved," she says. It is my personal nest egg I squirrel away funds in for pleasure spending. I had planned to surprise my husband to be only he ended up surprising me." The distaste was apparent in her voice.

"Anyway, I've got a lot of credit cards I live off of. If I don't overdo it, it can take almost a year for the credit card company to finally nail me."

"So what happens in a year or so."

Trinity smiles knowingly. "I'll worry about that when it happens," she says trying to make light of the matter before changing the subject.

"Hey, let's go do something."

Parker looks at her questioningly.

"You know, she says irritably, "let's go on a date."

"A date."

Parker thinks about it for a minute and says. "What about a movie?"

"Sure, that's good." Trinity pauses. "I know let's go see Ghostbusters in 3D. The new one with Melissa McCarthy, Kristen Wiig, and Kate McKinnon. It'll be like blending the past with the present."

"I'm game."

A surprise expression appears on her face. "You mean, you're not going to say it's a girly flick?"

"No, I'm not."

Together they get up, testing themselves for sobriety. They each have had two glasses of wine, but that was several hours ago. The theater is in Gates, a thirty minute drive if they don't take the expressway, which is what he plans to do. In the kitchen they drink several glasses of water and giggling make each other walk the line. Five minutes later they determine themselves to be sober.

Parker helps Trinity into her jacket and soon they are on their way.

Everything is interesting and fun as they continue to enjoy each other's company. He's been here before--that trifecta of a romantic relationship — intense love, sexual desire. All of which is the opening stage for a long-term attachment which sadly can not materialize.

Parker says, "This time we'll pay for the tickets and go in the front way just to be different."

Trinity, who has been deep in thought looks at him and nods. She can't help thinking that the emotional energy between them is what leads to a lasting passion filled relationship. They are really enjoying each other, really. This frightens her.

When they pull into the parking lot, they see a line. "Do you think everyone is going to the same movie?" Trinity asks.

"I hope not."

Parker and Trinity get out of the car and meet in front of it where Parker puts his arm around her. They walk together. "We should have known. The last show of the evening at the only three-D theater…"

"I don't mind. Do you."

"Well, can we sit in the back row and neck," Trinity asked, giggling.

"No."

"Why not."

"Because this is only are first date," Parker says kiddingly. Besides, by the time we get to the ticket booth all seats will be taken."

Trinity grabs his arm and squeezes it. The line moves surprisingly fast and soon they enter the dark theater.

Once the movie begins, from start to finish there is laughter in the theater. The movie is hilarious. At one point Trinity leans over and in Parker's ear says, "I almost peed my pants." Parker replied back, "I did."

The movie over, they join the others in the aisles, making their way to the exit. When they are finally in the parking lot, they stop and look at each other.

"Want to do something else?"

"Sure, what do you have in mind?"

Park thinks for a minute. "Let's go walk out on the pier. It won't be too crowded, plus it's the only thing left to do this late."

Trinity is all in so they drive back to his house to park the car. Parker opens the garage and drives in. He goes to the shelf at the back of the garage and finds two flashlights. He gives one to Trinity. Soon they are on their way.

Several couples are out walking, but for the most part it feels like they are alone.

"Tell me, Parker, how did you get interested in kites?"

"How…" he starts, then remembers she saw the kite in the house and probably saw the books too.

He thinks for a moment and then tells her about the ITE Flight held in 2009 to celebrate the 175th birthday of Rochester. "If you can imagine the symmetry of hundreds of kites soaring on the beach. Different sizes, shapes, and colors and just the way they soar. I was hooked."

It is a perfect ending to a perfect day as they make their way back to Parker's house. Not saying a word, Trinity finds the bedroom and slips into the bathroom while Parker undresses and sits on the edge of the bed, naked from the waist up.

Trinity returns wearing one of his shirts and walks to the other side of the bed and lays down. Parker follows suit. He turns to look at her.

Soon they are in each other's arms and Parker wants only to please her. He has never felt this strongly for someone in a long time. Only it is not to be.

Frustrated he sits back up with his feet over the edge of the bed, feeling less of a man. He jumps when he feels Trinity's hand on his back.

"It's okay, Parker. It's okay."

"Is that what they tell you to say in those women magazines," He replies a little harshly.

Trinity pulls her hand back.

The silence between them now is far from comfortable. Parker finally turns to look at her. "Hey, I'm sorry. I shouldn't snap at you. It's not your fault. It's just that, well, something happened a few months ago, and I think it caused this to happen now." Hopefully that'll be the last surprise waiting for me." He tries to laugh it off, but it doesn't work.

"Parker," Trinity says, "holding is nice."

He smiles. The warmth in her voice relaxes him and he gets back under the covers and puts his arm around her shoulders. She snuggles close. Somewhat content, they fall asleep.

33

Parker wakes up the next morning and gazes at Trinity who is still sleeping soundly. She looks like an angel to him with her hair untidy and her long lashes casting a shadow on her cheekbones.

Finally he forces himself to get up and goes into the bathroom where he brushes his teeth, takes a shower and puts on his robe; the big fluffy white one that his sons gave him for Christmas one year. It always made him feel like a celebrity when he put it on. It was the kind that the fancy hotels have for their guest to use.

When he returns to the bedroom, Trinity is up, wrapped in the sheet, waiting for him to finish. Parker goes to the closet and pulls out a robe just like his; also given as a Christmas present by the boys to their mother.

"Really?"

"Believe me when I say, she never wore it. The boys gave it to her when they gave me this one," he says pulling the sides of the robe out in front of him. "She stuck it in the closet, but it was just not her style."

Trinity laughed, took the robe and heads to the bathroom. Parker linger a moment then goes to the kitchen to make his famous pancakes. By the time Trinity joins him he has a full breakfast ready. He pours her coffee and joins her at the island.

"This is great, Parker. You are a man of many talents."

"Well thank you milady."

"I remember once when a friend fixed me breakfast. It was a bowl of cereal. Good cereal, but it had a real problem. I happened to look down in my bowl and saw things moving in it that I thought were raisins."

"God, how awful."

"Well, that's not the awful part. The real problem with eating insects in your cereal is that once you've eaten all the bugs, well, all you have left is cereal…"

Trinity gets the reaction she hoped for; except of course the spray of coffee in her face. He gives Trinity a shock expression that soon turns into laughter. They continue to laugh together; each thinking they seem to be laughing a lot and laughter is fresh and new to both of them.

"Hey."

"What."

"Is there something you've always wanted to do. I mean like when you were a teenager and didn't know any better."

"Seriously?"

"Yeah.

Parker observes Trinity and can see she is serious so he thinks about it. Finally he says, "Well, when I was around fourteen I use to dream of hopping a freight train to see where it would take me. You know, the age-old dream of being a hobo."

Trinity leans into his shoulder and smiles. "So what's stopping us."

"You've got to be kidding."

"Do I look like I'm kidding."

"It's a beautiful day for hopping a train."

Parker stares out the window and then back at Trinity. "Well, the rules are…"

"Wait a minute, you studied the rules?"

"Yes, I was seriously going to do this at one point, but chickened out. Anyway they say find the local freight yard. There'll be a train leaving or coming through there eventually."

Playing along, Trinity asks, "So how do we do that?"

"We look for train yards in the forgotten part of town, the part of town with all the rough neighborhoods. The yard is usually near big industry, maybe near a river or port."

"Okay, let's do this. Say around noon."

"No, the rules say…"

"What?"

"Well, wait until dark and wear dark clothing?"

"Forget the rules. We are going in broad daylight when it is safer."

Parker can tell there is no way she is going to change her mind, so he remains quiet.

While Parker cleans the kitchen, Trinity goes in and gets dressed. When she returns, she gives him a kiss. "I'm going home to change and I will meet you back here in a couple hours."

Parker walks to the door with Trinity and after she leaves, he goes to get dressed. By the time Trinity returns, He has everything in order. He has packed a backpack with water and snacks. He has on a dark turtleneck sweater, black jeans, and a pair of sneakers. When Trinity sees him she has to stop herself from laughing. He looks like a burglar.

Her car is in the driveway in back of his so they take her car and head to a point where he knows he has seen a train going down the tracks. They find a place to park the car and get out, walking quickly.

The railroad tracks curve around a hill and there is a lot of bushes growing near the area. They are almost out of the city but not yet in the country.

"We're sure going to feel silly if a train doesn't come," Trinity says.

"We'll feel worse if it does."

"So what's in the backpack."

"Snacks and drinks," Parker says.

Trinity starts to say something, but decides to be quiet. He obviously plans on a long ride, she thinks and muffles a laugh.

Walking side by side, Parker asks, "What took you so long anyway."

"Well I couldn't figure out what to wear."

"You're kidding."

"No, I changed my clothes three times," Trinity says. "I've never hopped a train before."

Parker looks at her. She has on a gold football jersey, blue sneakers, a blue and red plaid scarf and a large bag over her shoulder. It's hard for him to fathom that her outfit was the one she settled on.

"So how do you plan on hopping a train with that big bag over your shoulder."

"Great minds think alike," she says. I thought if it doesn't pan out, we could have a picnic. I have a bag full of sandwiches and a small thermos of coffee. It has this shoulder strap," she says holding it out in front of her, "and I can use both hands to grab hold. So it's no problem."

"If we live through this we'll get arrested anyway. Might as well feed the homeless."

"Sure, don't whitewash everything just to keep my spirits up," she mumbles.

Parker stops, holding up his hand.

Trinity stops and listens. At first all she can hear is the sound of birds, but then she hears it. In the distance is the sound of a train coming and it gradually is getting louder.

They both slowly turn and look at each other, their excitement showing on their faces.

"Now what do we do." She finally says.

"I don't know but it's time to do something."

He steers her over to some bushes. They duck out of sight and peer down the tracks, both nervous and happy at the same time.

"Where do you suppose it's going," she whispers.

"Now you're getting it," Parker says. She smiles knowingly.

Finally they see it coming around the curve, tearing down the track toward them.

It's so loud that he knows Trinity won't hear him so he grabs her arm and holds it, ready to give her the signal. He waits until the engine is far up the tracks and luckily the train is long. He squeezes her arm.

Scared and excited they step out of the bushes. It is immense a giant rushing wall of steel and they are only 10 feet away.

"We want to watch for open boxcars, or the rear platform of a grainer or hopper; something where we can get a leg up."

Trinity only catches and understands part of what he is saying

"Looks pretty big, Trinity yells to Parker.

"We don't have to stop it," He yells back even though they are standing only a foot apart. "We just have to jump on the side of it."

The train is long and they move out to the side of the tracks so they will be ready. Parker looks down the length of the train and sees what he is waiting for. Coming their way is the traditional freight cars, complete with handrails on the side.

Now they need to run fast enough, time it just right, grab a handrail and grab tight, jump up and get their feet on the rail. A cake walk he hopes.

Parker nods and Trinity starts running along behind Parker who is running dangerously close to the tracks. His mind is running as fast as his feet as he contemplates that he can think of better ways to spend an afternoon than being dragged to death.

But he runs as fast as he can, anyway. Soon he is running out of breath and as he chances a look down the tracks he sees he is also running out of train.

"It's now or never," He says. He sticks out his hand and surprises himself when he grabs hold of the ladder. The motion of the train has his feet running faster than he can run, but he hangs on, gripping tightly, his feet dragging as he commits himself to jumping up.

His grip starts to slip, but he scrambles to get his other hand on the ladder. Now his feet are flailing in the wind. He pulls his body toward the ladder and finally he has both feet in place. Parker hangs on tight, feeling very alive.

At that point he remembers Trinity and looks back down the track and sees her.

She is exhausted, running as fast as she can, but falling back.

He quickly hooks his right arm around a rung, then extends his left hand out for Trinity who is probably forty feet back.

She sees his hand stretched out to help her and she tries running faster narrowing the distance between them, slowly but she is determined. She is 30 feet away, then 20.

She is reaching out her hand.

But the speeding train is relentlessly charging on not giving an inch to help. Trinity deliberates, "You either make it or you don't".

Trinity is being left behind.

She waves for him to go without her as she lapses in to a half walk completely spent.

Parker watches as she shrinks in the distance, putting his face to the wind as he savors the moment one last time. The ground looks farther away and more intimidating as he swallows hard then starts counting to three. On one he tucks his head to his chest. On two he starts releasing his grip, and on three he jumps.

34

Parker rolls over sideways across the graveled shoulders, down the raised side area and finally stops on the edge of the grassy slope with a miserable clump. His shoulders ache as he tries to uncurl his body, thankful he knew enough to tuck and roll. He slides down the embankment on his rear end, more than a little stunned.

Ignoring a pain in his ankle, Parker manages to focus on the last of the train as it goes roaring down the tracks. He is exhausted, sitting there in awe at the power of the freight cars pounding away. He shakes his head from side to side thinking proudly that he has done it, then allows his body to fall back in the grass.

As it disappeared down the track, Parker determines that he is at the most, a mile from where they started. He never even got out of the city, Parker thought, but Jesus, that was fun.

He lay there, panting, knowing, he'd be sore in the morning, but doesn't mind a bit. He turns and sees the panting figure of Trinity slowly jogging towards him. Parker tries to get up, but then decides to just lie there in the grass with the sunlight shining on his face.

He smiles as he thinks of what he has done then admits to himself that the nice thing about hopping a freight is that it feels so good when its's over.

Several minutes later, Trinity slowly staggers over to him and collapses in the grass. They are both panting as they half-crawl toward each other.

"I'm sorry Parker," Trinity says, trying to catch her breath. "I'm sorry."

Parker just grins at her, happily.

"I'm really sorry," she goes on, "I wanted you to make your train…"

Parker pulls her closer.

"Hey…I made it. Don't feel sad. I actually did it."

"So, you did."

He kisses her, and she kisses him back.

Their tender moment is interrupted by the sound of someone cackling. They look around and their eyes settle on an old man standing about twenty feet from them, pointing in their direction as he guffaws, slapping his knee and almost tumbling forward.

All they can do is stare.

The man wore a strange hat, torn clothes, and carried a mysteriously familiar backpack, along with a sack he clung possessively in his hand. At his side is a three-legged dog.

Parker and Trinity exchange glances, then get to their feet. The movement is too quick and too soon for Parker who suddenly winces in pain, unable to stop before yelling, "Ouch."

This sent the old hobo into another fit of laughter.

"What's the matter?" Trinity asked, as Parker leans on her.

"My ankle. I must have sprained it or..." Parker suddenly turned to the hobo. "What the hell are you laughing at?"

"You, ya damn fool. You try to jump off a moving train and fall on your ass doing it. Then you start smoochin. The hobo barely finishes when he starts cackling again.

Ignoring the man, Trinity asks, "can you walk?"

"No, but I can limp." Trinity helps Parker to his feet. She puts his arm around her for support. Then slowly and awkwardly he tries to limp along beside her.

The old man stops laughing and hurries toward them. When he is right in front of them, Parker recognizes his backpack.

"Hey, wait," the strange man says. "You won't get far on that bum ankle of yours. Maybe I can help."

"Like you helped yourself to my backpack?"

The hobo looks at the pack. "Didn't know it was yours. Found it laying in the grass. Sit down and let me help."

Having nothing to lose, Parker obeys. They watch as he begins pulling things out of his sack, mumbling to himself as he unloads a yo-yo, a cracked coffee cup, a plastic dish, a spoon and then stops.

"Think I got me a ol ace bandage," he mumbles as he looks into the bag."

Getting a little impatient, Trinity says "thanks, but I think…"

"Here it is." The old hobo suddenly produces an Ace bandage and miracles of miracles, it even looks clean. "Take off your shoe, young fella."

Parker carefully takes off his shoe. The old hobo moves in front of him and expertly begins to wrap the bandage. "Yeah, just looks sprained," he says.

"Never did them rails afore, have ya?"

"No, First time."

"I've' been a boarding the rails a long time now," the hobo says. "Had a son once, hell, had a whole family but that was a long time ago. After my wife died and the boys grew up, I had nothing…" There, that should do it."

"Thank you very much," Parker says, checking the bandage. It was wrapped good and tight."

Parker stands and walks around.

"I think we can make it back to the car now," Trinity says.

"Car." The old hobo stared in amazement. "You got a car and you jumped on a train?"

"Just thought we'd try it," Parker says, almost apologetically.

"Just thought you'd try it," the old hobo repeated the words, shaking his head.

As the old hobo stared off into the distance, Trinity turned to Parker.

"Let's see if you can walk,"

Parker manages to hobble a little, experimenting with how much weight he can put on his ankle. He takes several steps and then they turn to leave, saying first "Well thanks again."

"Glad I could help," the old hobo says. "How about givin me five dollars for my trouble?"

"What?"

"Parts, labor, my medical training… five bucks is dirt cheap and you damn well know it."

Parker and Trinity look at each other. "What about you give me my backpack first."

The hobo looked at it, sniffed it, then said, "Tell you what, what if I take the food and then give you the backpack."

Parker smiles. "That's a deal." They wait while the hobo takes out the food he had planned for them, glad to share it with the hobo.

They turn and slowly head back toward Trinity's car. The old hobo watches them go.

It wasn't that far to go, but in his state, it took much longer. By the time they reached the car, Parker is exhausted.

“You want to get it x rayed?” Trinity asked as they drove toward home.

“No, I’m sure it’s just sprained. That crazy old hobo wrapped it good, though.”

“Want to order a pizza tonight for dinner?”

“Sounds good.”

Trinity says, not looking at him. “Say, Parker?”

Before she says it, Parker senses he’s not going to like what she has to say.

“What?”

“I don’t know if we should be seeing so much of each other,” she adds.

“We’re having that conversation again, Trinity? In the last thirty seconds, we’ve gone from caring enough to want to take me for an x-ray, to pizza to I hope we’ll always be friends.

“I’m serious, Parker.”

They drove along in silence. Parker can’t handle it.

“Are you sure?” Parker says adamantly.

“I’m not sure of anything.”

“Okay, we’ll talk about it.”

When they arrive at his house, Trinity helps him inside. Parker asks, “Will you order the pizza?” I want to take a shower. Trinity nods her head.

Parker hobbles to the bedroom and strips in the bathroom, waiting for the shower water to warm. He steps gingerly in, taking his time and allowing the water to run over his sore ankle and his aching bones. It feels good as he limbs around letting the water pour over him.

The room fills with steam and he remembers that he has company.

Sadly Parker forces himself to turn off the water and step out. He dries himself off, then takes the towel and wraps it around him. In the bedroom he first goes to the doorway and yells, “Pizza here yet?”

“No.” Trinity yelled from the next room.

Parker stuck his head back in the room, hesitates and leans forward again. “I think I’m going to climb in the tub and soak my ankle”

“Great,” hollered Trinity.

Trinity is still dressed in her freight hopping clothes and is wandering around, bored.

No nothing’s wrong, she thought to herself, except I’m too weak to run any more so we’re getting closer, which scares the hell out of me. That’s all. Otherwise, everything’s just peachy keen.

Trinity wanders over to Parker’s bookshelf where he is in the habit of leaving his keys and change. She picks up his key chain, studying the leather key chain top with what looks like a stainless steel tag hanging from it. She studies it closely and sees that it’s a gift for being a groomsmen. There is a date stamped on it.

The water has stopped running so she can hear him clearly.

“I like your key chain,” she says.

“I do too. It was a practical gift”, he says.

Trinity puts it down, and begins looking through Parker’s paperbacks while Parker talks about the keychain.

“I got it from my brother’s wedding so it is special to me.” With a grimace she hears him say, “Ouch.”

“Parker, are you in the tub?”

“Yes. I was sitting on the edge and put too much weight on the ankle. I guess it’s best for me to just put my whole body in.”

“Yes that’s best. The hot water is going to help that ankle and your body. If you don’t soak you won’t be moving much tomorrow.”

Parker knows she's right. Carefully he slides his body down into the tub. He leans his back against the tub and closes his eyes.

Trinity walks idly around the room stopping to look at a picture of a scenic view that she imagines hangs in most homes on the lake. It is that picture of the two white Adirondack chairs sitting cozily on the shore and the sun casting a shadow replica in the sand. It makes her smile.

She continues her survey of the room, stopping at an end table where she picks up a family photo of two boys standing with kites snuggly held against their bodies. This too makes her smile.

She knows that Parker is married, but he says they are separated and have been for some time. She believes him. He couldn't lie about having a wife because the exquisite decorating she sees around the rooms are definitely wifely skills.

It is a big room and she senses that the paraphernalia laying around on tables and chairs is far from the normal aura of the room. Again, she smiles.

Trinity slowly twirls around, pausing as she spots the bookcase. One can learn much about a person from the books they read, she thinks to herself. She walks over and sees that the books are paperbacks which tells her that this is more a vacation residence than a permanent one. She picks up one paperback to inspect it closer.

That does not make sense, she thinks as she leans forward. Behind the paperbacks there are hardcover books. Who puts paperbacks in front of hardcover books!

Curious she pushes the paperbacks aside and a sense of numbness comes over her as she pulls out and reads first the title of the book she has exposed. "Questions and Answers on Death and Dying: A Companion Volume to On Death and Dying, by Elisabeth Kubler-Ross."

Trinity pulls out another. "In the Face of Death: Professionals Who Care for the Dying and the Bereaved, by Danai Papadatou."

Unable to stop she grabs and reads another title, "Spiritual Perspectives on Death and Dying, by Bernice H. Hill, Ph.D."

Stunned into silence she stares at the book spines. She cannot move from the spot as she focuses on the books until something snaps in her head. "What the hell…!"

Trinity stares at the books she holds in her hands. At first, she is paralyzed by what they insinuate, but then she is infuriated. She rotates and heads toward the master bedroom, rushing toward the bathroom door.

Parker is in the tub ignorantly soaping away happily when Trinity kicks the bathroom door open.

"How could you," she screams. "How the hell did you find out. Who gave you the right to snoop around in my life!"

Shock is written all over Parker's face as he turns quickly, losing his balance and almost hitting his head on the back of the tub as his heels slide forward toward the faucet. "What are you talking about?"

Trinity ignores his reply. "Why did you do it? I loved you, you sneaky bastard and here you were playing some sick sympathy game."

Trinity, her arms laden with the heavy books, shifts them to one side as she throws them one by one at a stunned Parker. Her message delivered, she runs out the bathroom.

Dodging to avoid getting clobbered, Parker reaches over the side of the tub to pick up one of the books. He reads the title and pales. It doesn't take much for him to realize why Trinity is upset.

"Let me explain, please." But his words fall on death ears as he hears the sound of the front door slamming shut.

Trinity is gone, and he is sure she isn't coming back.

Parker confused about what has just happened is instantly sure of one thing. Trinity is definitely gone.

Parker rushes into the bedroom and grabs a pair of pants, forgetting the pain in his ankle as he quickly walks, putting one leg after the other into his pants. By the time he reaches the living room he is pulling up his pants and hooking them. He grabs his jacket, swings it over his head and slips his arms into the sleeves leaning hard to one side and wincing from the pain in his ankle.

He hurries out into the night, his hair and body still covered with soapy wet water, and looks around wildly. Her car is still in the driveway.

He moves as quickly as he can on his sore ankle. She's not out front, nor along the sides of the house. Where can she be.

Shivering in the night air and trying to ignore the pain, Parker limps up the street, peering into the darkness.

"Trinity, Trinity. He yells. "Where are you?"

He limps back in the other direction, toward the beach, frantically gawking around.

"Trinity"

No answer. He can't see her anywhere. Panic sets in.

"Trinity."

Nothing. She is gone.

Desperate but not knowing what else to do, Parker starts to turn and head toward the house when out of the corner of his eye, he sees a figure out on the sand, heading across the beach. Ignoring his ankle frantically he hurries after the figure, hoping it is she.

35

Trinity marches across the sand, traveling in the opposite direction as she ignores Parker calling out to her. She has to constantly rub the tears from her eyes so that she can see where she is going.

Fifty feet behind her, Parker is still limping after her.

"Trinity," he yells. "Will you wait a minute."

She doesn't answer or look back. She just keeps walking as fast as she can through the sand.

"Trinity, please."

He is getting closer now.

"Go to hell, Parker."

What happened. What..."

"Go hang around another death person, you creep" she screamed over her shoulder.

"I don't know what..."

"Get yourself some other loser."

Parker tries to hurry but can't trudge through the sand without feeling his badly swollen, purple ankle impeding every step.

"Trinity. Wait." There is desperation in his voice. "I don't know what is happening here."

Trinity doesn't stop as she yells back over her shoulder, her anger causing her whole body to shake and her growing embarrassment as she thinks what an idiot she has been. "You know I'm dying you... you."

Her voice starts to crack. "Leave me alone." She wants to leave and go home, but she doesn't want to close the distance between them because he will see how deeply he has hurt her.

Parker halts. He stands there in the sand, his ankle screaming at him and his whole body shocked by what Trinity has said. He had to mishear her words. He hasn't a clue why she is so upset.

He doesn't want to lose her. He can't let her go. When in doubt, speak the truth, he whispers to himself. Then aloud he yells, "Trinity, you aren't the one whose dying. I am."

Trinity stops in her track wondering if she has heard him right. What is this, some kind of sick game he's playing. Pretending it's all about him now. Her feet are literally caught in the sand, unable to move her forward.

Parker slowly limbs forward until he is right behind Trinity. He grabs her, loses his balance and they both pitch forward into the sand.

He takes her by surprise and thought exhausted, Trinity attacks him ferociously, pounding and kicking.

"Stop it," Parker says as he manages to grab hold of her wrists.

"Goddam you". She screams, as she struggles in his grip.

"Trinity stop it," he says, keeping a firm hold on her. "I'm not going to let you go until you tell me what the hell is going on."

Angrily, Trinity twists and turns trying to free herself, but Parker manages to hold fast, laying on top of her now and using the weight of his body to control her movements.

She wiggles her limps and gets a leg free and before he can stop her, she kicks him on his sprained ankle.

Pain radiates through his body and Parker loses his grip. "Ow," he says.

Trinity doesn't hesitate as she wrenches an arm free from his grip. But Parker is desperate now. He ignores the pain and moving quickly gets a hold of her wrist.

There is not much fight left in either of them. Parker can feel Trinity's efforts subsiding as she glares up at him, his full weight resting on her body.

The only sound to be heard now is the waves coming into shore and the sounds of heavy breathing.

"How can you act like you don't know." Trinity says in a tearful voice.

"Don't know what."

"That I've got cancer. What the hell else are those books for if you don't know."

Parker looks at her, stunned. "Cancer…"

He let go of her arms and leaned off to one side of her. There is something very believable about his amazed tone of voice and his stunned expression which confused Trinity even more.

"Goddamit Parker, if you didn't know how come you've got those books and how come you've been so nice to me."

Quietly, still stupefied, Parker gave the only answer he could speaking very softly and very slowly.

"I don't know whether to laugh or cry, Trinity, those books are for me because my gut is full of cancer, and I haven't been nice to you. I love you."

It is Trinity's turn to have a stunned expression, her anger perishes as she feels sad and confused. This can't be happening. She has been worried about starting up a relationship because she is dying… She has fallen for him, hard, and now it's a race to the finish line for both of them.

Parker is still letting it all settle in. What kind of sick joke is this, he meditates as he looks skyward. Are you fooling with me.

He feels Trinity's gaze and he looks at her. Her expression is raw with pain and sorrow and he wishes he could say something to comfort her. But what can he say.

Trinity hesitantly reaches out for Parker, gently touching him as though he might break.

Parker watches her trembling hand as it comes toward him. He feels her gentle touch.

He suddenly reaches out and pulls her in close to him and they lay still on the cool sandy beach, hanging on for dear life.

"Oh god," she heard herself saying. "what are we going to do."

Parker answers softly, "I guess we're going to die."

Trinity raises up and rests her head on her hand as she stares down at this strange man who has taken hold of her heart.

They remain in that pose for several minutes, their eyes locked and in silence.

Then, Parker sees it. The corners of Trinity's mouth push up into a smirk. At first he is confused, but then he can feel his mouth doing the same.

Trinity snickers then her whole body begins to rock, back and forth uncontrollably. Just watching her, Parker is helplessly caught up. His laughter pitches higher and higher as his body becomes more animated.

They fall on their backs, their legs and arms flailing about frenziedly and if a passerby were to see them now they would think these two persons were having seizures.

36

It has been a powerfully enlightening evening for both of them as they slowly control their laughter.

Unspoken, they realize they are learning to see and appreciate what they have instead of what they've lost.

Trinity gets up from the sand and reaches down to help Parker to his feet. Their bodies ache, making it twice as hard to walk across the sand, but what is important is they are doing it together. Their minds fill with a deeper sense of each other. They are at peace.

A comfortable silence comes over them as they walk with arms around each other back to Parker's house. With one hand on the railing and the other around their waists, they manage to conquer the steps until finally entering through the sliding back doors.

Inside Trinity heads to the Livingroom and drops down into the overstuffed chair. She can't remember feeling this tired, even after a long run.

Parker smiles at her as he limps to the kitchen. From her chair she watches as he gets out two clean dishes, wine glasses and napkins. She observes as he arranges them on the island, then joins her in the Livingroom.

Seeing him winch from the pain of walking on his ankle, she starts to say something, then checks herself, knowing he is fully aware that he needs to get off that foot.

Trinity smiles as Parker stretches out on the sofa. We are alive, she reflects and therefore we will die. It is a simple, most obvious truth of existence. A few days ago this would have been an upsetting idea, but now sharing it with Parker it seems kind of dreamy.

Trinity turns her attention to the glass blown winged horse on the bookshelf. When she was a child and well into her teens she loved horses. The first time she rode a horse was at her grandfather's stables when she was around seven years old.

Her mother hadn't gotten along with her father, so Trinity had not seen him until that day when her mother took her there. It was the first time she had been up close to a horse. As she walked into the barn next to her grandfather she yanked on his hand to stop him. He looked down and said, “What is it little one?”

As she stared up at him he could see she was frightened and picked her up and placing her on his shoulders said, “That’s better. Now you’re bigger than the horse.”

She never forgot that act of kindness that changed the way she felt about horses. If he had forced her to continue their approach, he would have changed her love for horses into one of fear.

Regretfully she never saw him again and just like everything else about her mother she couldn’t understand, she never asked why. From the time she was able to talk she had learned that what her mother did was not to be questioned, whether it affected her or not.

Now as she stares at the glass horse she remembers drawing wings on some of her horses when she was a child.

Trinity gets up from the chair and moves nearer. Now she can see the unusual details of the mane, tail and fetlocks are all created by hundreds of air bubbles.

She leans forward, admiring the detail when headlights flash through the window and fall on the figurine creating the illusion of volume and mass as shadows are casts from one side than another.

Mesmerized Trinity reaches out to touch the figurine when her motion is interrupted by the sound of the doorbell. She stops her hand in midair as she recoils, startled by the sound.

Parker has been watching her. The intenseness of her emotions is one of the things he is growing to admire. It makes him think how he has wanted to keep the blinds shut, closing off life and has been known to repeat the mantra, ‘Been there, done that.’ The truth is, watching Trinity he realizes that every experience is new, and it’s up to us to open our eyes and see beyond the obvious.

He sees Trinity's reaction when the doorbell rings and kiddingly says, "It won't bite." He then goes over and looks through the peep hole. "Pizza's here".

"Great," I'm starving.

"Me too."

While Parker pays the delivery guy, Trinity makes her way to the kitchen. By the time the delivery guy has removed the pizza from the warming bag and handed it to Parker, she is seated at the island.

Parker stands across from her and sits the pizza box down. He flips open the top and before the lid falls completely open, Trinity's hand is the box, pulling off a slice.

"Hungry," he says laughing.

Trinity nods, her mouth full with the first bite of her pizza.

Parker wiggles a slice free and holds it up. "Cheers."

Trinity giggles and touches the edge of her pizza to his. "Cheers."

Silently they finish off a slice each before Parker goes over to the cabinet to get a bottle of wine.

Trinity works out another slice as she watches Parker pour the wine and by the time he places a glass in front of her, she has polished off her second wedge.

"You better hurry," she says, "I could eat the whole thing."

"I can see that."

Smiling he goes around the island and sits down on the stool next to her. They manage to eat all but two slices before leaning back and taking a deep breath.

"That's it for me." Trinity says.

"Me to."

Parker stands and puts the last two pieces in a Tupperware container he takes out of the cabinet. While he does that Trinity swallows the last few sips of wine in her glass before getting up and clearing off the island. She is about to wipe the top when she is surprised by Parker putting the leftover pizza in the refrigerator.

"What are you doing?"

Parker turns around. "Huh?"

"You put them in the refrigerator?"

"Yes, we can have these two pieces later."

"Cold?"

Parker stares at her. "Yes, everyone knows that cold pizza is the best."

"Not me. No. I prefer my pizza fresh and hot, thank you. Those two are for you."

Parker, discombobulated by her announcement, isn't sure what she expects him to do with the slices, but it doesn't matter. His mind wanders elsewhere.

They have filled the day and evening and now awkwardly wait for what comes next. He doesn't want to ruin this newfound closeness, so he ponders exactly what to say. Finally he makes his move by saying, "We should turn in."

Trinity nods. Putting a little humor into the moment, she sashays her way to the bedroom. When he enters, limping, she pauses.

"Parker, sit down and let me see that ankle."

He obeys. Trinity sits on the floor in front of him and unwraps the ankle to get a good look. She's not a nurse, but it seems to be better. She gently wiggles his foot. "Does that hurt."

"A little."

"Well the swelling has gone down. I'll rewrap it but if it is still bothering you in the morning, maybe you should have it looked at."

"Why don't you shower first, Parker."

"Okay. The water might help."

She watches as he walks into the bathroom, limpingy less than he did before. That's a good sign.

While Parker is in the shower, Trinity gets a fresh ace bandage from the bathroom and takes it into the bedroom where she opens the dresser drawer and pulls out a shirt. She carries it into the bathroom and holding the shirt up says, "Parker, is this okay for me to wear?"

Parker wipes the steam off the shower door so that he can see her.

"Yes, that's fine."

Back in the bedroom she waits until Parker returns, then she quickly goes into the bathroom, brushes her teeth and climbs into the shower.

When Trinity returns to the bedroom Parker is sitting on the edge of the bed waiting for her. She smiles at him and then sits down to expertly rewrap his ankle.

Parker thought it would be easier now that their secrets were out in the open, but he feels awkward.

Trinity asks, "Which side do you sleep on?"

"Huh? Oh, you're fine, there," he says as he walks to the other side.

They finally climb into bed. Parker lays on his back staring up at the ceiling, while Trinity lays on her side, staring at the wall. Exhaustion takes over and they fall fast asleep.

The next morning when Trinity opens her eyes, she reaches over to find that she is alone in the bed. Looking around the bedroom, she doesn't see Parker anywhere. She calls out his name. There is no answer. She calls him again. Still no answer.

Quickly she jumps out of bed, hurrying into the bathroom fearing the worse. Only he isn't in there.

Now frantic she practically falls down the stairs as she searches the house and checks the garage. The car is there, but no Parker.

Trinity tries to calm herself as she continues her frenzied search.

She knows why she is so freaked out but pushes that thought to the back of her mind as she rushes upstairs and back in the bedroom she opens the window. She leans out and sees a figure that she recognizes. It's Parker. He is on the beach trying to get a kite in the air.

Trinity falls back on the edge of the bed and takes a deep breathe. Now that she knows his secret, she wonders, will it always be this way. The minute he is out of her sight will she worry he is dying?

She wants to cry but forces herself to hold the tears back until she goes into the bathroom. In the shower she allows her tears to flow unchecked and by the time she comes out, she feels much better.

She gets dressed in the clothes she wore the day before and feeling slightly grimy she goes downstairs and fixes herself a cup of coffee.

Trinity bites down hard on her lip to keep from crying, her eyes squeezing shut with the pain. Her one thought is to live during the time she has left, but can she do that while living for the time he has left too.

It would be soothing to be able to have a little guidance from someone close to her, but all she has is Parker and he has his own conundrums to face.

Trinity wandered around the house, feeling hollower than ever. She now understood why her doctor encouraged her to see someone; that being a licensed psychologist, or psychiatrist, and to join a support group. Sharing her feelings was not big on her agenda, but now…

Her cup empty, Trinity stands up and goes to the window again to watch Parker, thinking for the thousandth time since last night. He is going to die.

She allows that to roll around her brain, wondering what type of cancer he has. Neither one has told the other anything beyond it was terminal.

Inside Trinity looks out the window than turns away and walks over to sit in the Livingroom chair. She wants to feel happy and enjoy the feeling of being in love even if it is destine to be short, but how can she go about doing that.

Parker a hundred yards away is agitating the sand, trying to get his stupid kite in the air. But the kite wasn't gaining any altitude, no matter how hard he tries.

The day is perfect. Flying kites is most fun when the wind is medium, so you can do more than just hold on. He should be able to make his kite dance across the sky by pulling in and letting out the line, but it wasn't working.

He stood with his back to the wind, holding the kite up by the bridle point and letting the line out. He wet his finger and held it up, finding there to be sufficient wind. So why wasn't his kite going right up. The longer he tried without success, the more agitated he became.

Parker is yanking on the kite string when suddenly his stride falters. A shock expression appears on his handsome face as pain radiates from his upper-right abdomen to his pelvic.

He stops running, mouth agape, gasping for breath. He bends at the waist, the excruciating pain growing making it hard to breathe or for that matter stay upright. His eyes tear. He has never felt this level of pain, ever, and for the first time he is panic-stricken as he presses his right hand against his side.

Inside, Trinity studies the room, looks at her watch then smiles at herself for the unconscious gesture. Now more than ever, time means nothing. She takes off her watch and walks into the kitchen to put it on the counter.

She has decided to stop worrying and try to see and appreciate what she has oppose to giving too much attention to what she may lose. She heads determinedly back to the window.

Parker has moved closer to the house and she sees him clearly now. He stands there on the beach with his back to her, letting the kite swirl down toward the water.

"Parker, dammit, the kite." She says to herself. "Don't just stand there and watch it. Come on, try."

Swooping and falling in jerky motions the kite is just above the water.

"Come on Parker," Trinity says louder. "Don't you quit on me."

Without thinking, Trinity hurries over to the door, throws it open and runs outside. As she dashes down the stairs to the beach, she cups her hands around her mouth and starts yelling. "Parker. Your kites about to fall in the water. Get movin will ya."

He barely hears her as the pain takes over his body, then as she moves closer he catches her last words, and with effort repeats them, "Get movin will ya".

At that instance, Trinity becomes more important than the pain and reaching deep down he manages to force his grimace into a smile.

"Come on team," she yells. "Fight, fight, fight." She is smiling as she sees that his ankle is indeed better. Parker is actually able to jog on it. That makes her happy.

The pain has waned, but Parker is hesitant as he slowly straightens his body, little by little until he manages to straighten up. Testily he breathes deeply. He feels no pain.

His confidence grows as he finally remembers his kite, now almost in the water. Slowly he begins reeling in the line, changing its direction so that it is once more on its way upward. He is finally in command of the kite and his body as he starts jogging down the beach.

Only the pain comes again. This time sharper than before and Parker stumbles on the sand, almost falling. Aware that Trinity is watching, he forces himself to move forward, pushing in on his side as if he can hold the pain away.

Close on his heels now he can hear Trinity as she continues her ridiculous cheer.

"Give me a P, Give me an A, Give me an R…"

"Oh, wow, oh wow," Parker says as he grits his teeth, his face distorted and each breath dangerously hollow. All he wants to do is fall down on the sand and curl his body into a fetal position, but he can't. He mustn't scare Trinity.

That desire somehow gives him the strength to pick up his pace as he lets go of the bridle and starts letting some of the line out until it is taut with a little give to it. He pulls on the line to point the kite up, his concentration overpowering the pain until finally the kite climbs higher and higher into the air.

Closer now he hears Trinity. "Give me a K, Give me an E, Give me an R. What does that spell. PARKER…."

He can't let her see him like this. He can feel the sweat dripping down his face, his eyes almost squeezed tight shut and his mouth so tightly clenched that he can't feel his lips, He needs time so he moves faster away from her.

Trinity can see how hard he is trying now and exhausted she allows herself to drop to her knees in the sand. "Come on Parker," she whispers to his receding form. "You can do it."

Up ahead the kite dances in the breeze, way above the lake.

Parker continues to pick up his pace, panting hard as though trying to outrun the pain. His face is almost white with beads of perspiration on his forehead. The sand seems thicker as it engulfs his feet making it even harder to run in in his weakened condition, but he keeps going from sheer willpower.

Motionless, Trinity sits in the sand, whispering, "You can do it."

The pain radiates making it hard to ignore. His speed continues to slow making it tough to keep the kite airborne. Parker sees the kite is only two feet above the water now. A whitecap splashes water on it and the white cloth tail of the kite dips it's end in the water.

Parker digs down deep and runs like hell, his face contorted. While Trinity still on her knees, watches intently, mentally with him every step of the way.

The kite dips a few more inches down toward the water, then the string tightens a little, the wind catches it and it moves triumphantly into the air again, climbing higher and higher.

Trinity unable to control herself, grabs a handful of sand and getting up from her knees throws it in the air. As it falls around her, she is the second happiest person in the world.

Parker is the first.

The worse is behind him now. The pain is gone and he freely moves across the sand, keeping the kite up effortlessly. He is ecstatic as he turns to wave at Trinity. That's when he sees there is someone else watching him.

Recognition comes to him as he realizes this is the same old man he observed before seated on the bench. At that same moment, the old man notices Parker staring at him and he smiles. Then, majestically the old man gets to his feet and begins to applaud Parker.

It was like a validation to his success in overcoming the kite and the pain so Parker smiles and waves at him. He turns around and smiles in the direction of Trinity and though she is at a distance away, he knows she is smiling too.

Parker squints up at his kite in the bright sunlight. It is soaring now, high in the blue sky. He has passed his first test in his ability to overcome the pain and to fly his kite.

Happy and content, Trinity makes a decision. She goes back in the house, finds a piece of paper and writes a note to Parker. Smiling she heads out the front door, climbs into her car and heads home. There she packs some clothes and her toiletries and when she returns she finds Parker standing in the kitchen, waiting for her.

37

Life is beautiful since accepting. Parker and Trinity feel good on the whole even though things aren't going their way. They know emotional freedom and for them, that is enough. That along with trying something new, keeps their minds busy as they talk about what they have always wanted to experience.

It was one of those discussions that lead to the morning Parker, Trinity, among several others stand on a hill above Lake Ontario. It is a sunny afternoon and all eyes are glued to a man who soars overhead in a hang glider. He gracefully catches each new air current looking right at home in the sky with passing seagulls that ignore his presence.

The brochure had taunted them. Parker had seen it at the kite store and one evening he shared it with Trinity.

"Our most popular one day experience! The Introductory Experience is the best introduction to hang gliding. You will fly your first flights in a controlled environment, surfing the slopes of our small hills, only about 5 to 10 feet off the ground. You will get five opportunities to fly from our small hill with a certified instructor guiding you step by step."

Parker sat his coffee cup down and stared at Trinity. "Go ahead, continue," she said.

"After your morning session you will fly tandem with an instructor by your side to an altitude of either 1,500 feet or 3,000 feet above beautiful Ontario Beach. Because of your experience on the training hills, you will have more opportunity to and success in piloting the glider during your tandem." Parker pauses looks up beaming mischiefly.

"What is it."

"Moderate exertion will be required."

Parker starts laughing and Trinity joins him.

"Moderate my ass…" Trinity says, "But I'm game if you are."

"Let's do it. Let's experience the joy of flight and scratch one more item from our bucket list."

Trinity takes their cups over to the sink, rinses them and places them in the dishwasher while Parker makes the call that leads to them being perched on the cliff to watch an expert at hang gliding.

They could have gone for lessons and started slowly, but they both agreed they didn't have time to waste. So here they were.

They weren't stupid enough to think it would be a piece of cake so they opted for the most popular one day experience! They would each fly their first flights at the hang glide school mastering the small hills with a certified instructor.

That had gone well and they felt comfortable after the morning sessions. As prearranged they are taken out to the cliff where they stand amongst other eager participants.

When it came his turn, Parker walks with confidence over to the hang glider. He looks over at Trinity and gave her a thumbs up.

Standing on the rounded hilltop feeling a soft breeze on his face, Parker looks down the gentle, grassy slope in front of him. He steps forward toward the slope, letting gravity pull him from a walk to a gentle run. Within a few steps, he is lifted; the ground falls away beneath his feet and he is running on air.

He is not more than a few feet above the ground on his first flight with an instructor by his side making his flight less scary or intimidating.

It is a sensational experience of thrills until it comes time to land. As the glider drops downward, Parker is at first consumed with fear, wondering if his pilot sees they are over the lake. He wants to scream out, but that would be admitting his fright, so he sucks in his breath and closes his eyes.

The only thing keeping him from yelling out is the fact that he knows they both carried a parachute in their harnesses.

Thankfully there is nothing to worry about as the hang glider instructor makes a long final, come in with sufficient speed, using the basebar, and avoiding turning too close. They land lightly with their feet on the ground.

While Parker works his way out of the harness Trinity makes her way down the cliff and over to the landing site. When she reaches him he can see by the expression on her face she is not happy.

"What's wrong Trinity?"

"Nothing."

"Come on, tell me."

"I'm a chicken. I wanted to do this, really I did, but I'm chickening out."

"It's okay. We only have to do what we want." This is my bucket list item and I did it. You don't have to do it, but I wanted you to be apart of it.

Sobbing, Trinity falls into his arms. "What is it? What did I say?"

Slowly she pulls back and looking in his face replies, "You are perfect. Where have you been all my life."

They walk arm and arm back to the car. Trinity chews on the inside of her jaw before finally leaning close to him and saying, "Do me a favor will you."

"Anything."

"Let's not talk about this a lot, but I want you to promise me that if I go first…"

"Stop!" He doesn't know what to say or do beyond those words. He just doesn't want her to say anything more.

Trinity doesn't stop. "I don't want you to come to the hospital, the funeral or visit my grave. Okay."

"Jesus Christ, Trinity."

"Let me finish. I just want to say this once and we'll never talk about it again. When I think it's time I'll just disappear and do it alone." She pauses, then adds, "You can do what you need to do, like go see your family, but forget about me."

"Why are you saying this."

"Because it's what I want."

While Parker ponders what to say to this, Trinity says with austere, "I'm ready for beer and a hamburger now."

Parker wants to express his opinon, but can tell that Trinity is done with the matter. She looks happy and he wants to keep her content so he says, "Okay, let's go."

38

The next day, Parker has an appointment with his doctor. Earlier Parker and Trinity made a pact to just share fun stuff with each other so that their illness did not interfere with their happiness.

It wasn't what Parker wanted, but Trinity was a private person and was not comfortable with verbally dealing with their situation. Besides, she would say, they had to discuss their illness regularly with their doctors, so why let it invade their time together. Parker had agreed.

So this morning he had a cup of coffee with Trinity and then told her he would be back shortly. She didn't question why.

###

"So, doc, what's the verdict?"

“Remission is impossible at this point, you know that, don’t you?”

He did. “I am not expecting any miracles here. I have had a good life and been lucky to have lived this long, being a stock broker and all,” he adds jokingly. “Besides, I am obsessed with making my remaining time the best—however long it may be.” He smiles and adds. “Or short, I guess I should say.”

“I’m your doctor and your friend, Parker and wish I could give you some hope. All I can say is slow down, take it easy, and enjoy the time you have.”

Parker nods.

“Have you started going to any group meetings?”

“Yes, I have. I go to Gilda’s Club; funny name for it, but great people are there. I have to admit I feel comfortable there.”

“What about talking with the family or friends.”

That I find to be difficult. It makes me feel as though I am abandoning the family and coping with other people’s emotions is difficult for me. You know how it is. They feel awkward and don’t know what to say and sometimes can blurt out inappropriate or unhelpful things, particularly if they see you look well. Then they find it hard to grasp that I could be so ill.”

“I know Parker, but think about it.”

“I will.”

“So what can I do for you?”

“Just give me something for the pain. I had a chance to experience the pain and I don’t want to feel it again.”

Without hesitation the doctor writes out a prescription. Before he hands it to Parker he says, “I wish I could do more, but since you refuse hospitalization, this is it.”

"Sorry Martin, I know you want to help. I just don't want to spend the time I have left in the hospital."

On his way back, Parker makes one more stop, then heads home. When he enters the house, he calls out to Trinity, but there is no answer. He begins a top and bottom search of the house, but she is not there.

Parker tries to remain calm as he goes out the back door and scans the beach. Still no Trinity.

He takes a walk up the beach in case she has ventured out of sight, but doesn't find her.

"Okay, man, remain calm," he says in a whisper, before the worry consumes him.

Parker returns to the house and sits on the deck to calm himself. When he hears the sound of the front door opening, he stands up quietly, then forces himself to walk slowly into the house.

"Well, hello, sir, I was wondering when you would get home."

Parker smiles and walks over to give her a hug.

"Hey, you're squeezing me too tight."

"Sorry. Just glad to see you."

She kisses him and he helps her unpack the bag she is carrying. She has purchased prepared meals from Wegmans and they heat them up.

Late that night Parker stands and stares out of his bedroom window, the view of the lake that use to comfort him doesn't work. He sees it now as a reminder that it goes on and on, but not him.

"Parker?"

He keeps his back toward Trinity. "What?"

"You know, it doesn't matter."

Parker turns to face her. “It does matter and you know it.” He waits until he is calmer. “For us, it matters a whole lot.”

Parker turns back toward the window. “I went to see a shrink.”

Trinity is silent. Parker turns back to face her again, wondering what she is thinking.

“Why didn’t you tell me?”

“Because, that is not part of our relationship, remember.”

“No, that is different. That, you should tell me.”

“Well, I’m telling you now. After all the mumbo-jumble he tells me that cancer can affect a man's erections, his ability to ejaculate and a man’s fertility. In other words verification of why I went to see him in the first place.”

Trinity stares at Parker and finally asks, “So, what did it cost to learn that?”

“One hundred and twenty-four bucks for an hour and any part thereof.”

“Come to bed, Parker. It won’t cost a cent.”

That’s what he liked most about her. How easily she made every situation less stressful.

39

The fall weather can change drastically so Trinity and Parker work their days around it.

It is Trinity’s turn to pick something interesting to do. She has established a pattern and Parker has been a trooper about it. When they first decided to make the most of each day, Trinity had shared with him that she had always wanted to go to the festivals and visit the flower gardens around the area, just never seemed to find the time.

Parker readily agreed. At first because he wanted to please her, but she could tell later he was enjoying it as much as she did. They would start out in the morning and keep going until the evening on the days of her choice which wasn't much different to the days when they did what he chose. It was their nemeses to fill the days they had left.

In June they went to the Xerox Rochester International Jazz Festival and the Corn Hill Arts Festival in July. They had gone to the Garden tours at the George Eastman Museum and even the Sonnenberg Mansion & Gardens State Historic Park to see the nine themed gardens in Canandaigua.

The weather was on their side as August finished the summer months off on a warm and slightly wet note, but the above normal temperatures made up for the rainy days. Each day Parker and Trinity woke feeling blessed.

The weather seemed to cooperate with their plans as the Fall finished as the third warmest Fall on record for the area with temperatures averaging in the 50s.

Winter 2016

40

The plan today is to visit the Bausch & Lomb's Winter Garden where 775 large panes of glass enclose trees, shrubs and other plants plus a small pool and cascading waterfall...right in the center of the city. Then on to the Amerks Game.

Over breakfast as she tells Parker what she has in store for them. Parker sighs happily and pats his stomach. Trinity smiles. “Want more?”

“You must be kidding. You want me to walk around all day with a full stomach. I can’t fit another bite in me.”

Trinity laughs.

“What’s so funny?”

“I was thinking of a joke I read. A Texan, a Russian and a New Yorker go to a restaurant in London. The waiter tells them, Excuse me -- if you were going to order the steak, I'm afraid there's a shortage due to the mad cow disease. The Texan says, What's a shortage? The Russian says, What's a steak? The New Yorker says, What's 'Excuse Me'?

Trinity sees the question mark expression on Parkers face.

“You have to think about it a bit.” She adds, “It’s stupid, I know. It just popped into my head is all.”

Parker clicks his tongue. “It’s not that I don’t get it. I get it.” He tries hard not to let her see him laugh, but he can’t hold back any longer. The laughter bursts out.

“Oh, you.” Is all Trinity can think to say as she laughs with him.

When they are finally ready to leave, the weather is on their side as they go downtown and park in the ramp to visit the Winter Gardens at the Bausch and Lomb building. Warm sunshine fills the room as they walk hand and hand.

“It’s breathtaking, really breathtaking.”

“I’m glad you like it,” says a strange voice, causing them both to jump.

“Sorry, didn’t mean to startle you. Are you two wanting to set up a reception here.”

"Huh?" they say in unison.

"Your wedding reception, or special party?"

Trinity and Parker look at each other and play along. "Yes, sure, we would be interested in something, say, next week."

The man looks flabbergasted. "Ah, we can't do anything that fast. Our next available dates are at the end of next year."

"Well, then, no, we're not interested." They turn and hurry away so that he can't hear them laughing.

They walk for a while longer on this level and then take the escalators up to check out the rest of the building. When they have seen each floor and each exhibit they make their way back to the parking lot.

"So, what time does the game start?"

"The doors will open around 6:30 this evening so we have time yet."

"They're playing the Wilkes-Barre Scranton Penguins. That's usually a pretty good game."

Parker is thoughtful as they drive to the stadium.

Trinity on the other hand, chats away. "Well you'll enjoy. They have beer there…"

Parker reaches over to squeeze her thigh.

They park the car and climb out; grabbing their coats from the back seat.

The stadium is packed as they make their way to their seats. Parker looks around at the crowd wondering if they really like sitting in the cold, but once the teams come on the ice he finds that he does. He's watched the games on television but never in person.

His eyes follow the puck as it slides across the ice and the athletic ability of the players is astonishing. They move effortlessly and not even a bump against the wall can knock them down.

Soon he is jumping up and cheering along with Trinity. "I'm so glad you had this on your bucket list," he screams.

It's a slow process getting out of the building. As they make their way to the entry, she is surprised to see vendors out in the open area. There are booths with jewelry, clothing and of course food.

"Do you mind," Trinity asks.

"No, let's check it out."

They walk around the perimeter, with Trinity stopping to admire items up close. She picks up a few trinkets, taking several minutes to decide and steals at glance in Parkers direction. He smiles at her and she finds herself wishing she had met him a long time ago; back before.... She shakes her head refusing to think of anything sad.

"Hey Trinity, want to go hear the band over there?" Parker asks.

"Sure", she replies, "But if you are hoping to get a seat, forget it." Parker follows her sight line and can tell the chances of sitting is nil. All the same he grabs her hand as they head to the area, pushing gently through the crowds until they at least are able to see the band. They stay for several songs, then are about to leave when a troupe of dancers take the stage.

"What do you think?" Parker asks.

"Let's watch."

They are amazed; especially when the troupe is introduced as Garth Fagan Dancers.

When they finally are ready to leave, the crowd is so thick it is almost impossible to find passage.

Then it comes. Parker is taken by surprise as the pain starts just above his groin and radiates up the side of his body all the way to his arm pit. He can't move. He can barely stand as he leans into someone who is standing next to him.

At that moment Parker is afraid; afraid that this is it and his life is going to end in a crowd on Main Street. He will fall down and the crowd will walk all over him before anyone realizes there's a person underfoot.

The pain pounds against his ribs as if it is alive and wants to be set free. Parker can't think as he is consumed. All he wants is for it to stop. "Please God, please," he whispers. "Not here, not like this."

Slowly he gains the strength to stand on his own, thankful now for the crowd that unknowingly gave him support when he needed it. By the time they emerge from the mass, Parker is able to deal with the remaining pain that comes in weak waves now. As soon as he has space, he reaches in his pocket and pulls out his prescription. He swallows the pill dry. A few minutes later, he is himself again.

Trinity is unaware of what was happening to Parker and when they finally reach the edge of the crowd she says, "Are you all right? What a struggle that was, huh?"

"You have no idea."

Trinity smiles at Parker as he reaches for her hand.

"Are you hungry?" Parker asks.

"I'm starving."

Parker takes her arm and maneuvers her toward a sandwich place just up the street. Trinity has heard of the place. "Parker, this is perfect. You must try their hot relish/pickled jalapenos/red pepper aioli."

"They're, what?"

"They are hot relish/pickled jalapenos/red pepper aioli." She repeats.

"You have it. I know what I want right now and it's not something that will burn my insides out."

They find a table and he sits across from her, glad to be off his feet.

"So what's the plan after this?"

"Let you know when I know," she says amused.

It doesn't matter because he is happy and as far as he can tell, Trinity is too.

###

Parker has grown accustomed to not talking about their cancer; though they both are going to meetings at Gilda's Club together.

At first it seems weird to not share with each other when they listen to others sharing their thoughts and concerns. Somehow they manage to just listen and somehow that is enough. When they leave the meeting, Parker does feel a sense of peace knowing that he is not alone in this awful journey of death. Even though they don't speak about it, he thinks Trinity is gaining something too. At least he knows she will have a place to go to help her through after he is gone. Because he now knows that he will be first.

They live their own crazy none routine days starting out sometimes before dawn to get the most out of it or on other days, sleeping in until late afternoon then eating breakfast at sundown after a night filled with whatever entertainment meets their needs.

They were explorers venturing into new territory with each other discovering what might really be done with something as precious as time. They were together and they were happy and it continually amazed him how much life could be squeezed out of a night with only love and a couple dollars.

After another beautiful day of exploration they opt to spend the evening at home and enjoy the sunset together.

Trinity sat on the sand close to the lake, facing a small fire and waiting for the sunset. Two hot dogs were stuck on the roasting fork that she held over the flame, waiting for Parker to join her.

Parker trudged through the sand behind her carrying a magnum of champagne wrapped in a napkin and some plastic wine glasses. Still a safe distance from her, he stopped and smiled to himself.

"So, do you want to impress her or do you want to surprise her." An evil smile comes over his face as he whispers. "I vote for surprise."

Parker stops a distance away from Trinity and puts the glasses down in the sand. The bottle of champagne has been properly chilled to the perfect temperature so the pressure inside the bottle will not cause the cork to release quickly. He reaches in his pocket and takes out the wine key to use in cutting the foil below the large lip of the bottle.

That done, Parker takes a cloth napkin and places it over the cage and the cork to prevent the cork from flying off like a bullet. He untwist the cage counterclockwise, putting pressure on the cork to keep it from popping out prematurely as he holds the bottle at a 45-degree angle.

Parker is ready.

Trinity is alone on the beach as the evening is cool and windy, keeping most people inside. Carefully, Parker aims the cork to pop off somewhere near her so that it startles her. He starts laughing, but the sound of the waves muffles any sounds he makes.

But not the cork popping out because it's obvious Trinity hears it and turns to see it fall far behind her in the sand. Parker gives her a sheepish grin as she yells, "Come on slow poke, your hot dog's ready."

His entrance not as dramatic as he had hoped, he walks back and picks up the glasses and continues toward the fire.

He is a short distance away, staring at her back as she leans toward the fire twisting the hotdogs when the pain comes. It is so bad that it feels like someone shoved a fist through the left side of his thoracic back area and is squeezing his insides tightly.

He drops the bottle and glasses, groping his side and staggering a few feet to one side. It radiates through his body, feeling like someone has shoved a dull knife deep inside him.

Tears blur his vision as he stares ahead at Trinity, praying she doesn't turn around. He prays breathlessly. "Please, don't let her turn around."

41

Parker fights to control the pain, only it is too powerful. His mind fills with random thoughts linked by steady waves of torture. He recalls one person, he thinks her name was Tamara or something like that, sharing about her experience at a meeting at Gilda's Club. She said that pain can come and go. It can stay put in a single place. It can move through the body, so that it is everywhere, circulating like blood.

At the time he had trouble understanding what she said, but now he is a believer. It hurt all over.

With his hands quavering he fumbled in his pocket for his pills. When his hand grasps the little bottle, he pulls it out of his pocket and twists the cap slowly with fumbling fingers. He wants to get at the pills quickly, but if he spills them in the sand, he will be out of luck.

He hates the child proof caps that are adult proof too, but finally he gets the cap off and pops two pills into his mouth, washing them down with a swig of champagne. Then he waits.

It takes longer this time for him to feel the effects of the meds so not wanting to take the chance of Trinity seeing him like this, he turns and heads back toward the house.

Trinity wonders what is taking Parker so long and turns back around to see him heading back toward the house.

"Hey you," she yells. "You're going the wrong way. Get over here."

He hears her, but he can't turn around just yet. It surprises him how quickly his mind manages to work as he says, "Nap.." but it hurts to speak and he can't finish the word or communicate loud enough for her to hear.

"Parker," Trinity says with worry apparent in her voice.

He has to reply. He forces the word out, "Napkins..."

"I've got the napkins. Come on, get your butt over here," she says relaxing. "Get over here and share that champagne, you guzzler."

Parker manages to change directions, slowly and is grateful to find that the pain has lessened. He moves forward, afraid of an onslaught of pain, but it doesn't come.

His body, more erect he moves easily across the sand now until he is close to Trinity.

"Just my luck to end up with a wino. I saw you taking a swig."

"Hey little miss, you're the one who said we needed a magnum of champagne with our hot dogs. Not me."

Parker is in the moment, sitting by Trinity and watching the sun set while enjoying hotdogs and champagne.

"Parker," Trinity says thoughtfully, "Did you know that in the North and South Pole the sun never sets for six months and never rises for six months?"

"No, I didn't know that."

"It's true. The sun rises from the east and when it reaches the west it does not set but it rises again."

Parker moves closer to Trinity, wondering why she is sharing this piece of trivia. Then he thinks, that's just Trinity. He feels her as she lays her head on his shoulder. They sit in silence watching as the sun disappears below the horizon.

"Trinity," Parker says as he caresses her head. "I want to give you a present."

"A present."

"Yeah."

"Why."

Parker stalls, taking another drink as he watches the color changes in the sky, then lays his head on top of hers.

"Because you gave me a train."

Though he can't see her face, he knows she is smiling. "Tell me what I can give you that you always wanted."

"I don't know." She adds, "Nothing, really, Parker. You are everything I ever wanted."

"I'm serious. Please tell me."

"I am serious." But Trinity knows this is important to Parker, only she can't come up with anything. She is about to say this to him when it pops into her head.

"Promise you won't laugh."

"Why would I laugh?"

"Because it's really silly," she said.

"What is it?"

"Well…."

"Please, Trinity, tell me."

She tells him.

42

"So tell me Parker, what is it that draws you to trains."

"Well, let me see, there's the sheer power of motion, and speed. And, oh yes, sound is awesome. The sound of the wheels clacking, the size of the box cars and flat cars…"

"So, everything, huh."

"Yeah," Parker says smiling as they arrive at their destination and he smartly pulls the car off the road and up into the brush that runs behind the grassy area.

"We're here."

Trinity climbs out of the car and Parker follows. They stand there looking off in the distance at the large spherical water tower supported by its steel legs.

Once hearing her fantasy, they had run like kids back into the house to prepare for the adventure. They dressed in dark clothing and found paint and paint brushes in the garage that they put in the car, along with other necessities before heading out.

Now, as they stare at the tower, Parker says, "You sure you want to do this?"

Trinity can't remember it being so tall, but it doesn't matter.

"Yes, I'm sure."

They meet at the back of the car and each takes out a can of paint and a brush.

"Okay, your turn."

"My turn, what?"

"Why do you want to climb this thing."

Trinity smiles. "Because…"

"That's not an answer."

Trinity is thoughtful. "Parker, most people assume that water towers exist to store water. That they are no more than above ground vessels filled with water. But that's not their purpose."

Parker is thoughtful. "What is their purpose."

"To pressurize water for distribution."

"Interesting, but…"

"Parker, they're becoming a thing of the past. They are dying Parker. I want to be a part of their history."

He is about to let her know he now understands, but Trinity interrupts. "Look up Parker, look at the lights at the top of the tiny catwalk. I want to go up there."

He follows her eyes to stare up above. His heart leaps in his chest. He wonders if he can go through with this.

"How do you suppose we get up there. We didn't bring a ladder and the steel legs are going to take an acrobat to scramble through."

"Silly, look." Parker follows as Trinity moves forward to the far side of the structure. "See, there's the ladder." She points up to the catwalk. "It extends all the way down one side. How do you think the kids actually climb up the damn thing. Or did you think they had wings," she says teasingly.

"Parker, you haven't done this before?"

"No"

"That surprises me. You look like the type."

Turning toward her he says, "The type who has a death wish…"

As soon as the words were out, he wanted to pull them back.

Trinity doesn't react, so Parker relaxes, watching as she goes back to the car and gets a flashlight out of the glove compartment. She turns it on, making sure it is working before joining up with him again.

Together they work their way through the overbrush as they head toward the water tower.

Parker can't help it. He is really getting into it now. They are like kids giddy from the excitement ignoring the brush as it slaps against their bodies, and then their progress halts.

"Now what," Parker says.

In front of them is a high, barbed-wire fence surrounding the base of the tower. Trinity looks at Parker and says. "We can't be the first ones. Look up there at all the graffiti. There has to be a hole somewhere."

Slowly they walk the perimeter, pushing against the fence.

"Found it," Trinity announces in a loud whisper.

The pause in their progress knocks some sense into his head and Parker wishes she hadn't found an opening. He lets out an audible sigh and works his way along the fence to joins her. One by one they squeeze through the opening.

On the other side of the fence the area is cleared of brush, making it easy to get up close to the tower. They walk cautiously as if expecting to be caught at any moment, but they are very much alone.

Then they are there, right in front of it. Simultaneously they both look up and then turn to look at each other.

Parker again asks, "Are you absolutely, positively sure you want to do this?"

"Come on. It's imposing, but we can do this."

Doubting the possibility, Parker tells himself that she didn't actually give up on hopping a train for him, so he has to see it through.

Trinity stands by the ladder, motioning to him and when he gets there he sees that the bottom rung must be nine feet above the ground. Just one more obstacle to surmount.

Parker can see Trinity's disappointment and comes up with an idea.

"Trinity, come on. I'll crouch down so that you can climb on my shoulders."

Trinity's face lights up and eagerly transitions to his shoulders, a little wobbly at first, but able to grab hold of the railing on the ladder.

"Got it," she says.

"Pull yourself up and get your feet on the ladder."

He can feel her struggling, her weight seeming to get heavier as she tries to get her leg up.

"I don't know if I can do this," she says sadly.

"It's your water tower, lady."

"Okay, okay." With determination Trinity grits her teeth and pulls herself up until she has one foot on the rung, then sliding her hand up higher manages to get the other foot in place. Carefully, she pulls herself toward the ladder, hooks her arms around the railing and laughs. “I did it.”

Once she is in place, Parker hands her the paint and the brushes and waits while she balances them on a rung, above her.

“Now me.”

“How…” she starts, then looks as Parker backs up, runs and jumps surprising himself as he grabs the bottom rung on the first try, then with Trinity’s help he gets his body on the ladder.

They rest a bit, leaning against the side rails, catching their breath and determination before each positions a paint brush and paint can. They slowly begin the climb.

Trinity is up front and keeps looking up wondering just how far they have to go. When it appears that they have climbed three quarters of the way, she finally says, “Want to stop and rest a bit?”

“Better believe it. Thought you’d never ask.”

They lean into the ladder and pressing the paint can between their body and the rail, they relieve the pressure on their arms.

Suddenly a strong gust of wind smacks them roughly into the ladder. It knocks the wind out of Parker as he tries to speak. The ladder rattles and fearing it will break loose, he attempts to reach out to Trinity. Only he can’t move.

As quickly as it came, the wind calms. “Are you all right?”

“Yes, are you?”

“Yes. Hope the ladder is too.”

“It was probably designed just to hold the weight of only one person.”

“Thanks for that insight, my dear.”

Trinity begins moving up the ladder and Parker follows, keeping close behind her so that if she should lose her footing she can fall back against him.

"If I tell you now that I'm afraid of heights, Parker, what would you say," she asks.

The higher they go, the harder it is for him to hear Trinity so he stops trying. Parker wants to look at his watch to see how much time has passed, but he remembers he stopped wearing it.

His legs ache and the weight of the handle of the paint can digs into his palm. He tries to switch it to the other hand, but that means he has to lean back and there's no one there to catch him so he sucks it up and continues to put one foot up on the next step, pull with his hands and then bring the other foot up.

He can't take it anymore and decides he has to switch hands. Carefully he leans back.

Parker yells up at Trinity, "Look."

Trinity has been concentrating on the climb when she hears him. Carefully lowering her head so he can hear her, she says, "What did you say?"

Parker is pointing upwards. Trinity leans back to try and look over the base of the tower that obstructs her view, but she can see nothing.

"What is it?"

"We made it, Trinity. We made it."

At that moment, Trinity reaches up and finds there is no more steps above her. She can hear the pride in Parkers voice as she takes the last rungs on the ladder and plants her feet on the catwalk. "Piece of cake."

Her hand is numb from the handle of the paint pressing into it, but she ignores it as she moves down a ways, giving Parker room.

Parker steps up on the catwalk beside her, thankful for the metal bars that run behind them.

It is hard to hear each other speak above the sound of the wind as it vibrates and propagates as an audible wave of pressure all around them now. It's cold, but they ignore that too.

It doesn't matter. All they care about now is they made it.

At the base of the water tower, unnoticed by Parker or Trinity, a police car has slowly pulled in, stopped, turned off his lights and now waits.

Up on the tower Parker and Trinity pry the tops off their paint cans. They had been surprised to learn that there are two types of glo paint—one that is visible only at night and one that is visible daytime and nighttime. They purchased Daytime Orange Glow Paint. The salesman told them that it was a durable, long lasting, solvent-based acrylic phosphorescent paint that has both an orange color in a lit room and an orange glow in a darkened room.

Carefully now, they balance themselves and kiss before starting to paint their names in a huge heart. They work together getting the feel of it and when done, they look at it and smile.

They go in opposite directions creating the heart with their names at several positions on the tower. When Trinity runs out of paint she works her way back to where they started, expecting Parker to join her. When he doesn't she yells out,

"Parker, what are you doing."

"Painting." He yells back. "Want to make sure everyone gets a chance to see it."

Trinity is laughing and holding tightly to the rail. "You're enjoying this, huh."

"Yes I am. Never knew it, but I always wanted to do this too. Almost done."

Trinity savors the time alone by looking up at the stars that seem so close up here. When Parker returns, he takes Trinity's brush and the can of paint, walks further back and tosses them over the railing. He watches to see where they land so they know where to retrieve them later.

That done, he rejoins Trinity. Face to face they look at each other, and then they are in each other's arms, kissing and hugging. "I am so happy Parker."

"Me too. Me too."

"Now I have my very own water tower," she says. "Just what I always wanted."

Parker hugs her again, grinning from ear to ear.

They stay like that until the wind reminds them where they are. "This is all very nice, except that we have to climb back down…"

Parker looks over the edge, taking in the distance to the bottom.

"You know how to bring a person down to earth, my friend," she said. "You…" she starts and then sees him. "uh-oh."

"What?"

This time it is Parker drawing his eyes in the direction of Trinity's pointing arm. He sees the tiny police car below. From the height of the tower, it all looks like a toy town of tiny trees, roads and the ominous police car. And they are sure that inside that little toy is a little police officer too and he wants to escort them to a real, full size, police station.

"Got a plan?"

"Let's just get down and I'll think on the way."

Trinity steps off the catwalk and slides her foot down trying to find the first rung of the ladder when a fierce wind swings her to the side, followed by rain that forces her hand and her foot to slip. She clings for dear life.

Parker hugs the railing, looking down at Trinity. “Don’t let go, baby. Hold on tight, please. Hold on tight.”

Time is at a standstill while they pray for their safety and as suddenly as it came, the wind and rain recedes.

Slowly and cautiously, Trinity pushes her body over so that she is once again centered on the ladder with both hands and feet in position. She looks up at Parker who is slowly recovering.

“Are you all right,” he asks.

“Yes, I’m fine. But let’s get off this damn tower. I have had enough.”

“Right behind you sweetie.”

Slowly they move down the ladder that is now very slippery as well as steep. Neither one says a word, conserving their energy, but also concentrating on each placement of their feet on the rungs. When they reach what seems like the halfway mark, they pause to catch their breath.

“I am exhausted,” Trinity said as she leans her body against the ladder.”

At first, wanting to appear macho, Parker starts to say, “No problem…” Then thinking better of it, added, “I’m glad you stopped.”

Trinity manages a smile and in a few minutes is stepping back down. Parker follows her lead, too busy to think about the issue that awaits them at the bottom.

When Trinity reaches the bottom rung she looks up at Parker, who has already seen the police officer standing below her.

"Okay Ma'am, let go and I'll catch you," he says.

Trinity shrugs her shoulders and allows her body to propel into the officer's arms. He then puts her down next to him and waits for Parker to make his final steps. "I think if you can hang onto that last rung, I can reach your legs and help you down."

Parker obeys.

There they are side by side with Mr. Police Officer. Now what, Parker wonders.

"Let's get outside the fence guys," he said. "You want to tell me what you were doing up there before I read you your rights."

"We were recapturing our lost youth officer," Parker says with a straight face, helping Trinity through the fence. They stand a little apart from the officer. "Have you been drinking?"

"No officer," they say in unison.

He looks at them and makes a decision. "Wait here, I am going to get the breathalyzer."

He leaves them, walking with his back to them as he heads for his car. When he turns back around, they are gone.

As soon as the officer turns, Parker pulls Trinity by the hand and they start running as fast as they can through the bushes, laughing so hard tears are running down their cheeks.

"What," Parker says, turning around but keeping his pace. "The idiot is chasing us. Can you believe that."

"Just run old man."

They had a good lead on him to start, but he is catching up to them. "Let go of my hand and save yourself," Trinity says.

"Not on your life. You go down, I go down," Parker replies through puffs.

Parker sees a thick clump of bushes ahead and as if of one mind, they leap over the edge so as not to disturb the wall of coverage. The landing on the other side is hard, but their bodies are so consumed with laughter they barely feel it.

Parker puts a hand over Trinity's mouth and she does the same to him. They can hear the sound of the officer's footsteps getting closer until he is right next to where they are hiding. Peering through the bush they can see his shoes and hear him panting for breath. They dare not move as he stands there and yells out, "Come back here, damn you?"

Then there is the sound of him moving further ahead leaving them nearly in hysterics.

"That was close," Trinity manages to say giggling.

"Damn close," Parker responds.

All they can do now is wait until the officer turns back around and then wait for the sound of him driving away. Then, and only then do they dare to leave their hiding place, retrieve the paint cans and brushes and make their escape in the car.

The little thicket is quite comfortable with the pine needles under them. Trinity, still giggling, leans over and gives Parker a kiss. He kisses her back. Suddenly they stare into each other's eyes, no longer giggling. They kiss deeply, holding each other tightly, allowing the feelings to take over their bodies. Wantonly ignoring the cold, they strip off their clothes and like wild animals they are at each other with a passion they have never felt before.

Finally sated, they lay on their backs waiting for their breathing to calm down. They never heard the officer drive away.

43

The drive home is long and arduous as they try to focus on anything except the passion between them. When they finally arrive at the beach house, neither one wants to move too directly or drastically even though they now feel a part of each other.

But their attraction is poignantly strong, propelling them forward. They hurry up the stairs and into the bedroom, striping the clothes off each other as the tension heightens between them.

That night in bed they make passionate love, different from the experience in the bushes, because this time they are not in a hurry.

The next morning they wake and look at each other with knowing smiles on their face. Trinity makes the first move and soon their bodies unite again.

Parker is so happy knowing that whatever caused his sexual shutdown was not a problem anymore. The sex is great and the realization that he loves Trinity and wants to share everything with her doesn't scare him. He turns on his side and looks at her laying there beside him.

She feels his eyes on her and stretches her arms above her head before turning towards him.

"I feel really good. I feel wonderfully fulfilled in more than just a sex way," she says with a pouty stare.

"Do you know how happy I am right now?" Trinity adds.

"Yes, I think I do know. Now get up and get dressed," he adds flippantly.

After a quick cup of coffee, Trinity and Parker go for a long walk on the beach. They walk with their bodies touching, their hands held tightly looking every bit like a couple in love. They talk about simple things like the sun shining on the water and the feel of the sand under their feet.

They continue comfortably enjoying each other until Trinity announces. "Parker, I'm starving."

Parker looked at his watch. It is already past noon.

"Me too. There's a pizza place up ahead."

"Sound good."

Quickening their pace they are soon walking through the doors of the pizza parlor. While Parker finds a table, Trinity heads for the lady's room.

While in the stall she can hear someone crying. When she comes out she goes to the sink to wash her hands and sees two sinks down a youngest figure. Her hair falls forward over her face and she sobs uncontrollably.

"Honey are you okay?" Trinity asks as she dries her hands and moves closer.

Through choking tears the girl replies, "Yes, I'm okay… no, I'm not," her sobbing mounting.

Trinity gets another paper towel, wets it and hands it to her as she asks, "Can I help?"

"I just got stood up." She bawls. "I really liked him. I thought he liked me too."

Trinity, not use to being in situations like this, awkwardly patted the girl on the back, then, not knowing what to say she said what she thought.

"Listen, sweetie, I've been there. It will happen many times. I've been stood up by the best of them and the worst of them and I lived through it. Want to know one thing you can always count on with men?"

"Yes," she whimpered.

"I would, too."

The girl looks up, startled. Even with the swollen eyes from crying Trinity can see how pretty she is.

The girl continues looking a bit puzzled and then she understands. Slowly the corners of her mouth turn up and then she laughs as hard as she cried. Her laughter is contagious and soon Trinity laughs along with her.

"Are you okay, now?"

"Yes, thank you."

They hugged and Trinity went back to join Parker.

Parker has been waiting for her, the pizza in front of him. "Want to sit outside?" he asked.

"That would be perfect."

Parker picks up the pizza and steps aside to allow Trinity to move ahead of him. He follows behind as she picks out a seat in a sunny area.

"Everything all right," he asks once they are seated.

"Yes, nothing is wrong, I just did a good deed inside the ladies room. I think we should label this our good deed day. What do you think?"

"Sounds like a plan."

At that moment they noticed a young man sitting all alone on the patio. They look at each other, pick up their pizza and go over to join him.

"Hello," they say in unison.

Taken aback, the man looks up and hesitates before responding, "Hello."

"Can we join you."

They can see he is wondering what is happening here so to put him at ease they tell him they live around here and hadn't seen him before. "This is a friendly neighborhood and we like to welcome strangers."

"Please, have a seat." Forgive me, but I live in New York City and I'm not use to strangers being so friendly."

"Understood."

Parker seats Trinity and then walks on the other side of her to sit. As soon as he is seated he opens the pizza box and offers their new friend a piece before they take a piece.

"Cheers," Parker says moving his slice to the center of the table. Trinity and the man do the same.

They make small talk and out of the corner of her eye, Trinity sees the girl from the bathroom exiting the pizza place. She stands and walks over to her.

"Glad to see you moving on," she says. "By the way I never told you my name. It's Trinity."

"Hi, Trinity. I don't know how to thank you. You made me feel much better. My name is Alexa."

"That's a lovely name. Come with me, I want to introduce you to my wonderful man," she said leading Alexa toward Parker.

"Parker, this is Alexa. Alexa, this is Parker."

"Hi Alexa. Nice to meet you. This is my friend, Samuel. he's new here and could really use a friend to show him around."

"I… "Alexa started, but stopped when Samuel looked up and smiled at her. "I'd love to show you around if you like."

"I would."

Trinity grabbed Parker by the hand and hurried him away. The two would have to take it from there.

44

It comes without warning. They had a wonderful day of non-routine enjoying each other and filling every moment until exhausted they turned in for the night.

One moment Parker and Trinity are sleeping. The bedroom window open, the curtains stirring from the breeze and shadows playing on the walls in the light from the moon. The gentle slapping of the waves on Lake Ontario lulls them into a deep sleep. Everything is still and quiet.

Trinity screams at the top of her lungs, Parker is startled awake and sees Trinity roll out of the bed with a look of pure fear on her face as she scrambles to the corner of the room and crouches there, whimpering.

Parker jumps out of the bed and looks around trying to ascertain what has frightened her but sees nothing. He moves over to Trinity and lowers his head so that their eyes meet. He peers into her eyes and from her expression he can tell she doesn't recognize him.

"Trinity, its Parker, baby." He says softly. "Trinity, it's okay… everything is all right." He slowly reaches over and touches her shoulder to draw her near.

Trinity reacts violently to his touch, screaming and getting up. She runs across the room and crashes into the wall hitting her head and arm, but she doesn't feel anything. She is caught up in the terror and nothing or anyone can save her.

Parker is on his feet quickly moving toward her, but moaning she turns and runs to the opposite side of the bedroom. He follows and almost catches her, but she lets out a piercing scream, spins around and ends up in front of the closet where she tries to open the door, but can't. She begins pounding on the door, screaming, crying, and choking.

Parker grabs her shoulders. He shakes her.

"Trinity!"

"No, don't!" she screams slipping out of his reach and scrambling across the floor until she is in another corner of the room by the dresser. Her terrified whimpers fill the room.

Parker shocked by the episode that is unfolding, finally manages to grab hold of her and this time tightens his grip.

He holds her securely against him whispering in her ear consoling words of comfort. She struggles against him, but he holds her tight against his chest, sliding down the wall until they are sitting on the floor.

They sit like that until her shrieking finally diminishes into sobs. He lets her cry. When she is finally worn out she goes limp in his arms.

He rocks her gently back and forth, soothing her like a child, speaking softly as her breath comes in gasps from all the yelling and sobbing she has done.

Cautiously he finally asks, "What was it Trinity? What frightened you so?"

"I had a nightmare." She grabs his arm so tightly, squeezing the skin between her fingers that he almost screams out in pain. It hurts, but he ignores the pain.

"It was awful Parker."

"Can you talk about it."

Her voice barely above a whisper, Trinity begins to tell him.

"I dreamed I died and they put me in a coffin so that everyone could see me. They touched me and cried over me, but I wasn't really dead. I saw them and tried to yell out that I wasn't dead, but no one heard me. I laid there in that coffin for three days and I could see them as they sorted through my things and took what they wanted, and I tried to scream out to let my stuff alone. I tried to make someone hear me, so they would know I wasn't dead. But they didn't hear me, and they closed the lid of the coffin and…."

Parker could feel her shaking in his arms and trying to console her said. "I won't let that happen."

When Trinity is calm, Parker helps her back in the bed, laying close to her until she falls asleep. It seems important now for Trinity and him to see more of the psychiatrist. Parker is so worried by the episode of that night he can see no alternative for them but to have help because now he knows that Trinity is scared of dying and he doesn't know what to say or do.

Parker can't sleep the rest of the night. Instead he lays there watching the bedroom curtains float slowly against the wall and then out in tune with the breeze coming through the open window. He hears the waves on the lake that normally relax him, but now only perform a symphony for his unsettled mind. When morning comes Parker gets up and heads for the bathroom. He is in the shower when Trinity comes in and joins him.

It's like nothing has happened as they shower together and Parker thinks, this is the happiest he has ever been and maybe he should leave well enough alone.

Trinity climbs out of the shower and through the shower doors he observes as she blow dries her hair, standing there with the terry cloth towel wrapped around her.

He continues to watch her until she turns, waves with a finger, and then leaves the bathroom.

Parker is alone in the bathroom now and in the midst of washing his body it dawns on him that he needs to see his family. He needs to hug them and let them know he loves them before…

He can't bring himself to think about it as he dries himself off. He gets dressed and joins Trinity downstairs in the kitchen.

She looks up and smiles, then returns to her bowl of cereal.

That morning over breakfast, Parker carefully broaches the subject. "Trinity, I have something I want to discuss with you."

Trinity hearing the seriousness in his voice, stops eating her cereal and looked at Parker. "What is it."

"Well, I don't want you to think I think you're crazy or anything, but I think we need help… mentally."

"Go on."

Quickly, before he chickens out, Parker says. "I think we need to see a psychiatrist."

Trinity is quiet, just looking at him. She takes her spoon and sucks on it, then smiles. "I think so too."

"Oh Trinity, thank you, thank you," he says as he goes over and hugs her.

"But not together. We see our own psychiatrist and we go alone. And like our rules, we don't discuss our visits, when we visit or ask each other anything. Okay?"

"Yes, okay."

Parker feels much better now, knowing that Trinity wouldn't lie to him and will see a psychiatrist. He has his already and unbeknownst to Parker, Trinity does too.

45

Trinity sat in her psychiatrist office staring at her fingernails. Dr. Paterson, use to her silence, waited. He knew that Trinity was not going to blurt out just anything without giving it thought.

"You know doc, I use to think I was lucky…not in love, but life. That is how I felt until I learned I had a rare, incurable cancer."

Silence again.

Dr. Paterson doesn't say a word as he looks at her.

"Well, now I have two."

He starts to ask what she means by two, but before he can, she clarifies her statement.

"Now I have a brain tumor."

She says it so matter-of-factly that he is barely able to control his reaction.

"It's funny Doc. At first I thought it was a side affect of the drugs but when I told my doctor and he ran tests, I found out differently."

Trinity has a Kleenex in her lap and is fingering it as she talks. "I had a nightmare that scared me and my friend almost to death. It was shortly after that episode that I first noticed something strange." She pauses.

This time the pause lingers and Dr. Paterson says, "Go on. I'm listening Trinity."

"I am in a strange place I've never seen before. People are running about pushing and shoving and not acknowledging what they do. I move with the crowd because they force me to go forward and then the crowd moves ahead faster and faster and I can no longer keep up. I find myself alone. I turn and see a dark figure behind me. I can't make out the face or even whether it's a man or a woman, but something inside me says, run."

"I run as fast as I can. Sweating and gasping for breath, I scream out for help. And then I stumble and fall. Whimpering I see a hand reaching down and it grabs me. At first I feel grateful to have help, but when I look up, it's the face of the stranger and he has an evil grin on his face as he pushes me back. I let out a loud piercing scream that shakes me awake, but my body still reacts as though it is in the dream."

"So what do you thing that is about, Doc?"

"A lot of people feel over stimulated at times, Trinity."

"Oh, if only that was all it was. Since having that nightmare I avoid going anywhere alone. I used to love going out for a run in the morning, but the thought of doing that frightens me."

With a nervous laugh, Trinity adds, “So anyway, I guess you need to change my meds.”

Dr. Paterson gets up and goes to the water cooler. He returns to hand Trinity a glass of water before sitting back down.

“So, what has happened recently that may be the reason for this nightmare and this change, Trinity?”

She is thoughtful, wondering what to say. “Well, Dr. Proctor my cancer doctor sent his latest medical results to my medical doctor, Dr. Scott who shared the news with me that I have a brain tumor. Can you believe it, I have cancer and now if that wasn’t enough, I have a brain tumor.”

Out comes that nervous laugh again. “Here I was thinking it was the cancer causing my hallucinations, but it wasn’t the cancer’s fault at all. It is my brain that can't handle the flow of information and gets overloaded and this causes irritation, headaches and nightmares.”

“Any advice, Doc.”

Dr. Paterson looks at his patient and says, “When you find yourself speeding up and stressing out, pause, and take a deep breath. Take a couple more. Really feel the air coming into your body, and feel the stress going out. By fully focusing on each breath, you bring yourself back to the present, and slow yourself down.”

“Good advice. Thank you.”

Dr. Paterson walks Trinity to the door. He feels better knowing that she feels better.

It surprises Trinity to realize she had been so shocked by this latest news she actually needed to tell someone how she felt and what she was experiencing. She couldn’t tell Parker so Dr. Paterson became the scapegoat.

And that done, she feels better as she smiles at the doctor wondering how long he can survive with the weight of all his patients' problems on his shoulders.

46

Parker is finally ready to see his family. Where Trinity and he used to be able to go all day long, they have been winding down earlier these days, not because they can't think of things to do, but because their bodies won't allow it. Now as they sit at home he says matter of factly, "I want to go see my family."

"That's good, Parker. When?"

"I was thinking now is a good time. I'll call and see if they're going to be home first."

Trinity is quiet while Parker calls his wife. When he says, "Hello," she smiles at him and leaves the room.

In a few minutes, Parker joins her in the living room. "I don't know how long I'll be."

"No, stop it. This you have to do. I'll be fine. I have something I need to take care of too. I'll see you back here. Maybe I'll fix you a wonderful dinner."

"I'd like that. Love you."

"Me too."

Trinity hugs him, kisses her finger and touches it to his cheek. She stands at the doorway to the garage as he grabs a coat and heads out.

There it is, Parker thought as he sat in his car outside his home, or what use to be his home, trying to figure out what to say. He's glad that he will have some time with Cameron before the boys get home.

"Okay man, you can do this," He whispers as he climbs out of the car and makes his way to the front door. Cameron opens it before he even rings the doorbell.

"Parker, I'm so sorry."

"I know, Cameron." She moves aside and lets him enter the house first, then joins him.

"I need to talk to you before the boys get home."

"Come on in, have a seat in the living room and I'll get us some wine. Are you hungry?"

"No, but I'll take that wine."

While she gets their drinks Parker looks around the familiar room. He goes over to the fireplace and sees that the same family pictures are there with all four of them. It makes him happy.

He senses he is not alone and turns to see Cameron holding two glasses of wine. He takes one and they move over to the sofa.

Parker takes a sip of the wine and follows with a deep breath. "It's hard to start this conversation. I don't want to sound ominous and I don't want to upset you, but we need to talk about the pink elephant in the room."

That last part is hopefully to make Cameron comfortable. She smiles, but only with her mouth, not her eyes.

"I'm very ill. We both know that and so you need to know a few things."

"I'm listening," Cameron says softly, reaching over to lay her hand on mine.

That touch makes it easier for him to continue. Knowing Cameron so well, it has always been her way of letting him know she is with him.

"I know that talking about these things is never easy and I'm sorry I didn't tell you earlier." He pauses. "I guess I took the chicken's way out, letting the doctors do my dirty work."

"Stop it Parker, it was probably the best way for you to handle it. I know you and talking seriously is not one of your strong points…"

Parker has to smile. "So do you have any questions for me?"

"Well, I…Does it hurt, Parker?"

"No, it doesn't hurt and that makes it hard to believe that I am dying." Seeing the look of despondency come over her face, he adds, "It's okay. I've adjusted to that fact."

"I told the boys and they took it hard, but they seem to be doing okay now. I think they will feel better seeing you."

"Again, I'm sorry that it fell on your shoulders. I should have been here to help you tell them. It's just that.."

Cameron gets up. "More wine?" she asks and he can hear tears in her voice.

"Yes, please."

He gives her the time she needs and when she returns he hands her the Letter of Final Wishes he has prepared and gives her a copy of his safe deposit key where he has his will and ancillary documents stored.

"What about… I mean…"

"Yes, Cameron, I have written out what I want for my final arrangements. That is sealed and in the safe deposit box too.

Cameron nods. She sips her wine and then turns to him. "Parker, I want you to know that I still love you and the boys love you too. It's just that…"

"You don't have to explain yourself to me. I know. And I'm happy that you have someone in your life too. It will make it easier for you and the boys."

To ease the tension, Parker points out changes she has made to the room. “I like it like this,” he says. Cameron relaxes glad that topic has changed. They are in the midst of sharing niceties when they both are startled. The door flies open and in unison, Jonathan and Nolan yell, “Dad!”

They cover the distance to the sofa and plop down beside him. Parker wants to make plans with them, but isn’t sure how much time he has so he remains quiet. Instead he sits with them and catches up on what they have been up to. He listens and smiles at their eagerness to tell him everything. When there is a lull he finally asks them, “Do you have any questions you want to ask me about my illness?”

His sons look at him and he can see they are holding back their tears. Each one shakes their head and hugs him so tightly he can barely breathe.

At that moment Cameron breaks the tension in the room when she returns carrying a plate of sandwiches.

It’s surprisingly comfortable as they laugh and talk together. It feels as though they haven’t been separated at all until the door opens again.

Parker stands and shakes hands with Cameron’s friend, Alexander.

“Well boys, I’ve got to go.”

“No dad, stay a while longer.”

“Don’t leave on my account, Parker.”

“No, Alexander, I was getting ready to leave.”

“Dad, when will we see you again,” Jonathan asks.

“I’ll see you soon, pal. Take care of each other.”

He hugs them, then waves at Cameron before turning and walking out the door, proud of himself for managing to take care of what needed to be done. He knows that his lawyer could have handled it, but he wanted to be with them just one more time.

Back in his car, he waves at his sons who are waving at him and then he starts the engine and drives to his new home and the woman who is awaiting him.

While Parker is gone, Trinity keeps an appointment with her psychiatrist. Dr. Paterson was surprised when she called for another appointment so soon after the last. He tells her to come right in.

Seated in the doctor's office, Trinity doesn't waste time telling him in detail her reason for being there.

His expression remains unreadable. "So doc, what do you think?"

He's silent so Trinity takes a deep breath. If she wants his help she needs to lay it on the line.

"Doc, I had another appointment with Dr. Scott a week ago." She pauses then quickly adds, "I have developed extreme aphasia. I am experiencing double vision, and blinding headaches so I won't be able to do much driving. At times I am clearly very confused and can barely utter an intelligible word. Dr. Scott says it's because the tumor is growing.

Trinity fumbles in her purse and finally finds what she's looking for. She takes it out, but her fingers aren't working well and it drops on the floor. The doctor starts to get up, but Trinity motions at him. "Don't, I can do it."

Dr. Paterson watches as Trinity leans over, holding tightly to the edge of his desk and retrieves the flash drive. She stands, not moving for a moment and then turns toward him and says, "Here. This is for you to hang on to. It contains everything that needs to be shared when I am gone."

Dr. Paterson starts to talk, but Trinity holds up a finger. I'm asking you to be, well, like my Power of Attorney, putting this in the right hands at the right time. And, I'm asking you not to view it until that time."

"What, I don't understand."

"The doctors spelled out my situation in no uncertain terms which I am thankful for. I have more likely weeks than months to live. They gave me a prescription to help stabilize me, but it is only a matter of time."

Trinity gives the doctor a pleading look. "I don't know how many more sane days I have. I will gradually sleep more and more, eventually losing consciousness and not wake. It doesn't sound like a bad way to go."

"Isn't there a family member you can share this with?"

"That's it Dr. Paterson. My parents are deceased, and I was an only child. I have a friend, Monique, but she has her hands full with her family and I wouldn't put this pressure on her. I do have a male friend, but his time is limited too. You are all I have doc.

Dr. Paterson is thoughtful, then says, "Well, if you are giving me such a big personal responsibility, you need to call me Thomas."

47

There is a knock at the door. Parker looks at Trinity and Trinity looks at Parker and smiles. "I'm not expecting anyone."

"Me neither."

Trinity watches as Parker walks to the door and opens it. Framed in the doorway is a very pretty little girl about six years old with brown hair and a nervous smile as she tugs nervously at her dress. She holds a piece of paper in her hand and when she looks up at Parker, her eyes are big and wondering.

"Are you the man with the kite," she asks.

The question takes Parker by surprise. "Am I?" Parker is confused, then it dawns on him. "Well, yes, I guess I am the man with the kite."

The little girl takes a deep breath as she looks right at Parker and begins.

"My grampa says that if you're the man with the kite that I, uh, that I..."

Parker just stands there. Trinity can see that the little girl could use some help so she joins Parker at the door.

"Hello, my name's Trinity," she says, smiling and bending close. "What's your name."

The little girl visibly relaxes. "My name is Audrey."

"Hello, Audrey. This is Parker, ah, the kite man. Do you have something to tell him?"

Audrey settleas down and says, "Yes. My grampa says that if you're the man with the kite that he wants you to come to his birthday party." She thrust out the piece of paper she has in her hand. "And this is the address."

Parker takes it. "Thank you little miss."

Parker and Trinity watch as Audrey turns and starts down the deck steps. Suddenly she turns back and runs up on the deck. Looking at Trinity she says, "You can come too." Then she runs back down the steps and heads up the beach.

It looks like a family gathering that spills out on the deck and on to the beach. Just outside there seems to be at least thirty people and as they make their way up to the back door, they can see the house is filled to capacity with people wandering around laughing and drinking.

Parker and Trinity stand at the back door which they find is open and peer inside. There are tables of food; enough to feed an army.

Slowly, Parker steps through the open door wondering who is throwing the party and why he was invited. Parker unfolds the piece of paper to check the address. They are at the right place. He reaches back and grabs Trinity's hand.

They step aside as people come and go through the door and then, moving further into the house, Parker sees a familiar face.

Through the crowd he recognizes the same old man from the beach who always wore a green scarf. At the same instance, the old man sees him and his face lit up. He gestures for them to enter and Parker and Trinity move through the crowd to join him.

"Hello, thank you for coming. My name is Billy Barker." From behind him he ushers Audrey forward. "And this pretty little miss is my granddaughter, Audrey."

"Hi again Audrey," Parker says. He turns to Mr. Barker and says, "Thank you for inviting us. This is, my friend, Trinity."

Trinity steps forward and shakes hands with Mr. Barker.

"Aren't you a pretty one," Mr. Barker says. "But you need to call me Billy. Everyone does."

Everybody is so friendly; most are relatives, but some are just friends like Trinity and Parker. They drink, eat and talk, happy they accepted the invitation. Then there is an announcement to move into the living room and join Billy as he opens his presents.

It is easy to see that Billy is having the time of his life as he thanks each person for their gift. Finally, he has the gift from Parker in his hand. Trinity looks around to see Parker and feels him squeeze her hand. They watch as

Billy opens the present. It's a brand new kite and string. The card says, 'Its more fun to fly than to watch.'

"This is wonderful, Parker. I didn't expect a gift from my brand new friends. Thank you."

"You are so welcome. Now I can watch you fly a kite."

The room filled with laughter. As the crowd dispersed around Billy, Trinity moved Parker over to the side of the room and whispered. "You are special."

"Me?"

"Yes, have I mentioned how much I like you?"

"You do?"

"You know I love you, but this is the first time I am telling you that I like you too. I like you a lot."

Parker responds, "I like you a lot too."

Trinity giggles and they make their way to the table that holds the cake, where the rest of the party has now gathered. Billy stands behind the table and the friends and family members yell, "Speech, Speech."

It is quiet as Billy clears his throat.

"Well, I am ninety years old today and I am so grateful to have friends and family members such as you. You all being here lets me know how special my life has been."

Billy clears his through again. "To have friends and family such as you speaks for itself. You are the good in my life along with my wife, Anna. He motions for his wife to join him. When she is by his side, he gently kisses her.

There is loud applause, handshakes and kisses. Parker and Trinity join in, avoiding eye contact as each realizes that they are seeing two people who have the luxury of loving and growing old together.

Music begins to fill the room and Parker hears Trinity say, "Ah, a waltz."

He watches as she leaves him and goes over to Mr. Barker. From the smile on Billy's face, Parker knows she has asked him to dance.

Soon they are in the middle of the room, dancing expertly across the floor; both looking like accomplished dancers as they float expertly around the room. When the music stops, Trinity gives the old man a kiss on the cheek and he hugs her in return.

Others follow suit until the space is full of dancing couples. Not wanting to be out staged, Parker looks around the room and sees a woman who is standing alone, tapping her foot. He approaches and says, "Can I have this dance?"

Flustered, she nods and soon they are on the dance floor.

Trinity and Parker have a dance together and then decide it is time to leave. They go over and thank their host for a lovely evening and wish Billy Barker a Happy Birthday.

48

December ended 2016 on a relatively cool but wet note. Temperatures were above normal for the start and end of the month, but a cold stretch at mid month brought the monthly average down considerably. The coldest day came on the 18th with a high of only -2 and a low or -25 but it didn't stop Parker and Trinity who knew that it could be worst and they didn't have to wait long. The big snow maker was a winter storm that dropped 8.3 inches the week before Christmas. While there was snow on the ground Christmas morning, it didn't necessarily feel like Christmas with temperatures reaching near 40 degrees. On record it was said that a very strong El Nino in the early part of the year gave us a mild winter. A weak La Nina helped out to make the fall very warm.

Several things happened to make the time special. It began with Trinity dragging him from store to store until he had made all his purchases for the holiday. She then helped him with the wrapping, laughing at how much difficulty he had making the presents presentable.

That was followed by hot chocolate and trimming a tree at the beach house, followed by a nice glass of wine in front of the finished tree.

Parker spent Christmas morning with his family and the rest of the day with the woman he loved.

But more amazing was the energy they were experiencing. It could be from changes in their medication or maybe they were experiencing personal highs. In any case as Parker and Trinity weathered the winter months they began crossing off items on their bucket list.

Trinity, who lived in the neighborhood, had not taken time to visit the Rochester Museum & Science Center so, on one of her choice days, she suggested they spend the day between the museum and the George Eastman House.

Nothing was off limits as they checked off places of interest. Parker surprised her when he didn't balk at going to see the Rochester City Ballet perform and Trinity was open to making the trek to Brooklyn New York to visit the Transit Museum where all the old subway cars, busses, and trolleys rested.

It was fun to do all the things they planned on doing but hadn't gotten around to. What added to the fun was they were doing it together. Parker could not remember when he had enjoyed himself so much.

Eventually the weather takes a nasty turn keeping Parker and Trinity indoors most days. Somedays they spend bundled up and sitting on the front porch watching neighbors and the Rochester Public Works doing their job. Rochesterians make the best of winter since it drops a lot of that fluffy stuff and lingers on for months and months. As the snow piles up, people are seen pulling sleds tied to their snow blower, trying to entertain restless little kids. Others are out on cross country skis and snow shoes either for exercise or ease of transportation.

Parker keeps the sidewalk and driveway cleared, while Trinity cheers him on from the porch. On days they need to shop, Trinity stands in the garage, protected while Parker throws snow from one side to the next, trying keep his viewing area clear for backing out of the garage.

In the end everyone grows impatient for March 20, the first day of Spring.

SPRING 2017

49

Trinity stands in the kitchen listening to the news. "Winter Storm Stella is hammering the Northeast with heavy snow, intensifying winds, even some accumulating ice, which will lead to major travel disruption." A frown is on her face as she goes about putting breakfast together.

Upstairs, Parker is anxiously getting dressed. He plans to shovel the drive so that they can go out for breakfast. When he is halfway downstairs, the aroma of coffee greets him and when he enters the kitchen he sees Trinity at work.

"Ah, Sweetie, I was going to take you out for breakfast."

Trinity points to the tv and continues working on breakfast. The announcer says, "Blizzard warnings continue for parts of nine states in the Northeast, from Pennsylvania to Maine. This major nor'easter is taking shape as a strong area of low pressure off the East Coast …"

"Okay, change of plans."

"It's no problem, we have plenty of food and drugs to keep us going."

"It's not that, I wanted us to get out for a bit. Maybe we could trudge down the beach."

"Well, we could, but already two feet of snow has piled up on the three feet out on the beach. If you think walking through the sand is hard, walking through that mess will be even worse."

Parker goes to the front window and looks out hoping to see less snow. He pulls back the curtain and observes trees bending in the strong winds.

"Parker, accept it, we are staying in today. This is a bad winter storm. They even gave it a name.

"They did?"

"Yes. Its Stella. Like in the Brando Movie, A Streetcar Named Desire."

Together they mock Brando, "Hey Stella!"

The nor'easter slams Rochester. Strong winds in combination with the weight of the snow have downed tree branches and intense snowfall rates are observed with 4.5 inches in one hour

They lose power. Parker who thought installing a generator in a house they only used once or twice a year, outrageous is now thankful Cameron talked him into it.

Outside it becomes a wintry wonderland. When the sun comes out, it reflects off the snow with tiny little diamonds glittering all over the surface.

Fallen trees are covered with ice and snow looking like sculptures against the white backdrop and there are few footprints or car tracks to be seen.

Parker and Trinity feel as though the world around them has disappeared as they spend day after day in the warmth of their home reading, playing checkers and putting puzzles together.

One morning they rise to the sound of power equipment. Trinity leaps out the bed and goes over to the window. She looks up and down the beach but can see nothing.

She rushes over to the bed and shakes Parker. "Get up, somethings happening outside," she says.

Parker stretches and manages to open one eye. "Come on, sleepy head! Get up!" Trinity jumps up and down almost pouncing him off the bed.

"Okay, okay. I'm up."

Trinity grabs Parker by the hand and leads him down the stairs. At the front door, she hurriedly puts on her coat and slips her barefeet into her boots then patiently waits while Parker does the same.

Outside, they step down into the snow that comes up over their boots as they make their way slowly across the porch and down the few steps to the walkway. They cling together pulling one foot after the other up out of the snow. Finally, they reach the sidewalk.

Trinity finds it funny and starts laughing. Parker joins in.

"Listen. Hear it?" Trinity says.

In the distance they can hear the sound of the plows making their way towards them.

"Look up there."

Parker follows her arm and sees a sidewalk plow trudging through the snow.

Carefully he helps Trinity back to the house. "Open the garage for me," he says.

Trinity stays inside while Parker begins clearing out the driveway. When he finishes, he starts clearing the sidewalk, the walkway and the porch. He works diligently throwing shovel after shovel of snow off the porch and when he finishes, he comes in the door, exhausted and soaked through his clothes.

Parker, surprisingly has not had any further episodes. In the beginning he worried he'd be caught off guard with one of those excruciating episodes, but thankfully the new pills his doctor gave him seem to be working.

"Want to go out for breakfast?"

Trinity is thoughtful, but before she can answer, Parker's cell rings.

She sits on the steps while Parker talks on the cell. When he disconnects, he says, "That was my brother Paul. He wants to meet me for breakfast. Want to join us."

"Ah, no. I think you have some serious information to discuss with him and I don't want to be serious today."

Parker nods. He ruffles her hair as he goes up the stairs to get ready.

In the shower he goes over what he will say to his brother. He climbs out and dries himself. As he stands wiping the steam from the mirror, he considers how much he needs to share with Paul and if Paul will take it well. By the time he is dressed and ready, he has a game plan.

He kisses Trinity. "I won't be long. Can I get you anything."

"Just come back to me. That's what I want."

He smiles and heads out to the car.

The roads are clear with little traffic as he makes his way toward downtown and over to Park Avenue. There are piles of snow along the roadway so he searches for an open place to park; somewhere safe from the snow throwing plows.

He makes his way across the stree to the Frog Pond, a place he and his brother go often. Over the years they decided because they liked going here so much, might as well make it their place. It also was fun to say they were going to the Frog Pond.

Parker stalls, standing in front of the door, just staring at the place and remembering. He wonders if he will have time to come back again or if this is the last time he will see this place.

Someone behind him says, “Excuse me,” and abruptly Parker jolts back to the present, opens the door and steps inside.

He doesn’t see his brother at first, but as he scans the room a second time he catches sight of Paul waving at him.

Paul is the handsome one of the family. Parker knows he is good looking, but Paul has it over him. His younger brother has a square jawline that women identify with strength. His blue eyes accentuate his black hair making people take a doubletake when they walk by. He even has full lips and a caramel complexion. Yeah, Parker thinks, he has it all.

Before he reaches the table, Paul is on his feet and coming around to give him a bear hug. “I’ve missed you bro.”

“I’ve missed you too.”

They sit down and Parker stares at his brother as if trying to burn his face into memory. They have always been close even though there is almost ten years between them. At first, he was Paul’s protector, then later the one who gave him the advice he needed to make it through the teenage years. Beyond that he became Paul’s confidante to discuss matters with.

“So, Parker, how are you feeling.”

“Well, quite well actually.” It was the truth, he tells himself, but thankful when the waitress arrives.

They both order the famous Frog Pond Frittata, picking almost the same fixings.

Parker manages to steer the conversation on Paul and what he has been up to these days. He listens intently as Paul fills him in.

Their breakfast comes and the conversation halts while they eat.

When Paul leans back patting his flat stomach, Parker knows the time has come.

"Paul, I have something important to talk to you about. You know, I have cancer, but you need to know that it is incurable." Paul starts to speak, but Parker needs to get it all out.

"I am dying. I may not look like I am, but I am and you have to accept that now. Otherwise it will only be harder to accept later."

Paul keeps his head down and doesn't say a word.

"Paul, I don't want to upset you. Please."

Paul clears his throat, then slowly raises his head. "I know. It's just I'm having a hard time hearing this. Why you. You are my best friend. I can't imagine finding anyone who loves me more or knows me well enough to give me advice. What will I do without you."

Being emotional, Parker was right to tell him in a public place. If they weren't in public, Paul would manage to make him downplay the situation by showing how much it hurt to hear this. He was the protector after all.

"You are strong Paul and you can handle this. I need you to tell me that you will be all right. That you will not let this interfere with your life. You have a wonderful family and they will be your focus."

"Yes, but…"

Parker is quiet. Finally he says, to Paul, "I have someone who you might find interesting to talk to."

"No, Parker, you mean a psychiatrist? I don't need one."

“Well, do you remember my friend Martin Henderson?”

Paul thinks for a moment. “Yes, the guy who you befriended in high school and I use to follow you and him around like a puppy.”

Parker laughs, “Yes, that’s him. He is now a doctor—not a psychiatrist—and a friend.”

Parker can tell that Paul is thinking about it. “Well, I always liked him.” He pauses and looks at his brother.

“I have his card right here.” Parker takes out his wallet and finds Martin’s card. He hands it to Paul.

“I may take you up on that. Thanks Parker.”

“You are welcomed. I have already mentioned to Martin that you might be calling.

Over coffee Parker shares most of the details that he covered with his wife. Then he broaches the final subject. “Paul, I want to ask you something.”

Paul leans toward him and smiles, “Shoot.”

“Will you be my Power of Attorney. I could ask my lawyer or Cameron, but I am not sure they will follow my wishes to the letter like I know you will do. So Please.”

Paul is speechless as he grasps what his brother is saying. He’s talking final arrangements and Paul is not ready, but he can’t refuse his brother.

“Sure, but why are you moving so fast. You have a lot of time left. A lot of time.” Even as he says it, Parker can tell Paul doesn’t believe it.

Not planned, but happening at the right time, Parker’s face goes red and he leans forward, pressing against his side.

“Hey, brother, are you all right Parker?” Paul is on his feet and by his side.

It’s too hard to speak so Parker nods his head as he fumbles in his pocket for his pills and tosses a couple in his mouth.

Paul hands him his water. The worry apparent on his face as he stares at his brother.

Minutes later and he feels like himself again. The meds work and Parker finally says, "I guess God wanted to make sure you know that I don't have a lot of time."

"I'm sorry," Paul says.

"You have nothing to be sorry about."

The check arrives and Parker stands up straight, still breathing a little heavily. Actually, the pain hadn't been the worst he has experienced. It just came on so unexpectedly.

"Sure you okay?"

Parker nods. "I'm okay. If you have the time Paul, can we go get the papers notarized?"

Without hesitation, Paul says, "Yes."

"Oh, something else that will help?"

Paul turns toward his brother. Anything, Parker, anything at all.

"You paying the check." Parker says chuckling as he walks out the door and waits.

With the business with Paul handled, Parker returns home with a surprise for Trinity. He gets out of the car and hurries up the step to the front door. He has the gift wrapped and it looks pretty.

He bursts into the house roaring and pounding his chest, trying to scare the royal bejesus out of ol' Trinity. But she isn't in the living room.

"Hey, I got a new sexy nightgown for you," he yells hurrying into the bedroom. But she isn't there.

Parker goes back into the living room and peeks out the window. He can't see her on the beach or the porch. He then turns back around and sees it.

Across the room, there is a small note attached to the refrigerator door. Trinity is a note writer. He knows that. She'd leave him notes all the time. Once he even found one in the freezer. But he knows this one is different, and he knows he doesn't want to read it.

Parker tries to calm himself but he can't. Trinity writes notes for the simple stuff. If it's serious she texts or calls.

"Come on old man, pull yourself together."

His hands shake as he reaches over and touches the note. Slowly he takes it in his hands and looks up to compose himself, then he lowers his head and reads:

It's time for you to go spend time with your family. Tell you kids to catch their freight trains. I've been in a lot of pain but haven't wanted you to know. Remember what you promised about not looking for me. God, I love you.

Trinity

Stunned and shaken not knowing what to do, Parker turns and looks around, knowing she isn't there. He calls out to her in a whisper.

"Trinity"

He slowly sinks into the chair his head bowed and begins hugging the note tightly to his chest.

50

It is a toss up where she'd end up. Would they consider her a brain patient or a cancer patient. Trinity giggled, drawing stares from the attendants who not knowing what else to do, smiled at her. That made her giggle more.

Such a grand entry way, she thinks as she drives in and decides to park in front of the entrance instead of the ramp garage. No second hand entry for her. No sooner has she stopped when a staff member comes up to the passenger side window. She rolls it down.

"Ma'am, can I help you?"

"Yes, I'd like you to park my car."

"No problem. Turn your vehicle off and follow me."

Now this is nice, she thinks as she walks under the green pergola held up by four red brick columns. At the main entrance glass doors, she pauses behind the attendant and waits patiently. He turns and hands her a ticket.

"Now, when you come out, just show this and someone will get your car for you."

"She giggles again." Why am I doing this, she says to herself, then out loud, "Thank you sir." She barely gets it out before she giggles again.

The floor echos each step as she walks down the wide hallway entrance, taking it all in. It feels like she is in a high end hotel as she makes her way down the corridor. Except that is for the signs that spell out locations in the hospital and what color to follow.

Eventually she makes it to the admittance desk.

"Good morning, honey. Can I help you."

"Yes," she says suppressing another giggle. I'm here to check in. My name is Trinity Hunter."

Trinity stands patiently waiting. "Ah, yes, Dr. Proctor's patient."

Trinity is thoughtful. "Dr. Proctor, Dr. Scott…whoever wants credit."

"Excuse me?"

"Oh, I'm sorry, I have a brain tumor you see, so don't listen to me. I don't seem to be able to make much sense."

Trinity giggled thinking, that's a plus. She can blame her actions on her little friend the brain tumor.

The receptionist makes a call and in a few minutes an attendant arrives with a wheelchair. She's young, pretty and full of life. She even walks with a bounce in her step.

"I hate her," Trinity thinks.

"Good morning Ms. Hunter. I am going to take you to your room."

She tries to help her into the wheelchair. "I can do it, but thank you." she giggles, "I appreciate it."

There is no reaction from this one. She must have seen and heard it all. Young and pretty, she is probably the first one called to wheelchair duty.

She has been to this hospital many times and waited for an elevator to take her to the floor. Now, for this perky little lady, it's like the elevators are at her command and arrive almost as soon as she pushes the button.

"Wow," Trinity says giggling again.

“Sorry, what did you say?”

"Oh, nothing."

In no time they arrive at her room. "Here we are Ms. Hunter."

She starts to climb out of the wheelchair.

No, please stay seated. She is about to say something else when she hears her say, "Ah, here you are. This is Ms. Hunter. Ms. Hunter, this is Melanie.” Trinity turns to see Melanie. “She will be attending to your needs."

Now that’s more like it, Trinity thinks to herself as she stares at Melanie. Melanie wears her hair pulled back into a bun at the nape of her neck. She has great skin and doesn’t seem to be wearing any make up. She has a nice, ‘you can trust me’ face.

Melanie moves in front of the wheelchair and Trinity turns around. Her wheelchair friend has one more thing to say before she leaves. “And, this is your room.”

Trinity looks up and can’t help it. She leans over laughing. When she gets control of herself, she sits up straight and lets out a shy smile. “I like the room.” Trinity looks around aware that all RGH rooms are private. “Its quite sizable and nicely decorated.”

She starts to get out of the wheelchair, then looks at Melanie to see if it's okay,

"Come on, I'll put your things away while you change into something more comfortable."

Trinity nods and heads for the bathroom where she finds a hospital gown waiting for her and socks with runner strips on them. She laughs loudly.

"Are you all right in there."

"Oops. Oh yes, I'm fine."

Ready, she steps into the room.

Melanie helps her into the bed while Trinity looks around at the equipment she has placed in the once near empty room. While she hooks Trinity up, she explains what she is doing and that makes her comfortable.

“Okay, now on to the important things,” Melanie says.

“As you can see, you have a television. I have called down to have it turned on. And this,” she says picking up the gray box on the bed, “is how you change the channels, lower and raise the sound, and it also controls the bed positions.”

She points out the storage areas and opens the desk drawers to display my toothbrush and toothpaste as well as other grooming paraphernalia. “Now, you can have a phone if you like, but most tend to use their cells. What do you prefer?”

“My cell is fine, Melanie.”

"Good. If you need help, the call button is also on this," she picks up the gray box again. "There is also a call button in the bathroom."

"Do you smoke?"

"No."

"Good. No smoking allowed anywhere in the building or the Hospital campus."

"I think that's it for now, Ms. Hunter. Do you have any questions for me?"

"No, I think you covered everything."

At that moment Dr. Scott enters, smiles at Melanie and then turns to Trinity. "How's it going?"

"Find doctor, but I do have some questions for you."

"Go ahead."

She asks about what she can expect at this stage of the game and if he knows how long it will be. To both questions, he tells her that everyone has different experiences and time.

"Well, can you tell me if it will be soon. I'm ready."

"Yes, it will be."

"For now we will make you comfortable and medicate you so that you are not feeling pain. How does that sound?"

"Good. Now, what time do I get to eat."

Dr Scott smiles and looks at his watch. That will be soon too."

She is alone now. She lays on her back, her head turned away, facing the wall. She knows and accepts that she is in the last stages of her fight against her cancer.

When she first heard she had this thing called Desmoplastic small-round-cell tumor, it had floored her to learn she had cancer, let alone one that was rarely found in women. Leave it to her to have a rare one.

During her last visit with Dr. Scott he told her she needed to be hospitalized so he could help with the pain.

Ah, the pain. There should be another word for it because it was beyond what should be called by a one syllable word.

She had fantasized she could endure until the very end outside the hospital walls, but that fantasy died several weeks ago. She'd been having upper abdominal pain for almost a year now but the meds had helped.

It was embarrassing when the burping started, but she could laugh that off. Then came the bouts of nausea and the pain in the middle of her back making it hard to sleep. But she survived it and kept it secret. Now the tumor made it impossible to pretend she could cover up the progression of her illness.

At one point she gave into treatment beyond the meds, but the tumors just kept spreading. There was no recourse but to check into the hospital.

It has been several days now and she can feel the change. Trinity reaches over and picks up the hand mirror on the stand next to her bed. She stares at her reflection. Her skin is dry and she has nasal oxygen prongs in her nose. Her hair is a mess from lack of care and sweating.

Next to her hospital bed is an IV stand with three plastic bags that connect to a tube in the back of her hand. She is glad no one knows she is here...

Instinctly, Trinity turns her head and sees a figure looking at her from the doorway. Her face screws up in anguish. She tries to yell but it comes out a whisper.

"Oh god I told you not to do this."

Slowly guiltily, Parker comes in the room. He rushes across the tiled floor and buries his face in her side as he leans over her bed.

Trinity rolls her head from side to side on her pillow weakly moving only as much as the tubes in her nose would allow. Her hand goes to his hair and plays with it.

"I told you not to do this," she says softly. Parker never raises his face from her side, but his hand gropes for her hand and when he finds it he holds it tightly.

"How did you find me."

Parker clears his throat and raising his head says, "It wasn't easy. I didn't know if you would be at one of the hospitals, or a hospice, or a fancy hotel. But I couldn't give up. I had to find you. I'm so sorry."

"Oh, god, this is exactly what I didn't want to happen." Trinity again rolls her head from side to side unhappily. "Go Parker, please leave."

Trinity tries to push him away but she is too weak. They look into each other's eyes, but Trinity quickly turns away.

"What are going to do". Her voice gets louder and starts to crack. "You gonna buy me flowers." She puffs air, "Make some small talk. You want me to save you a seat."

"I just wanted to see you."

"Okay, you've seen me. Please Parker, please. Just go."

Their hands are intertwined but Trinity desperately tries to pull hers away. When she succeeds she pushes weakly against his chest. Frantically she stops pushing and doubling up her hand, she beats against his chest.

"Go... please..."

Parker takes a step back but can't go any further. He takes a step forward and suddenly bends at the waist. Slowly he puts his hands on either side of her face, turning it toward him as he leans down closer to kiss her on the lips. As he starts to rise, he feels Trinity as she pulls him back to her and kisses him hard before turning her head away.

"Get out of here, Parker." She softly cries into her pillow. "And don't come back."

In a daze Parker freezes as he gazes at the woman he loves until finally he finds the strength to turn and leave the room.

Trinity's hands curl up in a tight fist, twisting part of the bedsheet in a ball. The fierce grip continues well into the night until sleep forces her fingers to relax.

SUMMER 2017

51

Parker in a suit and tie leans against his car his hands in his pockets feeling the breeze on his face and thinking.

Loneliness does not surprise him, but it's not just loneliness because what he is feeling needs a stronger word to express it. He misses the sound of two glasses clinking together in celebration of their accomplishment. He misses someone breathing soundly next to him as he goes to sleep at night. His brother and even Cameron have tried to get him going out again by inviting him to social gatherings and he has gone, but still feels alone.

His friends and family have been wonderful. He can call any number of people and they would come and just hang out or show him a good time. But inside his heart he will still be alone. Funny, but what has helped him get back into his life and jumpstart his career has been strangers.

One day he sat down and found a support website. He has chatted with strangers who don't know him but are as close as he can come to confiding in people who know exactly what he's been through. He openly tells these strangers some of the most intimate details of his live, and the crazy things he has done. No one says, “You did what? You’re crazy!” Maybe because, we have crazy in common.

Parker doesn’t think that most people who haven’t experienced loss truly understand. The person who cared when something really great or really bad happened is missing. The person who was just as invested in his live and the decisions they made is now gone while he’s left to slug it out down here on his own.

Yes, it took some time to make it here, but he did make it. He actually remembers the moment he decided to come. He had been walking on the beach with the sun shining brightly over his left shoulder, feeling like just walking out into the water and disappearing when he heard a voice. He can’t remember what the voice said, but he did recognize it. It was an audible thump that had reality crashing down on him.

Parker looks up and smiles, shading his eyes from the bright sunlight. The grief has softened over time, but he knows that the month of June will always trigger flashbacks to the hospital and the last day he saw her.

He stares across the street. Finally ignoring the traffic, he walks across then down the sidewalk and pass a fountain just inside the entrance to the cemetery.

Parker wanders around expressionless toward the area, ignoring the manicured trees, green grass, and gray headstones.

He almost walks pass it, then half turns, stops and stares. It’s a simple and elegant headstone design. Parker chuckles as he looks around at all the white marble, then turns back to the black granite gravestone that marks her grave.

He runs his hand across the stone then leans down to read the engraving.

Trinity Hunter

1983-2017

(Hi, Parker, thought you would drop by.)

Parkers face shows his emotion as he starts to laugh. He laughs deeply, tears flowing from his eyes and his body jerking as each spasm of laughter takes control.

He shakes his head in disbelief as he turns away and then turns back again.

"You idiot," he says fondly.

It is several hours before he manages to draw himself away. Parker walks slowly through the cemetery, wiping his eyes with a Kleenex, then blows his nose.

When he is on the path to the exit, the groundskeeper turns on the sprinklers.

Parker stops and turns around to see rainbows forming above the green grass and suddenly he is enraged. He tries desperately to suppress the feeling, but the anger boils up inside.

Turning back toward the exit, he stiffly walks out the entrance and crosses the street, but instead of lessening, the feeling grows. When he reaches his car, he goes to the back and opens the trunk. There laying on the carpet is an old tire iron. His dad had given it to him years ago and he just hung on to it. He picks it up liking the feel of it in his hands.

Parker is out of control as he raises the tire iron and in one smooth powerful motion smashes it down into his own windshield, watching a characteristic "spider web" cracking pattern appear. He swings the tire rod again, this time piercing the glass.

He looks ahead and sees a small car parked in front of his. He walks up to it and looking in the window he sees the reflection of a madman in mid swing. Parker moves forward and smashes the back window of the car. He moves to the side and swings again.

He can't stop as both hands methodically continue the motion as he moves from one car to another using the same powerful strokes and getting the same results.

There are no pedestrians and only a light trickle of traffic going by, but Parker doesn't care whether anyone sees him or not. His anger is so powerful it is in total control.

He continues down the row of cars, his face distorted with anger, his body soaked with sweat until his shoulders ache and he can't swing anymore.

Parker calmly walks back to his car. He takes out his keys and unlocks the door. Slowly he climbs in behind the wheel taking a moment to catch his breath. Then without warning he sobs uncontrollably, beating the steering wheel until finally, sated he starts the car and pulls out of the parking space and heads toward home.

52

At the beach house, Paul walks around the kitchen wondering what to do and finally goes to the refrigerator and takes out a beer. He carries it with him into the office.

He takes a swig of the beer while waiting for the computer to come to life and when it does Paul puts in the password and takes another swallow.

Finally, he is in. Paul leans forward looking at the screen and notices a folder on the desktop named, Trinity. He stares at it and then questioningly opens it.

Paul begins reading.

Dearest Parker, death is nothing at all. It does not count. I have only slipped away into the next room. Nothing else has happened. Everything remains exactly as it was. I am still me and you are still you and the old life that we lived so wonderfully together is untouched and unchanged. Whatever we were to each other that we are still.

Call me by the old familiar name. Speak of me in the easy way which you always used. Put no difference into your tone. Wear no forced air of solemnity or sorrow. Laugh as we always laughed at the little jokes that we enjoyed together. Play, smile, think of me, pray for me. Let it be spoken without an effort, without the ghost of a shadow upon it. Life means all that it ever meant. It is the same as it ever was. There is absolute and unbroken continuity. What is this death but a negligible accident. Why should I be out of mind because I am out of sight. I am but waiting for you, for an interval, somewhere very near, just around the corner. All is well.

Love

Trinity

Paul Parker wipes the moisture from his eyes and closes down the letter; feeling like a snoop, but unable to stop reading.

Who is this Trinity and what happened to her, he wonders. And then a sad expression covers his face. Did his brother know that the letter was there? Did he have a chance to read it? Paul is still sobbing as he moves across the room and sits on his brother's overstuffed chair. A kite lays on the seat and he picks it up.

Beyond the room he can hear the sound of the waves as they hit the shoreline. He takes a final swallow from the can of beer crushes it with uncharacteristic strength and reaching over the arm of the chair, drops it in the waste basket.

Paul stares at the small redwood box he has carried with him. It sits on the sofa near the cardboard boxes of Parker's belongings. He goes over to the box opens it and takes out a small Brass urn. He frowns at it.

Suddenly he chuckles, remembering something his brother had said to him when he had neared the end. He had said, "Remember, I am counting on you to ignore what anyone says, and just carry out my wishes." His brother had paused and added, "Okay, instead of a cardboard box, I will allow you to purchase a brass urn, a very small, the smallest my ashes will fit in, brass urn."

"So tacky," Paul says.

Laughing and cradling the urn to his chest Paul strolls out of the house.

The helicopter is easy to rent, and the pilot is even easier to bribe and before long Paul is nudging the pilot and pointing down at the train tracks below.

Expertly, the pilot drops down lower as they fly a path above the tracks until the train comes into sight. In the passenger seat, Paul works quickly, opening the urn. Then leans out the window holding the urn tightly as he tips it just above the moving train below, allowing the ashes to flow from car to car. When the urn is empty, Paul holds it up, kisses it and then releases it.

The helicopter veers away gaining altitude as it heads back home.

Along the flight path they fly over a large water tower. On the narrow catwalk at the top of the water tower a man in overalls is using a long roller to apply dull gray paint.

Inches away from the back side of the tower where Parker had been alone, there is a heart with an arrow through it and inside is written, Drake Parker loves Trinity Hunter.

If one could see the man's face they would recognize a look of disgust on his face as he grumbles, "Goddam kids," then wetting the roller in the paint, he covers the drawing until it is no longer visible.

THE END

www.ingramcontent.com/pod-product-compliance
Lightning Source LLC
LaVergne TN
LVHW091030080826
845145LV00002B/429